"What th   in my room, Carl?"

Joanna took a step toward him, then stopped, suddenly aware she was wearing nothing beneath her robe.

"Checking the window," Carl replied. "How would you feel about my setting my camera here?"

"Would you have to be behind it?"

"Only while I'm focusing it. And I'd have to check the tape each day."

Joanna shrugged. "I guess it wouldn't be too inconvenient." She pulled her robe closed at the neck, although there was nothing of her body exposed and the room was uncommonly warm. "I can handle it."

Carl looked at her quizzically. "Sure *you* can handle it, Mrs. Keller," he said softly. "But that makes only one of us...."

ABOUT THE AUTHOR

Molly Rice has loved writing since she was a child. However, she only "came out of the closet" with her writing in 1982 at the age of fortysomething, when a friend invited her to a Romance Writers of America meeting. *Chance Encounter* is her second Superromance novel and is set in her hometown of St. Paul, Minnesota, where she lives with her husband. They have four children.

Books by Molly Rice

HARLEQUIN SUPERROMANCE
440–WHERE THE RIVER RUNS

Chance Encounter

MOLLY RICE

Harlequin Books

TORONTO • NEW YORK • LONDON
AMSTERDAM • PARIS • SYDNEY • HAMBURG
STOCKHOLM • ATHENS • TOKYO • MILAN
MADRID • WARSAW • BUDAPEST • AUCKLAND

Published March 1992

ISBN 0-373-70490-9

CHANCE ENCOUNTER

This book is dedicated to family:

First to my husband, Eugene, who in his own way is always there for all of us.

> To Tracy and Carl, Dana and Joseph
> Barrie, Katie and Robby
> Lincoln and Adele, and Chianne
> Heather and David, Krystal, Beau and DJ

And to friends, because good friends *are* family:

> Joanne and Rick
> Sue and Bob
> Carol and John
> and Pj

With all my love and gratitude.

PROLOGUE

IT WAS MIDNIGHT. There was no moon to light the path from the beach to the abandoned lighthouse. Augustus Mueller used a pencil-thin flashlight to guide his steps over rocks, driftwood and the crocus corm that had begun to grow wild in unexpected places all over the island. Behind Mueller, another man followed closely.

The door to the lighthouse was padlocked, but Mueller was prepared. He drew a long, thin instrument from a leather case and, with a practiced gesture, used it to pop the lock.

Then he used the pocket flashlight to lead the other man behind the stairs to the only room on the ground floor. The room's single window faced the ocean. Only then did he switch to a larger, lantern-type flashlight, knowing its illumination could not be seen from shore.

There was no furniture in the room, but an old packing quilt on the floor was sufficient for their needs. Mueller gestured to the other man and the two of them lowered themselves to the floor, crouching close together so that neither would have to raise his voice.

"I have brought you here to tell you that you have had a considerable honor bestowed upon you, my young friend. The Committee has determined that you should be the one to carry out a very special mission."

The younger man's face betrayed none of his thoughts or feelings. He had learned early on that to obey without question was the first rule of behavior in the Party.

"It has been decided that our best method for over-throwing the government of Greenwich Island is to force the people to vote the existing administration out. We do not have the manpower to fight the army and navy but we do have the means by which to destroy the government's hold on the citizens."

"We are not going to stage a coup?" the other man asked, speaking for the first time.

"No. The Committee has come to the conclusion that we need something that will gain us the sympathy of the other governments around the world. What we plan will allow us to appear to win the election almost by default. A political ploy rather than a terrorist uprising will gar-ner us world sanction."

Mueller stopped to light a cigarette and then went on to explain the plan.

The younger man listened intently as his superior con-tinued.

"Some time ago, there was a small shipment of con-taminated grapes exported to America from Chile. When the cyanide was detected, all the grapes were recalled and Chile lost millions of dollars in revenue. This incident al-most destroyed the economy of the country.

"As you know," Mueller went on, "the economy of Greenwich Island depends on its worldwide export of saffron. We have devised a plan like the Chilean grape incident to further our cause. Only we will go them one better—we will not risk the saffron being examined in transit by American customs or the FDA. We will send a man to America after the shipments have cleared and he will poison the spice there."

For a moment the other man remained silent, his expression vacant. And then horror distorted his rugged features.

His voice was a ragged whisper as he said, "And I am to be that man?"

Mueller shrugged and studied his compatriot's face through the haze of smoke from his cigarette.

"You have a problem with that, my friend?"

"Augustus, if we do this thing, many innocent people will die."

"Innocent?" Mueller spat the word, his own face contorting in outrage. "Are the Americans not the very people who support our present regime, the people who espouse the warped standards of romanticism mixed with greed that we are fighting against?" His face reddened with his fury and his eyes seemed to bulge from his head. "We will no longer allow ourselves to be ruled by such a people, not even indirectly. It is time for us to return our people to the only sane form of government, one which sanctions the right of every man to rule his own life without responsibility for any other man's."

As he expected, the other man immediately fell under the spell of the Party's credo.

But as they were preparing to leave, always afraid of meeting too long in one place, Mueller's comrade had one last question.

"Augustus, saffron is the most expensive spice in the world. If we do this, how can we expect enough of it to be sold in time to do its job?"

Mueller laughed hoarsely and clapped the other man on the back.

"Ahhh, that's the beauty of the plan, dear boy. The poisoned saffron will only go into the kitchens of the rich and powerful, and who better to raise the hue and cry that will cause the entire saffron industry to collapse?"

CHAPTER ONE

A FINE MIST FORMED a silvery cone from the bulb of a lamppost to the steel floor of the bridge. Wet rivets glittered from the edges of beams, contrasting sharply against the dark caverns of shadow under the overhanging arches.

Special Agent Carl Donay crouched at the edge of an arch, squinting through the veils of darkness, mist and fog. His hearing, trained to recognize all manner of sound, was distracted by the dreary, repetitious drone of foghorns downriver. With vision and hearing limited, he hoped that on a night like this there'd be few people around.

He was about to emerge from his cover when a figure appeared out of the fog at the end of the bridge. All he could make out was a wide-brimmed hat and trench coat. He eased back into the shadows, almost holding his breath as the figure started across the bridge. Was this his contact? He would wait for the signal, the gesture that had been agreed upon as identification, before he revealed himself.

At the opposite end of the bridge, another man crouched against the embankment that abutted the leg of an arch, waiting for the woman, whom he'd seen just in time, to traverse the length of it and clear the area for his rendezvous. Dampness had beaded on the surface of the steel arch creating runnels of water that dripped down onto his bare head, chilling his skin, and running into his

eyes. He didn't know if he could stand the discomfort
much longer. Maybe he should leave—after all, he didn't
owe the government anything and the price they were offering wouldn't justify his catching pneumonia. He'd give
it five more minutes and then he'd be history.

Joanna Keller hesitated on her trek across the bridge,
breathing in the damp, clean air, enjoying the feeling of
hanging, suspended over the river. She was a lone senti-
nel in the night. Mark had scolded she'd catch cold on
such a night, but once his eyelids had closed heavily, in
surrender to his medication, the onslaught of night
claustrophobia had driven her out into the mist, to the
patent leather sheen of wet streets and buildings, the
mourn of foghorns symphonizing weather and time.

She loved these solitary, middle-of-the-night walks
along the wharf and down to the bridge that spanned the
Mississippi, especially in spring when the schizophrenic
weather offered a mixed bag of warmth, rain, cold and
sometimes even snow, with the promise of summer's heat
soon to follow.

She took another deep breath, sighed, and turned away
from the rail, knowing how quickly her two hours of
freedom could speed by. Mark's medication was good for
that long for sure, but after that his night became a series
of pain-induced waking and drifting and waking again.
She didn't like to leave him to face that alone.

The soft rain created sparkles of light all around her so
that when she caught the glimmer of something at the
edge of her vision, she almost ignored it. She looked back
over her shoulder just as her foot moved from the concrete shoulder to the steel floor and saw that there was indeed something different in the shape of light on the
parapet beyond the rail. She leaned forward, the metal rail
pressed against her middle, and squinted to see better. A

small circlet of gold. A wedding ring, she thought. Probably not valuable—even if it was truly gold. But what was it doing just there, in that most unlikely place? Had someone meant to toss it into the river and missed his mark? She turned away again.

Her imagination went into high gear. What if someone had jumped, or fallen, and the river had carried the body away? What if the ring was a clue? She stretched over the rail and when she still couldn't reach the ring, she knelt to push her arm through the rails. The ring lay just beyond her fingertips. She stood up and considered the height of the rail and the width of the parapet. Easy. Without another thought she lifted her leg over the top of the metal bar.

The man, peering up over the floor of the bridge watched the woman climb the rail. He wiped rain from his eyes and shook his head. Goddamned dumb broad was going to jump. Well, that did it for him, he was out of there. He slid down the embankment just as he heard the thunder of footsteps running overhead and heard a male voice shouting hysterically.

Carl Donay swore under his breath as he sprinted from his hiding place and tore down the length of the bridge, yelling, "Stop! Hey, lady, don't jump." He caught the woman's arm just as she knelt to fall forward into the water.

He was still yelling, unaware of what he was saying, as he jerked her over the rail to the floor of the bridge, mindless of her struggle to fight him off.

The unexpected screech from the end of the bridge, followed by a man emerging from the shadows and rushing down to attack her almost made Joanna lose her footing on the parapet and plummet into the icy river below. The maniac grabbed her and at first she thought he was trying to throw her into the water but suddenly she was yanked over the rail, as if she were as inanimate as a sack of potatoes, and flung to the ground.

"What the hell do you think you're doing?" she yelled.

"What the hell do you want to go and kill yourself for?" the man demanded.

"I wasn't—" she started to protest, but he wasn't listening.

"Nothing's worth killing yourself for," he interrupted, grabbing her by the arms and pulling her to her feet. His face was only inches from hers, screwed up in anger so that she couldn't determine what he really looked like. His hands were iron manacles around her arms. She realized she was on the verge of laughing and choked back the sound.

"Listen! There was this ring...I was only trying to—"

"You were trying to kill yourself over a hunk of jewelry? You yuppies are something else. Isn't your life more valuable than some hunk of gold?"

She tugged, uselessly, to pull free. "No. You don't understand—"

"Lady, you're the one who doesn't understand. I've seen people die and believe me, once it's over, it's over!"

She pulled again but his strength seemed almost superhuman. Maybe he was a maniac after all and she ought to be humoring him.

"I really didn't want to—"

"People like you really get my dander up. The first little sign of trouble and you wanna take a dive. Sister, you don't even know what trouble is!"

The laughter was like an itch at the base of her throat, begging to break free. She let a little of it out, a tiny giggle, and then the dam burst and she was laughing uproariously, her body shaking with the effort. The effect on the man was immediate: he let go of her wrists and his mouth fell open. The sight made her laugh all the harder.

Carl took a step backward. It was obvious the woman was hysterical. He looked around furtively. Maybe someone who could help would show up. He turned back and saw that she was leaning against the rail, still laughing, her arms clutched around her middle, tears rolling down her cheeks, babbling about that damn ring and something about walks and rain. The woman was making no sense at all.

He knew the drill—you were supposed to slap somebody who was hysterical, but something told him that would only make matters worse.

Daring fate he moved forward and put his arm around her shoulders. She was shaking, either from cold or laughter, he couldn't tell which. He drew her away from the rail. "Come on, there's a café with a bar, down on the dock. What you need is a shot of brandy and some hot coffee."

It was all happening so fast she couldn't seem to resist—not the man's propelling of her body along the bridge nor her own response to this absurd situation.

She tried to pull away from him, but the more concern he showed, the more the laughter welled up, weakening her. She stopped once, wanting to get some tissues from her pocket but he pulled her on, talking incessantly about the kinds of drinks that would make her feel better, insisting that he'd feel better when he got her off this damned bridge.

Her laughter had simmered down to a few giggles punctuated with hiccups by the time they reached the door of Mandy's Café. The neon sign that spelled out Food & Liquor cast a pink-and-green-striped glow across her captor's face. She supposed it did the same to her own.

"That's better," the man said. "We don't want to go in there and make a scene."

When fresh peals of laughter threatened, she quieted herself by taking deep breaths and holding her stomach. If she could just regain her composure, she could make him listen, she could explain calmly that he'd made a mistake.

He held the door open and stood back. She smiled weakly at him and led the way into the brightly lit, nearly empty café. The smells of stale beer, deep-fried foods, and dishwasher steam assailed her. She walked to the last booth in the row along the front windows and slid onto the bench, facing the front of the café.

He'd stopped at the counter, telling the woman there, with gestures, what he wanted. It gave Joanna a chance to study him.

No wonder he was able to overpower her; he was at least six-four, with shoulders that suggested he could have played football. The rain had dampened his clothes, making them cling to the solid, muscled flesh beneath his tailored slacks and brown leather topcoat. The same dampness flattened and darkened his hair against a well-shaped skull so that his profile seemed almost carved.

When he turned to face her as he walked toward the booth, her breath caught in her throat. His face was wonderful! He had gray eyes that crinkled at the corners, a nose that looked as if it had met with one fist too many, a wide mouth that curved upward as if smiling was second nature to him.

He gave her an example of that smile as he slid into the booth across from her and her heart gave a sudden start. This was no maniac. The one thing that shone in his face beyond anything else was *kindness*.

He appeared to have calmed down. Maybe this was the right moment to tell him what she'd really been doing on the bridge. But just as she was about to begin, the waitress came, bearing a tray with steaming cups of coffee and two glasses half-filled with a dark liquid that Joanna guessed was cheap brandy. She waited while the woman set the things down.

Carl used the moment to observe his companion at close range. The hat, a tan slouch that matched her trench coat, shadowed her face, but he could still determine that she was a beautiful woman. He'd noticed, on the walk down from the bridge, that she was tall—her shoulders fit comfortably under his arm.

Her features suited her height; large eyes, hazel, he thought, though they were shadowed by the hat so he couldn't be sure, and a long, classically straight nose. It was her mouth that appealed most, a wide mouth that suggested both humor and sensuality. He'd had a taste of that humor, erratic as it may have been. As to the sensuality, he could only speculate. The thought brought a surge of warmth to his chest, made him sad that such a woman would want to end her life.

The heavyset, middle-aged waitress grunted something at Carl and trudged off with her empty tray. Carl nodded at Joanna's glass and said, "Drink up, you'll feel better."

Joanna sipped obediently, found with surprise that it wasn't such a poor grade of brandy after all and drank the rest with relish. She followed it with a gulp of coffee and sat back, with a sigh of pleasure. Either the night had been colder than she'd realized and the dampness had finally penetrated her clothing, or the whole episode with this handsome stranger had sapped her strength. She thought of what Mark would say about all this. He was going to think this was one of her made-up stories, the kind she used to amuse and distract him. He'd never believe it had really happened. She gave a small giggle as she pictured his reaction.

"You're not getting upset again, are you?" Carl asked, leaning forward, his face creased with concern.

Then she did the strangest thing. She patted his hand, as if to comfort him. As she lifted her coffee cup, a small smile played at the corners of her lips.

He stared at her. Something was out of sync here.

"What's your name?" she asked as she lifted her hand to the brim of her hat.

"Don..." Carl's voice caught in his throat as the woman's hat came off and her hair tumbled to her shoulders. At that same moment her eyes became clearly visible to him. He'd been right about the eyes—large, hazel eyes, heavily lashed. And just as he was thinking they were the most exquisite thing about her, her magnificent hair caught his attention, crackling with electricity, shining under the café lights, framing her face in a mass of silver waves.

She didn't seem aware of the impact her looks had made on him. "Don?" she repeated. "Don what?" Her tone was gentle, her manner serene. They might have just met at a tea party.

"Not Don. It's Donay. Carl Donay." He felt as if he was stammering, maybe even flushing. She wasn't just a beautiful woman—she had style. She didn't act at all as if she were someone who'd just been on the verge of throwing in the towel. He had a sinking feeling that he'd walked into someone else's dream and was about to get a rude awakening.

She held her hand out and smiled. "I'm Joanna Keller." Her smile became a roguish grin. He took her hand in his; it fit nicely against his palm and created instant warmth there.

"Thank you for attempting to save my life, but I really wasn't planning to jump."

It occurred to him then that in "rescuing" her, he may have made a fool of himself. He let go of her hand and sank against the booth back with a groan.

"You see, I'd spotted what looked like a wedding band—on the parapet—and I got to thinking that it might belong to someone who *had* jumped and maybe it ought to be turned over to the police."

She laughed at another of his groans and then frowned as she said, "I never did get the ring, you know. You almost scared me into falling off that damned ledge and then you grabbed me before I could pick it up."

So he *had* made a fool of himself. But that wasn't the worst of it. For the first time in half an hour he remembered what he'd been doing on that bloody bridge in the first place. The chief was going to love hearing that he'd blown the meet and maybe set the case back about six weeks, which was how long it had taken to locate this contact—and all for a crisis that hadn't existed in the first place.

Hid mind replayed what he'd heard and seen before he'd peered out and noticed the woman climbing the rail. Had there been a sound at the other end of the bridge? A shadow that suggested another presence? If the guy had shown up and was so skittish he'd run off at the first sign of disturbance, he probably wouldn't be in any hurry to set up another meet.

"I'm sorry I gave you such a hard time," the woman—Joanna—was saying now. "I guess it must have been scary to see someone you think is about to take a dive off a bridge."

He nodded. "Not my idea of a perfect end to an otherwise rotten evening."

"What were you doing on the bridge, anyway? I got the impression you'd been hiding under one of the arches. You seemed to come tearing at me from out of nowhere."

"Hiding? No. No, of course not."

"But you were standing back under—"

"I was trying to light a cigarette," he improvised.

"Oh." A single word that carried a host of questions. "Well, if you want to smoke, go ahead."

Carl made a half-hearted gesture of patting his pockets. "That was my last smoke . . . I guess I tossed it when I ran for you."

Joanna smiled and nodded toward the woman at the cash register. "I'm sure they sell cigarettes here."

"Oh. Well, I really wanted to quit, anyway." She was testing him. Why? She couldn't know anything about him, who he was, what he did, why he was on the bridge. Unless . . .

"I quit about five years ago." She ran a finger around the rim of her cup and looked up at him with a sly grin. "One of the things I noticed about six months after I quit was how sensitive I'd become to the smell of smoke and tobacco on other people."

"Good for you," he said briskly. "And now, would you mind telling me what you were doing out there alone at this hour of the night?"

"Taking a walk." She was sure he'd deliberately changed the subject to distract her from his small but obvious lie.

"My God! You really are suicidal. Don't you realize how dangerous it is for a woman to be out alone . . ."

He was off on another of his tangents. She tuned out his words and concentrated on looking at and speculating about him. His hair was drying now and had lightened to a soft ash brown that had gold highlights and fell in a soft wave across his forehead and was clipped short around his ears. That errant wave reminded her of Mark's hair and, as she was used to doing with his, she was tempted to reach out and brush Carl's back from his forehead. Of course she didn't accede to the temptation.

His hands, which he used to emphasize his words, were nicely shaped and well-groomed; these were not the hands of a manual laborer. His sophisticated clothes and the ease with which he wore them added to the evidence that his work was probably something that required the use of his mind rather than his hands. What kind of job would have him hiding on a bridge in the middle of the night? And hiding was what she was sure he'd been doing.

"I can't get out much, or for long, during the day, so I go out at night for fresh air and exercise," she said when his lecture ended. "I've lived in this neighborhood all my life and I feel perfectly safe. Besides, I always have this in my pocket."

She pulled out a narrow can of Mace.

Carl flinched. "I guess I'm lucky you didn't use it on me, given the circumstances."

She gave him a level look. "Yes. You are." Suddenly she wondered why she hadn't used the Mace, especially in those first moments when she'd thought he was attacking her. Had some instinct been in place, even then, telling her he didn't really mean her harm?

"Would you like another brandy? More coffee?" Carl asked, wanting to prolong this time with her. The night was shot for him anyway, he wouldn't be able to begin to make restitution for it until morning. Joanna intrigued him. There was an air of mystery about her, a hint of sadness beneath the easy humor. Perhaps it was the romantic combination of the late hour, the rain and this deserted wharfside café, that sparked his imagination.

She glanced at her watch and shook her head, with a moue of disappointment. "I can't. I really have to get back to—" she coughed "—to get back." She picked her hat up from the bench beside her and rose. "It's been . . . well, you know what I mean."

He stood, too, and nodded. "Yeah. I'm sorry about the misunderstanding but I'm glad . . ."

They nodded in unison, each knowing they couldn't carry this moment into the future. When they said goodbye, it would be for forever.

Joanna swallowed, saddened by reminders that her life was on hold for now. She wasn't free to pursue a new relationship.

Carl lifted his hand, wanting to touch just one silken wave of Joanna's marvelous hair before she disappeared from his life. Common sense prevailed, halting his hand in midair. He put it to his own forehead and gave her a small salute. This wasn't the first time his career had prevented him from going after an attractive woman; it wouldn't be the last. The fact that it hurt a little more this time could be attributed as much to fatigue and stress as it could to her undeniable allure. He turned and led the way out of the café, stopping only long enough to place a bill on the counter.

Out in the street they faced each other again.

"I go that way," Joanna said, gesturing with her chin to her left.

He knew he should get to a phone, report the aborted meet. "I could see you safely home."

She shook her head. "It's not necessary." *No sense prolonging this.* And she really didn't think it wise to let him see where she lived, just in case he should want to try to see her.

He accepted her refusal with a shrug. *If I knew where you lived I'd probably be tempted to start something. Better to end it here.* "Well, good night then, Joanna Keller."

"Goodbye, Mr. Donay," she said firmly. She turned away and then, remembering, turned back. "The ring," she called out after him. "Do you suppose it might be important to the police?"

Carl glanced at his watch and shook his head. "Don't worry about it. I'll take care of it."

They looked at each other for one more moment and then waved and went in opposite directions.

JOANNA TIPTOED UP onto the porch of the little redbrick house and felt in her pockets for the key, looking up at the neighboring building as she did so. A light in a third-floor window caught her eye and she frowned. As far back as she could remember, there'd never been a night watchman at the Argylle Spice company. Surely nobody was working there this late at night? She wondered if she should call someone—maybe 911—and ask to have it checked. But then, what if it was only Mr. Argylle or one of the executives; they wouldn't thank a nosy neighbor for calling in the cops.

One false alarm a night ought to be enough. She shrugged and turned to unlock the door, telling herself a burglar wouldn't turn on a light and draw attention to himself.

Once inside the house, she slipped off her shoes and went right to Mark's room. He was just starting to stir, his head tossing on the pillow. She went to the adjoining bathroom, wet a washcloth with warm water and returned to the bed.

He opened his eyes as she wiped perspiration from his forehead. "Hi, Mom."

"Hi, hon. Have a good trip?" She sat on the edge of the bed, drawing her knees up to rest against his hip.

He grinned. "First-class. The stewardess wanted me to fly away with her but I told her I wasn't through raising you."

She punched him lightly on the shoulder and laughed. "People pay good money for hallucinatory drugs, and here you are riding for free."

"Yeah. Speaking of hallucinations, got any good ones for me, tonight?" He lifted himself onto one elbow and Joanna leaned forward to prop a second pillow behind his head.

"As a matter of fact, wise guy, I have had a real honest-to-God adventure and if you treat me with a little more respect, I might share it with you."

He began chuckling almost as soon as she began to relate her story of the episode on the bridge and by the time she finished he was weak from laughing. But his color was better and his eyes a little clearer so she decided the excitement had done him some good.

"Wouldn't it be easier to put an ad in the personals column of *The Reader*, or join one of those singles clubs to get a man, Mom?" Mark asked with a grin.

Joanna pretended to think about it. She shook her head, remembering the handsome man who'd thought he was coming to her rescue. "Uh-uh," she said, grinning sheepishly. "Taking a dive off a bridge is the perfect way to attract men."

"I gotta hand it to you, Mom, you can really spin a yarn. I don't know why you don't try your hand at writing."

She feigned indignation. "I'll have you know that was a true story, young man. And if I'd been able to get my hands on that ring, I could have proven it to you."

"Sure, Mom," he teased. "And if I could have got that stewardess's phone number we could double date."

"Oh you. That's what comes of my telling you stories to brighten your nights—when something *really* happens you don't believe me." She stood up and straightened his covers before returning the washcloth to the bathroom.

"Hey," he called after her, "you mean it really happened?"

"Never mind, if you want to think I made it up, go ahead. I just wonder how any kid of mine could have become so jaded in only seventeen years." She looked at herself in the mirror for a moment, wondering where Carl Donay was now and if he'd gone back for the ring.

"Mom, could you come here..."

Joanna ran at the sound of Mark's voice trailing away to a reedy cry. She was all economic motion and efficiency as she administered her son's medication, held his head while he swallowed water, removed the second pillow and gave him the oxygen mask that would ease his breathing. In a matter of minutes he was breathing easily and his pulse was restored to something near normal. She sank down beside him, taking the mask from him as she bent to turn off the flow of oxygen from the tank at his bedside.

"Better?" She brushed his limp blond hair from his forehead.

"Mmm." He managed a grin that tore at her heart and turned his head to stare out the window. "Thought I saw lights . . . Argylle," he said, speaking slowly to regain his strength.

"Me, too. Must be someone working late."

"Mom?" He turned his head so that he was looking up at her. "Mom, would this be easier for you if I went into a hospital?"

She let him see the truth in her face as she spoke, shaking her head. "No way, José. It's you and me together . . ."

"To the end," he finished the ritual words.

"Yeah." She squeezed his hand. They'd agreed a long time ago to always be honest about their feelings. But sometimes Mark tried to protect her. "Mark, would it be easier for you? They've got all those professionals there to wait on you hand and foot."

His laugh was hoarse. "Over my dead body. I'm not ready to cash it in—you still need work."

As if to justify his words he began to reach toward the book on his nightstand. Joanna anticipated his desire and handed him the paperback.

"You or me?" he asked, opening the book to a turned-down page.

"You, if you feel strong enough." She scooted down to the foot of the bed and propped a pillow between her back and the footboard. "Okay, go."

He managed to read three paragraphs before his medication kicked in and he fell asleep, his finger caught between the pages. She eased the book out of his hands and pulled the covers back up under his chin.

"To live is to sleep—to die is to awaken." The words he'd read from a metaphysical teaching rang in her mind. It was what Mark believed, and what she was trying to believe so that she could let him go without resentment. He wanted her to believe that life wasn't about dying but

about living, that it wasn't about pain but about joy. Not easy to accept, especially for a woman with her track record for losing loved ones but she was making the effort. It would be her last gift to her beloved and only child.

CHAPTER TWO

CARL SLOUCHED BACK in the wooden armchair, his long legs stretched out before him, his hands pushed into the pockets of his slacks.

On the other side of the desk, Harvey Wisher, the portly, balding section chief fingered the beaded chain of a rosary and squinted at Carl. After a moment he set the chain aside and cleared his throat. "So, you lost the catch." He shook his head, his eyes sad. "And for the purpose of saving a woman you thought was about to commit suicide, but who wasn't trying to jump off the bridge at all. Do I have that straight so far, Donay?"

Carl opened his mouth to defend himself, thought better of it and closed it, nodding instead.

Wisher let the younger agent stew a minute and then relented. He had a soft spot for Carl Donay though the younger man wasn't typical FBI material. Maybe it was the determination with which Donay clung to the job Wisher respected and that made him overlook the occasional screw-up on Donay's part.

"Well, your mistake may not be as costly as you feared. The fact is, we know where the shipments of saffron are headed." Wisher smiled at Carl.

"You do!" Carl shot forward, all senses alert.

Wisher chuckled, sobered, picked up the chain again. "I got a call late last night. We know the shipments are coming from Greenwich Island. Our informant across the water has narrowed it down to four distributing companies in the States." He paused for effect. "One of those companies is right here."

"And?" Carl almost held his breath. He wanted to stay with this one. He deserved it, despite his failure to connect with his contact the previous night. The agency didn't always sympathize with alibis based on extenuating circumstances, but the chief seemed to be taking Carl's story in stride.

"The company is Argylle Spice—they bottle and distribute all over the country."

Carl nodded. Argylle was a common brand—he probably had a couple of their products on the spice rack in his kitchen. "Do you think they're in on it?"

Wisher shook his head. "We're pretty sure the receiver companies are being used without their knowledge, but we're putting agents in place in each of them anyway. If nothing else, we need inside men to alert us when the shipments arrive."

"Undercover?" Carl could almost feel himself salivating. Damn! He wanted this one so badly he could taste it. He'd been with the FBI for six years and had yet to make his mark. He'd often wondered if he was really cut out for this work. Maybe he'd be better off starting his own law practice.

He suspected Wisher would probably agree. But Carl wanted something on his record to prove that he hadn't wasted the last six years; this job, if he handled it right, would provide that proof.

"Yes." Wisher put down the rosary, picked up a file folder, shuffled through it and said, "You'll be going into the shipping/receiving department as a temp. Report to a Jack Smythe." He looked up and smiled as Carl let his breath out on a long sigh of relief.

"Let me ask you something, Carl," he said, softening his tone and settling back with his hands behind his head. "How did you ever decide to apply to the service in the first place?"

Funny that Wisher should ask, when Carl had just been thinking along those lines. He wondered if his explanation would sound hokey to the older man and then decided to risk telling him anyway.

"When I was a freshman in high school, we had a guy come to talk to us on career day. Special Agent Tom Wilke." Carl's eyes grew dreamy, remembering.

"I was thirteen years old, fatherless, impressionable as hell. After his speech, I was one of the kids who met with him in a small question-and-answer group. He was—" Carl searched his mind for an apt description "—bigger than life." He cleared his throat. "For some reason, he singled me out, began to ask *me* questions. The whole scene was pretty exciting for a kid. Then later, when I was getting on my bike in the parking lot after school, he was just getting in his car and he called to me. Asked me if I'd like to go out for a cola, talk some more."

"A big thrill for a thirteen-year-old," Wisher muttered wryly.

"Yeah," Carl agreed. "But it turned out to be more than that. I found myself opening up to Tom in a way I'd never been able to do with anyone else. He was on temporary desk duty, recovering from surgery—wounded in the field—and he had a lot of time to spend with a kid who had no other male role model in his life. Tom took me to my first Vikings game, helped me get my first part-time job after school. Mostly though, he made me see that I could make my life go any way I wanted, just by giving my best efforts to whatever I was doing."

"Sort of a big brother," Wisher said, nodding.

"Oh yes. And surrogate dad, sort of. He was in and out of my life till I was seventeen. He'd bring me things when he came back from an overseas assignment and now and then I'd get postcards from him. He always seemed really interested in how I was doing. He knew how to listen, you know?"

"What happened to him?"

"He took a bullet to the heart." Carl waited for the moment to pass, making sure he could handle it. "The last time I saw him, we talked about my future. He said I had a good head for law and that with a law degree I'd be able to write my own ticket, even get into the FBI if I wanted."

"And that's what you wanted."

Carl shook his head. "I think I wanted to please Tom. And then after he died, maybe I wanted to avenge his death. Especially when it turned out he'd left me enough money for the first four years of my college tuition. Anyway, when I was graduating from law school, I heard the service was recruiting agents and that seemed like some kind of message from Tom. So I applied."

Wisher made a rumbling sound deep in his throat and picked up a file folder. "So the reason you came into the service was that you felt you owed it to Wilke. I guess that's no stranger than what motivates other recruits. What bothers me is I've never felt sure you were completely happy with your decision."

Carl shrugged. "Even though I have a law degree, I've never thought much about doing anything else. In the beginning, I guess I thought it would make me feel close to Tom again, that it would be a way of paying him back for helping me get through school. Maybe lately it's begun to feel like a debt I'll never be free of."

The older man winced. "I never knew your friend Wilke, but I'd bet my pension he wouldn't expect you to stay on if you wanted to try something else. I'd hate to lose you, you're a fine person, Carl, but I don't like to think you see your work as some kind of lifelong debt."

Carl chuckled, a little embarrassed at how much he'd revealed to his superior. "I'm probably just a little stressed out. I've got some leave coming, maybe I'll give myself some down time after this case is resolved."

Wisher saw Carl pulling back into himself. "Well, good luck and let's wrap this up as quickly as possible, Donay," he said gruffly. "I'm counting on you."

"You won't be sorry, Chief," Carl said, getting to his feet and putting out his hand. They shook and Wisher handed Carl the file.

"Here's the picture as we have it so far, including the stats about your job. There's a creative resumé in there—get it copied and take the copy with you to Argylle. They'll want it for their records."

The older man stood up. "I'll expect to hear from you on a daily basis whether you get any action or not."

Carl nodded, thanked his superior and left to get the paperwork done.

AN HOUR LATER he got his car out of the underground parking garage and drove toward the waterfront area where he'd missed his contact the night before.

On the way, his thoughts primed by the conversation he'd just had with Wisher, his mind wandered back to the past.

Deserted in babyhood by an irresponsible father and raised by an alcoholic mother, he'd learned early to fend for himself. He'd been the caregiver in that three-room apartment where his mother seldom moved from the living-room couch, except for forays to the liquor store when her welfare check came.

It had been Carl, himself, who saw that the food stamps were spent on groceries, before his mother could sell them on the street to buy more booze. He'd worked mornings before school, and evenings, at whatever jobs he could find so that there was some money for clothing and for the personal hygiene and cleaning supplies they needed.

When it came time for him to go to college, a soccer scholarship had augmented the money left to him by Tom Wilke. A shared dorm room with another soccer scholarship student, Danny Mondy, had provided the first real home he'd ever had. He and Danny hadn't become best friends—they were both too single-minded, too used to being loners—but they'd been amiable roommates for four years and compatible teammates on their school's championship soccer team.

He could honestly say that since Tom's death, the closest he'd come to friendship was with Mick Johnson, a fellow agent who'd been his partner on quite a few cases over the years.

He pulled his thoughts back to the present as he came to a red light and saw that he had only to turn the corner to reach his destination.

Argylle Spice was located just four blocks from the bridge and on this windy, spring day the whole area was scented with the spicy fragrances that came from the company.

Carl parked his car on the street, across from Argylle Spice, and looked over at the building that would be his place of employment for the next few weeks. His assignment wouldn't begin until the next morning, but he wanted to check out the area before he was absorbed into the system. In a minute he'd drive around the block and get a feel for the setup from another vantage point. You never knew when knowing the layout of the neighborhood would come in handy.

"Odd," Carl muttered aloud. There were three buildings on that side of the street, but only two of them, Argylle on the east corner and a coat outlet on the west, were commercial buildings.

Set back, between the two, was a redbrick house with black lacquered trim and a black wrought iron fence surrounding the small front yard. It was a little jewel of a house, with tall, mullioned windows and double-hung oak doors with beveled glass inserts. The larger commercial buildings towered over it on either side. But the house did not seem out of place and was obviously very much in use. The exterior was impeccable and lacy curtains hung at the windows. Carl hoped the occupants wouldn't find themselves in danger, should something unexpected go down at the spice company.

He lingered a moment longer, staring at the house, and then shrugged and started up the ignition. The chief had said they didn't suspect the distributors, so it was highly unlikely they'd be any trouble on the premises.

When he drove around the block, he could see that the back of the little house had a high wooden wall separating the property from the alley so that the yard was hidden from view.

The back of Argylle Spice, however, was open to the alley with a fair-sized parking area that fronted a loading dock at the back of the building. Two men were loading drums from a truck backed up to the dock, onto the shelf of a forklift. A third man was holding a clipboard, apparently checking off the shipment.

Carl watched for a while. Starting tomorrow he'd be part of that team. Eight hours a day of boring, uneventful work lay in store for him for the next few weeks, with maybe a few minutes of elation at the end. But that was the reality of his work. Not nearly as exciting as TV and movies portrayed it.

When the guy with the clipboard glanced over across the street to where Carl was parked, Carl knew it was time to move on. It'd look strange if he was recognized the next day as someone who'd been casing the place prior to coming to work there.

"COULD YOU CLOSE the window now, Mom?" Mark asked.

Joanna went to the window and lowered the sash. The warm spring air felt good, and most of the time she loved the spicy smell from the factory next door, but she knew the noise from the loading dock irritated Mark after a while.

"Sometimes I wonder what my grandparents were thinking of when they leased off the lots on either side of us to commercial buildings," she grumbled as she looked out at the three 18-wheelers backed up to the loading dock of Argylle Spice.

"They were probably thinking of the hefty inheritance they were going to be able to bequeath their granddaughter," Mark teased. "And at least we don't get anything but a brick wall on the other side."

"Yeah. Don't you wonder how the people who work in that place can stand not having any windows at all on that side of the building?" Mark didn't answer and she turned to see that he had drifted off again.

She pulled her rocker over to the window and sat down to finish her grocery list. If she called it in before noon, Crocus Hill Market would deliver her order to her, saving her a trip that would take her out of the house for too long. Sometimes, on Mark's really good days, and when she had only a few purchases to make, she'd walk the few blocks to the supermarket near the river.

She chewed on the eraser and stared, unseeing, out the window, as she tried to recall the things they needed. More of those little wafers that Mark liked. She could always entice him to eat one more spoonful of soup if she gave him a cheese wafer. She jotted down the item and looked up again.

One of the big trucks was just pulling away from the dock and a man was turning toward her, pushing a dolly stacked with boxes. He looked familiar. She squinted, leaned forward and then stood up, the list and pencil falling to the floor unheeded.

It couldn't be!

She fumbled in her apron pocket for her glasses, found them, put them on and looked again. The man was talking to another man whom she recognized as the foreman. It was Carl Donay.

Her mind cast back over the night they'd met and her speculations about the kind of work he did. Nothing she remembered supported the evidence before her eyes. She could feel, in memory, his palm against her own as they shook hands. A hard, masculine palm, but one unmarked by calluses. She'd have bet he didn't even have hobbies that required working with his hands. And now there he was, his muscles bunching under a blue chambray work shirt, nodding his head at something the foreman was saying, and wheeling the dolly toward the open dock doors.

She watched until he'd disappeared inside the building, waited ten minutes longer to see if he'd reappear and then retrieved her shopping list and left her observation post to call in her order.

All through the day her mind wandered back to Carl Donay. She went to the window so often that finally Mark commented on it.

"You're sure it's the same guy?" he asked, when she'd told him she'd seen Carl next door.

"Positive!"

"Were you wearing your glasses?" He laughed at the look on her face. Her one vanity was her eyesight. She carried her glasses more often than she wore them, refusing to admit she really needed them.

Sheepishly she admitted putting them on. "Just to make sure."

Mark grinned. "So what do you make of it?" He tried to pull a pillow over to raise his head.

Joanna helped him and sat down on the edge of the bed. "I don't know." She shook her head. "I'd have sworn he was a lawyer or a businessman—someone with some kind of desk job."

"Maybe he's out of work and took this on for the bucks."

Joanna thought about that and then shook her head. "He's too young to be out of a job. I mean, say he was an accountant and lost his job for some reason. He's young enough, and personable enough, so he'd be able to get another accounting job pretty quickly."

"Not if he did a little embezzling on the side," Mark said, letting his imagination go to work to make their little mystery more intriguing.

"Well, then he'd be in jail," Joanna disputed.

"Naw. He'd be out on bail until the trial."

"Oh. Right." She could see Carl's face as it had looked with only a table's width between them in the brightly lit café. "But he had such an intelligent, kindly face," she mused.

"And of course intelligent, kindly people don't ever commit white-collar crimes," her son taunted.

She laughed but sobered instantly. She didn't want Carl Donay to turn out to be a criminal, she realized. "Time to start dinner," she said, getting up. "Want anything before I lock myself in the lab?"

"No, thanks. And please don't concoct any more of those strange, gourmet-type formulas, Mom. I'm not very hungry and they take away what appetite I have."

"Just like your father," she grumbled, tweaking his hair. "Just a boring old meat-and-potatoes kind of guy."

As she went down the hall toward the kitchen, she thought what a long time it had been since Mark had been able to eat anything as hefty as meat and potatoes and she sighed sadly.

This wasn't the best time to be thinking about Sam, either, she knew. There wasn't any way to think of him without remembering that nightmare when he'd taken a bullet meant for his partner and had bled his life away on the steps of a house where an escaped convict had holed up. He'd received a posthumous medal, presented to his widow and young son, for the gallant act of jumping in front of his partner when he'd seen where the convict's revolver had been aimed.

It had taken years to get over the secret resentment, the conviction that her husband had cared more about saving his partner than about surviving for his family. She knew, intellectually, that her reasoning was convoluted and self-destructive, but the feeling had returned over and over to haunt her.

Some of that resentment had spilled over when she learned that Mark's cancer was now out of remission and was terminal. But it was Mark who had asked for New Age and spiritual books when she went to the library, and it was Mark who had insisted she learn, with him, to view life and death as temporary conditions chosen by souls for the purpose of gaining emotional and spiritual insight.

She got vegetables from the crisper in the fridge and lined them up for chopping on the board. She hadn't succeeded in assimilating Mark's philosophical acceptance of his impending death—maybe she never would, given the strict, orthodox religious training she'd grown up with. But at least she'd reached the point where she wasn't crying all the time when she thought of losing him or of him losing the rest of his life. He'd honestly come to believe that a lifetime was not a matter of years but a matter of love and that love was infinite. She could not argue the beauty of his philosophy nor let him think she wasn't willing to embrace it. Any other stance on her part would seem self-serving and grasping.

She added the vegetables to the simmering stock on the stove, partially covering the pot with a lid, and then leaned against the counter as a spasm of weakness overtook her body. How could a mother not be selfish, not want to grasp at her child's life and hang on tightly? How was it possible for her to let him go with a smile on her face and joy in her heart as he begged her to do?

She forced herself to breathe deeply, one of the helpful techniques she'd learned from her own reading, and finally felt her strength return and her emotions come under control. Not a minute too soon, she realized when she heard the tinkle of Mark's bedside bell summoning her.

"Can I sit by the window tomorrow, Mom?" he asked as she went around the room, picking up and putting away various items that cluttered the room.

She looked over at him, surprise widening her eyes. "Do you feel strong enough?"

He grinned happily. "I do. Maybe it's energy generated by your little intrigue, but suddenly I feel good, like I want to see the outside world, even if it's just the world outside my window."

Excitement and optimism filled her chest. She was almost in tears as she agreed, but they could be forgiven since they were so obviously tears of joy, the one emotion Mark most approved of.

"If you eat all your dinner and really feel well in the morning," she promised, bending to give him a hug.

"Some people will do anything to make you try their culinary experiments," Mark muttered against her hair.

She drew back and smiled at him. "Nothing experimental about chicken soup, kiddo. They've been using it to cure all the ills known to man, probably since the beginning of time."

"Or at least since the beginning of chickens," Mark called after her as she left the room.

"Smart-ass kid," she said, loudly enough for him to hear.

CARL HAD ALREADY BEEN working as a receiving clerk at Argylle Spice for two weeks, and now sauntered down the street, enjoying the pleasant weather, the comfort of a hot meal in his stomach, the knowledge that he had fifteen minutes to spare before he had to punch in his return from his lunch hour.

Knowing it was never acceptable to call in a report from a phone on the site of a job, he'd established a routine of going out to lunch every day instead of brown-bagging it the way the other guys in his crew did. They teased him a little about it, but no one seemed to think it all that odd, and it gave him a chance to make his report from a phone booth a block from the plant.

He was just crossing over to his building when his eyes were distracted by the sight of a woman coming down the street from the other end. He could only see her eyes and hair above the grocery bag in her arms but he'd have recognized both, anywhere.

Acting on instinct, he drew back at the side of the Argylle building, before she could look over and see him. He was prepared to turn and walk the other way if she rounded the corner. He waited, holding his breath, listening to the distant sound of her heels clicking on the sidewalk. And then the sound stopped, and he heard, faintly, the sound of a door closing. He stepped out and looked up the street. She was nowhere in sight. It took him only a second to realize that she had to have gone into the little house next door.

Shock and excitement heightened his breathing, twisted his innards. It was definitely *her*. Joanna. The woman from the bridge, the woman he'd thought about over and over during the past few weeks.

He stood a minute, thinking about the house she'd gone into. One afternoon, he'd looked from a window on the second floor of Argylle down into a window in the house. A young man, in his late teens he'd guessed, wearing pajamas and robe with an afghan around his shoulders, had been sitting near the window. The boy had been reading and Carl had drawn back, not wanting to be caught invading the privacy of the house.

Obviously the boy was sick. Was Joanna a nurse? The kid's nurse? Or a tutor, maybe? The boy was high-school age—maybe he was laid up and needed home tutoring.

He heard the bell from the grade school a few blocks away and realized he was almost late getting back. He hurried into the building to punch the time clock.

All afternoon he found himself glancing over toward the house but he couldn't see much from the loading dock. Finally, he made an excuse to go up to the second floor to the window from which he'd first spotted the boy. He watched, seeing no one, for a few minutes, and then just as he was about to return to his work area, a movement from below caught his eye. It was Joanna, sitting in a rocker just a foot or so from the partially open window. Her magnificent hair caught the sunlight, shooting slivers of silver all around her head.

Carl's breath caught in his throat and he made a soft moaning sound. What incredible, twisted act of fate had placed her back in his life and in the most undesirable proximity?

Over the next few days he made so many trips presumably to visit the men's room, but really to look out the second-floor window, that Jack, his foreman, took him aside and asked if he was having stomach trouble.

"The flu's been going around. You haven't caught it, have you?" the older man asked.

"Could be," Carl lied, wondering what excuse he'd come up with next if he couldn't stay away from that window. "But it's not bad enough to make me miss work."

"Well, you do your share, flu or not," Jack admitted. "But if it keeps up, maybe you'd better see a doctor."

Yeah, a shrink, Carl thought, as he stacked another drum marked Cumin onto his dolly. He had to be out of his mind. Why else would he be letting his fascination with the woman next door become such an obsession? Especially given the fact that he would never have a relationship with her or anyone else, not as long as he worked for the service. Some of the other agents married and even seemed to make their marriages work. Personally, he'd always thought it was selfish to ask a woman to share a life fraught with danger and marked by long separations.

Marriage looked like a full-time job, not easily conducted from a distance. And most field agents spent more time away from home than at home. He was one of those. Ergo, serious involvements were out of the question for him.

So why was he hanging out at that window, waiting for a glimpse of Joanna? When he saw her hugging the boy, touching his hair, bending to kiss his cheek, the scene somehow warmed him, made him want to know more about the relationship between woman and boy.

He thought she was the gentlest woman he'd ever seen. Her touch seemed butterfly soft when she caressed her son, her every gesture suggesting infinite tenderness. Sometimes he could hear the sound of them talking, though he couldn't make out the words. Often he heard their laughter, the boy's deeper than his frail appearance would warrant, Joanna's a flute sound that set Carl's pulse racing.

Since he never saw anyone else going in or out of the house, nor anyone else at the window, he'd determined the two lived there alone and were probably mother and son. His imagination came up with too many possibilities for the whereabouts of the father, and he quickly gave up trying to figure that out.

The toughest thing had been reporting to the chief that the woman in the house next to Argylle was the same woman he'd thought he was rescuing on the bridge. There'd been a long pause as Harvey Wisher considered the coincidence and its possible ramifications.

"No evidence yet that anyone from Argylle is in on the job—so my guess is there's no danger that the woman's recognizing you, should that happen, would be harmful to our case.''

Carl hadn't realized he'd been holding his breath until he let it out on a painful sigh. The last thing he wanted was to be taken off the case. And if he was to be ruthlessly honest with himself, he'd admit he didn't want to lose his chance to see Joanna, even from a distance.

Okay, so nothing was ever going to come of it, but somehow thoughts of her—and yes, even of her son, if the boy actually was her son—filled a lonely, empty place inside him that no short-term affair had ever been able to fill. When this case came to an end, when he was stationed somewhere far away, the memories of the woman and boy would be part of a mental photo album he could take out and study at will, like a make-believe family he could pretend was his own.

CHAPTER THREE

THEY MET on the street. Joanna was coming around the corner after making a quick trip to the drugstore.

Carl was standing with a group of Argylle workers who were discussing the merits of the new union contract.

They spotted each other immediately.

"Well," Joanna called out, smiling, "if it isn't my savior."

Before she knew what was happening, Carl had her by that familiar armhold and was rushing her back around the corner.

"What are you doing?" she demanded when he finally let go of her. She moved her package to her other hand so she could rub her arm and glared at him defiantly. "Am I wearing a sign that says, Manhandle Me or something?"

Carl kept his voice low and said urgently, "Please, Joanna, don't raise your voice."

"Why not?" she asked, but complying with his request, she had lowered her tone.

"I . . . I don't want the people from Argylle to know . . . well, it's hard to explain, out here on the street, but they don't know who I am."

She raised her eyebrow and studied his face. "Do I?"

"You know my name."

"And they don't?"

"Look, I don't want to have them start talking. Could we talk—somewhere else?"

She had no choice. Mark would never forgive her if he learned she'd had an opportunity to solve some of the mystery and hadn't taken advantage of it. "Do you want to come to my house?"

"Yes. But, I can't. I mean not now. Could I come after d...I mean, later tonight?"

She gave him a puzzled look but nodded her head. "Sure. My son and I live right next door to Argylle."

He almost said, "I know," but decided, on impulse, to keep that his secret.

He let her go first and then went the long way around to the street where his car was parked, figuring if he gave the guys a chance to rib him about Joanna, it would fix it more firmly in their minds.

He drove to his condo in the downtown skyway near the federal building, collected his mail from the lobby and took the elevator up to the tenth floor. He tossed the mail, which turned out to be nothing more than junk advertising, into a trash basket on his way to the shower.

Since he'd begun eating a hot meal at noon, he'd found he had little appetite for the evening meal. Tonight he fixed himself soup and a sandwich only to help pass the time until he could leave for Joanna's.

He watched TV as he ate, paying little attention to either the fare on his table or that on the tube. Then a news item caught his attention. He sat upright in his chair. The commentator was speaking about the Chilean grapes that had been contaminated by cyanide back in 1989. Economists had finally estimated Chile's loss at $800,000,000, enough to cripple the economy of a country twice its economic size. The journalist was reporting on Chile's slow climb back to solvency.

Carl sat back in his chair, thoughtfully. What would the dollar loss be to Greenwich Island if the contaminated saffron shipment slipped past the agency? The island's major industry was saffron, a costly spice that was processed from the purple-flowered crocus. Greenwich Island had important status for the U.S. because of its location on the Atlantic, between Great Britain and the U.S. Furthermore, it had been American agro-economists who had advised Greenwich that the climate and soil were perfect for the raising of the crocus and the processing of saffron highly profitable. The project had already improved the economy of the Island.

If terrorists succeeded in poisoning anyone with the contaminated saffron, all the saffron would have to be called back, destroying the economy of the island and totally discrediting the government in power there. And when he thought about all the thousands of people who would die as a result of ingesting the poisoned spice, he was gripped by bone-chilling terror.

Anxiety killed what little appetite Carl had left. He dumped the remains of his meal into the garbage disposal, rinsed his dishes, stacked them in the dishwasher and went to his room to stretch out for a while. It had been years since he'd done the kind of physical labor he was doing on the loading dock at Argylle. A nap would help to pass the time.

Sleep wouldn't come. His thoughts wouldn't leave him alone. So far, there'd been no sign of the shipment from Greenwich Island and no hint of collusion on the part of Argylle or any of its employees, but Carl had learned during his six years in the agency that the waiting was often as important as the action. Meanwhile, he asked subtle questions on the job and kept his eyes and ears on the alert.

When he wasn't thinking about Joanna. The thought seemed to pop into his head from out of nowhere, making him writhe uncomfortably on the bed. He stared up at the ceiling, realizing he'd have to come up with a plausible story for Joanna. He couldn't tell her the truth and he was going to hate lying to her, but this was one of those times when he had no choice.

He closed his eyes and racked his brain.

JOANNA TOOK the last batch of cookies off the aluminum sheet and placed them on a cooling rack on the counter. She didn't know anything about Carl Donay's tastes, but chocolate-chip peanut-butter cookies were universally a safe bet. They were certainly Mark's favorites, though she had to limit his intake of sweets in general, and chocolate in particular.

She'd told herself, as she changed from jeans and a sweatshirt to a light cotton sundress that she was only freshening up after a day of grubby housework, but the truth was that she was remembering the look of admiration in Carl's eyes and looked forward to seeing it there again. In fact, she'd thought of him ever since their meeting that afternoon, anticipating his visit with excitement. She and Mark didn't get many visitors these days, she rationalized.

He'd certainly piqued her curiosity. She couldn't wait to find out why he was working under an assumed name. She was surprised to discover she was hoping with all her might that he wasn't some kind of criminal.

She turned off the oven, wiped down the counter and started to take off her apron. The crinkling of paper in the pocket reminded her of the letter she'd stuck there when the mail had come at the same moment the stove timer had gone off, announcing the first batch of cookies were done.

She sat at the table and read the letter from her best friend, Claire Hanson, laughing out loud at the bits of Hanson humor and sighing sadly when Claire wrote of how she missed Joanna and Mark, now that she lived in New York City. She ordered Joanna to "give the kid a big hug and kiss from his Aunt Claire," and then went on to detail some of the trials and tribulations of owning an internationally famous modeling agency and the joys and stresses of living in the "Big Apple."

She took the letter in to Mark and was just commenting about the fact that it had taken Claire three months to answer their last letter when the doorbell chimed.

It was Carl, his tall figure looking particularly virile in jeans and a pale green cotton pullover with a V-neck that showed the neckline of a white T-shirt beneath. When she realized he was also giving her the once-over, she laughed and gestured him inside.

She led the way into the kitchen, saying over her shoulder, "Coffee will only take a few minutes. Unless you'd like something stronger?"

"Coffee would be great," he said.

With satisfaction she watched his reaction to her kitchen. It was a very large room, expanded by giving up the formal dining room she'd never used anyway. She'd kept the hardwood floors and the oak hutch and added custom-built cabinets with the same etched glass doors as the hutch. A Casablanca fan overhead had a tiffany light fixture that complemented the stained glass window over the sink. Whoever had done the work had obviously respected its original architectural integrity.

She busied herself with the coffeepot. "So, come on, Carl, I've waited all day to find out what you're doing over at Argylle and why you're using an assumed name," she said, getting straight to the point.

He cleared his throat and said, "I'm a P.I."

"You're a what?" Joanna turned from the coffeepot and stared at Carl.

"P.I. You know, a private investigator." He laughed sheepishly and avoided meeting her eyes. This was harder than he'd thought it would be. He cleared his throat. "I . . . um, well, I'm working for Mrs. Argylle's divorce attorney."

Joanna fixed him with those beautiful hazel eyes, the coffee forgotten. "Doing what?"

"Well, I'm sort of keeping surveillance over at the plant because Mrs. Argylle thinks Mr. Argylle is hiding some of his assets from her."

Joanna looked dubious. "Hiding them in the spice factory?" She giggled. "Like hiding diamonds in the sweet basil?"

Her humor irritated him when he was trying so hard to tell a convincing lie and didn't want to lie at all. "No! Just not reporting his revenue accurately."

"Well, isn't his income on record, with the IRS, for example? Can't they look at his books?"

"Books can be faked—altered."

"Hmm—I should think you'd have wanted a job in the office then. Doesn't seem likely you'd learn much about the books if you're working on the loading dock or in the shipping department."

"Are you saying you don't believe me?" He'd heard the best offense was a defense but he couldn't recall having to use it before. "Or that I don't know how to do my job?"

Joanna gave him a level look with those compelling eyes and Carl mumbled an apology. She turned back to the coffeepot.

"No, I'm sorry. I guess my overactive imagination sometimes leads me to ask lots of unnecessary questions. My son warns me I could easily become a real pain," she said, still standing with her back to him.

She had her hair pulled up in a ponytail and the back of her neck looked vulnerable as she bent over the coffee-pot. Carl fought the urge to kiss the soft skin above her collar.

"These things have to be done subtly, is all," he said now, finding it easier when she wasn't staring at him with those beautiful, searching eyes. He also thought it was time to change the subject.

"Tell me about your son."

She plugged in the pot and turned around, a tight smile on her face. "Mark. He's seventeen, bright, beautiful, the love of my life." She fussed with the belt of her dress.

And?...

The unspoken word hung between them.

He could see the decision in her face the moment she made it.

"Would you like to meet him?"

"Yes." Had he sounded too eager? She'd looked surprised. But then her smile softened and she gestured for him to follow her.

Carl knew he'd remember that meeting as long as he lived. Mark Keller was a remarkable kid with a gift for humor, a gift for life that most grown men would envy. As soon as Carl saw the oxygen tank he knew the boy was in serious trouble. But Mark, propped up on a couple of pillows, behaved as if he were receiving his guest in the front parlor and in mere minutes he'd managed to put Carl at ease.

Mark's eyes were remarkably like Joanna's but where hers reflected myriad emotions, the boy's shone with only two: humor and joy. Carl was sure that never before had he known another human being who seemed to have cornered the market on joy. It was particularly compelling in a young man who had so obviously been cheated by fate.

Carl and Joanna exchanged a look that told of his admiration for her son, her pride in the boy.

Joanna left the room, a smile of satisfaction on her face, and returned a few minutes later with a tray of coffee and homemade cookies. Mark and Carl were already deep in a discussion about the history of the house.

"Remember, just one cookie, kiddo," she said to Mark, but when her son sneaked a second one she pretended not to notice. Carl discovered he was hungry and ate four.

"Can't remember when I last had homemade cookies," he told Joanna. *Or homemade anything, for that matter.*

"Why don't you come for dinner some time," Mark suggested. "You can try one of Mom's lab experiments."

Carl's face betrayed his confusion and mother and son laughed. It was a great sound.

"He hates gourmet food," Joanna said.

"She thinks anything that's unfamiliar must be gourmet," Mark retorted.

"How do you like it over at Argylle?" Joanna asked, after making a face at her son.

"Nice people to work with," Carl said, "but I'm not sure I'd want to work in shipping for the rest of my life the way some of those guys will."

"Jack's been there since before I was born," Mark said. "He used to give me gum when I was playing in the front yard and he was passing by."

"Yeah. A good guy," Carl said. He wondered how long Mark had been sick but didn't like to ask. He glanced over at Joanna, who was curled up on the rocker by the window, smiling at the two of them.

"Tell Mark what you're really doing there, Carl. He'll love it."

It was even harder lying to the boy, who had his mother's clear, trusting, hazel eyes. But Mark only expressed excitement at the disclosure that Carl was a private investigator.

"My dad was a cop," he said proudly. "He died saving his partner's life."

There wasn't a trace of sadness in Mark's voice when he spoke of his father's death. Perhaps it had happened so long ago that it had no reality for the kid. But when he glanced at Joanna, Carl saw the spasm of pain cross her face as though it had happened recently.

"Oh! Say! That must have been you prowling around up on the third floor at Argylle late one night a couple of weeks ago, looking for evidence," said Mark.

Carl became instantly alert. A couple of weeks ago. "You saw someone?" he asked.

"No. But there was a light in one of the rooms up there and that's never happened before, except once a year when they do inventory and then the whole place is lit up."

"Maybe it was the cleaning crew?"

Joanna interceded. "Not at night. They come in around six in the morning." She frowned and then her eyes widened with surprise. "Carl, it was the night I met you. I remember now, I noticed it when I came up on the porch and then Mark commented on it when I went to check on him."

Could this incident be related to the saffron shipment? It was the same night the chief had heard that Argylle was one of the companies slated to receive the contaminated product. Had someone already moved in and begun some preliminary work on the job? That would mean there was someone working on the inside, someone trusted by Argylle. Here was something the chief would want to know. Clearly they'd need to do a more in-depth check on the employees of the spice company.

Mark drew Carl's attention back by wriggling higher on his pillows, his face alight with excitement.

"So there's a mystery for you to solve," Mark chortled. "Maybe it was Mr. Argylle, hiding the real books."

"Mark knows all about private eyes," Joanna said, getting up and fussing around the nightstand. "All he likes on television are detective shows."

Mark looked up at his mother, his face aglow with humor. "I like the soaps, Mom. I just don't want to get hooked on them and then never find out how the characters resolved their problems."

The blatant reference to the boy's mortality shocked Carl. He got up to refill his coffee cup, needing to hide his reaction. Joanna seemed to have taken Mark's comment in stride.

"Time for bed, honey-bunch. We don't want to use up all your strength in one visit."

"Will you come back?" Mark asked Carl, eagerness shining in his face.

"You bet. I'll even chance one of your mom's experiments."

"You wanna leave here alive?" the boy joked.

"Okay, that did it, kiddo. It's lights out for you."

Carl carried the tray back to the kitchen, giving mother and son the privacy he thought they'd want as Joanna prepared Mark for sleep. It gave him time to get a good look at the Keller house.

There was wonderful woodwork throughout the house, including the kitchen, and little details that made the house shimmer with style: leaded glass inserts in cabinets, built-in bookcases everywhere, a marble-front fireplace in the front parlor. It was a house that bespoke generations of comfort and care.

It fit Joanna. When she joined him in the kitchen the room seemed to come alive around her. She touched things lovingly, as he'd seen her touch her son, and he wondered how it would feel to make love to a woman with hands that caressed so tenderly, so freely.

"More coffee?" she asked.

He shook his head. "No, thanks. What do you usually do now, after Mark goes to sleep?"

"Little jobs that get neglected during the day. Nothing that requires long stretches of concentration though, because he doesn't sleep for very long. He won't take the heavy medication until around ten."

Which explained why she took her nightly walk so late.

She shrugged. "Sometimes I sit in the parlor and read. It's a room that gets lonely if it's unused for too long. And sometimes I go upstairs to my room and watch TV. The kind of shows Mark scoffs at." Her laugh was almost girlish. "I don't have my son's exalted taste in entertainment."

"Is he... does he..."

"He almost seems to look forward to going," Joanna said, interpreting his awkward unspoken query. She looked bemused. "He's been studying metaphysics, and he's convinced that there is no such thing as death, that it's merely a passing on to another dimension of life." She spread her hands and frowned. "I don't understand it all—I was raised differently—but I try to go along with it because it gives him such... peace."

Carl recalled the boy's manner when speaking of his father's death. "So that explains his attitude about your . . . his father?"

Joanna sat at the table, across from Carl, and folded her hands on her lap. "Yes. He says Sam, my husband, had done everything he needed to do here, and was ready to move on."

That might work for a teenage boy who had only a short time to live, but Carl could see it only added to Joanna's pain. Hard to accept that someone you loved would leave you by choice, even if that choice was made at some deeper, unconscious level.

He thought it was time to change the subject.

"Joanna, you understand, don't you, that it would cost me my job if anyone at Argylle found out I was there under false pretenses?"

"Of course, Carl. But there's something you need to know, too." Her eyes sparkled with amusement. "I'm having a hard time buying that story."

Carl heaved a frustrated sigh. What was he going to do with her? She was so damned forthright, so insightful—a dangerous combination for a man in his business. Maybe if he played it light he would come up with something better.

"Where did I lose you?"

She tilted her head to the side, one long, elegant finger tapping against her lips. "I think from the first words you spoke, when you called yourself a P.I."

He laughed uncomfortably. "So what should I have called myself?"

She shrugged. The gesture heightened his awareness of her body, and he found himself studying her again. For a tall woman, she had uncommonly delicate bone structure and her body movements were graceful.

"Maybe you should just have said you worked for a detective agency, or something simple like that, something less TV-ish." She grinned at him and Carl felt something unusual and, yes, frightening, happening in his heart.

What if he told her the truth? There were times that agents had to enlist the aid of civilians; sometimes with their knowledge and sometimes without. Would it help the case any for the Kellers to know what was going down? But if they knew, wouldn't they be in danger?

It seemed improbable. A sick youth and a mother who hardly ever left the house for very long were not apt to go snooping around over at Argylle. He decided to try honesty without going into too much detail. If more was needed later...

"Let's put it this way, Joanna. Without authorization from my superiors, I'm not in a position to tell you what I'm really doing over there. It's still true, though, that it's absolutely imperative no one at Argylle finds out my true identity. They mustn't know that I'm working there under false pretenses."

Even that much was too much. He could tell by the way her face paled and her lips tightened into a narrow line. He'd only meant to warn her, but he'd obviously frightened her, instead.

Joanna stared at Carl Donay, her stomach churning, heart pounding. He was a cop! Oh, maybe not a city cop, like Sam had been, but some kind of law enforcement officer, nevertheless.

He was sitting in her kitchen in blue jeans and a cotton sweater, his handsome face even now etching itself forever on her mind. But he was one of that fraternity who spent their lives courting injury and even death.

Carl watched Joanna's transformation come to completion. She looked bone-weary and a cool, distant expression shuttered her eyes. She stood up and her body language clearly implied the visit was over.

"You'd better go now, Carl. I still have some chores to do and I'm very tired."

"But we'll do this again?" Carl asked, hating the pleading sound in his voice, dreading her answer.

"I don't think that's a good idea," Joanna said. The implacable set of her chin and determined tone of her voice told him she meant it. "After all, you have your job to do—whatever that is—and I keep pretty occupied with Mark."

She was right. He had no business letting himself get distracted from the assignment. An agent's job didn't end when the time clock was punched as it did for the other dock workers at the plant. Even now he should be at home, going over the records the department had compiled, sifting through the profiles of the Argylle employees, looking for that one little discordant note that might lead to an important clue.

And after all, where would a friendship with Joanna lead, given his determination not to become involved with anyone on a long-term basis?

He stood up and held out his hand. "You're right, of course." They shook hands politely. "Thanks for tonight, anyway." He followed her down the hall to the front door, trying to quell the spasm of disappointment that made the back of his throat burn strangely.

When he stepped out onto the little porch and looked back at her, he thought he saw the same regret darkening her eyes.

CHAPTER FOUR

THEY MEANT to stay away from each other.

For fear of running into Carl, Joanna made sure she didn't run any errands in the neighborhood between noon and one o'clock, when she knew the employees were on lunch hour, or at around four when they were streaming out into the street at the end of their workday. She knew that there was always at least one man left on overtime if a shipment of goods was coming in after the plant closed for the day, but even if that someone was Carl, he'd have to use the back alley exit after accepting delivery.

Carl avoided looking over at the little redbrick house, and began using the men's room on the other side of the building so he wouldn't be tempted to look in on the Kellers from that second-floor window.

Joanna still took her lone late-night walks, but now she walked away from the wharf area rather than toward it; Carl was spending more and more time poring over the employee records to keep his mind from returning to the beckoning warmth and comfort of the Keller house.

After exhaustive research he still hadn't found anything that would even remotely indicate that any of Argylle's people were involved, but frustration hadn't yet set in. Carl was sure that this time he was going to succeed at his assignment.

It was Mark who unwittingly brought Carl and Joanna together. He'd been champing at the bit to get outdoors, and on a particularly warm day Joanna capitulated and wheeled him out to the small, enclosed backyard. She knew it had been a mistake to come out here the minute she looked up from tightening the brake on Mark's chair and met Carl's eyes across the distance between the two properties.

Standing on the concrete dock, Carl could see quite easily over the fence into the Keller yard. He'd always known that sooner or later she'd have to go out into the back garden, but nothing had prepared him for the actual physical shock of looking over the fence and actually seeing her there; his stomach lurched and the pulse at his throat changed from its normal rhythm and became erratic.

They made no gesture of recognition beyond what their eyes betrayed. It was Mark—unaware of the currents that flowed between the two adults—who raised his arm and called out to Carl.

"Great day, isn't it, mister?"

Carl almost sagged with relief as he realized Mark was making a point of pretending they were strangers. He was some kid, Carl thought, to have remembered that Carl was working at Argylle under an alias.

"Great," Carl called back, and then, nodding at Joanna, he merely said, "Ma'am."

Joanna nodded in return and hid her flustered feelings by bending to fuss over Mark, pulling the lapels of his robe closer, tucking the blanket around his legs more firmly into the sides of the chair.

In a low voice Mark said, "How come Carl hasn't been over again, Mom?"

She couldn't lie to Mark. "We agreed it wasn't a good idea."

Mark looked surprised and then worried. "Because of me? Mom, you know I don't want—"

"No, Son, no, of course not. It's got nothing to do with you. As a matter of fact, Carl was quite taken with you. And as for me, I choose to spend so much time with you because I love you, because you're the best company I could ask for." She smoothed his hair back from his forehead and bent to kiss him gently. He smelled of medication and the creams she used to keep his skin supple and her heart quickened at the thought of anything hurting his feelings.

She glanced over at Carl, busy unloading a semi, and wished there was some way she could have him over to visit Mark without letting her own feelings come into play. His visit had had such a wonderful, uplifting effect on Mark.

But even as she watched the muscles of Carl's back and forearms ripple with the effort of bending and lifting, she knew that keeping her feelings out of it would be impossible. He was a very attractive man. More than that, a very sexy man; she was not made of clay though she'd lived the last ten years, since her husband's death, in near celibacy and the last two, since Mark's illness had surfaced, in absolute celibacy. The sight of Carl, already tanned by the weak spring sun, was enough to set the blood thumping through her veins, her body stirring with liquid desire.

"It's because of Dad, then, isn't it, Mom? You're afraid Carl is some kind of cop."

Now how had the boy worked that out? She shook her head and ruffled his hair. "Have you taken up mind reading along with your other metaphysical studies, kiddo?"

He grinned and ducked his head. "Come on, Mom, you know he's no private dick checking up on Mr. Argylle's income. Any third grader with a TV set would have seen through that story." His face became serious and she could read the sadness he felt for her in his eyes.

"Mom, what if everything I'm learning is true? What if life's not a risk, but a plan—something that's been predetermined by each of us in advance of coming into it? Wouldn't it be a shame to waste any of the precious moments of it waiting for something bad to happen?"

If only she could believe, as Mark did, life would be a whole lot easier. Joanna wanted to embrace Mark's philosophy with all her heart, but something within her would not give way. She could not dispel the fear that etched her dreams or the sorrow that haunted her days.

"Will you be content with a book while I do some of the yard work?" she asked her son, evading his question as she looked around at the gardens she'd neglected so far this year.

There was a raised, rock-bordered garden around the elm tree in the far corner of the yard, planted with perennials that she'd covered with leaves the previous fall. She used a small hand rake to pull away the sodden leaves, and found the bright, lime-green shoots already thrusting out of the ground.

Near the back fence, lily of the valley was already budding and it took no effort to anticipate the familiar fragrance that their full bloom would bring.

She worked steadily, removing dead leaves, weeds, and the natural debris that found its way mysteriously through the winter snow into the small, enclosed area. Behind her, the sound of Mark's portable radio competed comfortably with the sounds that were a natural part of the activity at Argylle. She became less aware of Carl Donay as she became more aware of her awakening garden.

CARL SLOWED HIS MOVEMENTS just slightly, wanting to prolong his work outside on the loading dock so he could enjoy the scene in Joanna's backyard.

Today he was privy to things he'd never noticed before: Mark, wearing glasses to read, so that Carl suddenly saw him as he must have looked to his classmates when he was able to attend school, and Joanna in shorts, so that he could see the full length and curve of her long, lovely legs, her skin still white from a winter indoors but glowing in the sunshine with the promise of an easy tan in the days to come.

Joanna had that glorious platinum hair pulled up into a ponytail and she wore no makeup, which only emphasized her elegant bone structure all the more. She looked more like the boy's sister than his mother.

They were a beautiful family, each somehow frail and yet each with an inner glow of strength that made Carl's insides tremble as he observed them. They drew him into their little circle in some indefinable way, without a word or a glance, so that he, too, seemed to be working in slow motion, his body part of the scene at Argylle, while his inner self was frolicking through the little yard over the fence, smoothing Mark's hair from his forehead, patting Joanna's rounded bottom as she bent over her plants.

"You've slowed down a little today, Martin," Jack commented. "Haven't had a relapse, have you?"

Carl looked up. "Relapse?"

"That flu that struck you last week," his boss reminded.

Carl grinned. "No. Just a touch of spring fever today, I guess."

Jack followed Carl's gaze to the yard next door. He'd watched Joanna Manville Keller turn from a gawky, too-tall teenager into a gracious, lovely woman. He'd seen young Sam Keller come courting, seen him carry her over the threshold into the house that had been in Joanna's family through three generations. He'd watched Joanna, large with child, resting in the hammock in that yard and, months later, saw the happy couple bringing the newborn Samuel Marcus Keller, Jr. home from the hospital.

He'd been in that house twice: once to pay his respects when Katherine Manville, Joanna's mother, had died, and again for the wake following Sam Keller's death.

"A house of widows," Jack said softly.

"What's that?" Carl asked.

Jack scratched his head under his cap and then replaced it firmly on his head.

"Used to be called the Harton House. Mrs. Keller's grandparents. But the old man died when Katherine Harton was just a kid, and she and her mother lived there alone until Katherine married Sherman Manville. Sherm worked here, you know, up in purchasing. He was killed in an automobile accident the year I came to work here, leaving Katherine to care for her mother and a twelve-year-old daughter. Mrs. Harton died that same year— heart attack, I heard. Now, Joanna's there alone with her kid, a widow, just like her mother and grandmother."

"You knew the family pretty well?" Carl asked, lifting a drum, marked Cinnamon, to the dolly.

"Mostly from a distance and hearsay, you know. But Katherine Manville was one of those special people who didn't believe in barriers between people. Even after Sherm passed, she'd talk to us over the fence on summer days, and many's the time she'd come through the alley with a big thermos of hot cocoa and a box of homemade cookies during the winter when we were freezin' our asses off out here.''

"I guess it'd be hard not to feel as if you know that family when you can see into their yard so plainly every day," Carl said.

Jack gave him a bemused look. "I don't think that young woman could handle anything else on her plate right now. She's changed since Sam Keller died, and what with young Mark's illness—well, I'd say that's a lady who's right on the edge."

It sounded, uncomfortably, like a warning. Carl ducked his head and hoisted another drum from the tailgate of the truck. Had his preoccupation with the Kellers been so noticeable? If so, then he was losing his ability to keep his emotions at bay—something a good agent needed to do for personal as well as professional security. He'd wanted this assignment for the sole purpose of proving that he could be a good agent. He would have to concentrate on his job, not on the Widow Keller and her son.

Jack went off to choreograph the parking of an incoming 18-wheeler, and Carl doubled his efforts to finish the unloading of the cinnamon shipment without so much as a glance into the yard next door. But as he turned to wheel the loaded dolly into the building, he couldn't suppress the temptation to take a last look.

Joanna was nowhere in sight. Obviously she'd gone into the house for something. She'd done a fair job of raking the grass; the yard was a smooth expanse of pale green. Carl's eyes moved to Mark and saw that the boy was attempting to wheel his chair across the grass. The kid was doing all right until his front wheels hit the rock path that bisected the yard, and then suddenly the chair was tilting and Mark was crying out as he fell to the ground.

Carl was off the dock, around the alley and through the wooden door into the Keller's yard in a matter of seconds.

"Are you hurt?" he asked, lifting Mark's head gently, afraid to move the boy in case something was broken.

"No, no, I'm just... just shaken up," Mark assured, moving his limbs so Carl could see he was all right.

Carl lifted the boy in his arms, cradling him to his chest, and pushed the chair upright with his foot. His heart lurched painfully as he became aware of Mark's frailty; the boy seemed weightless in his arms. He set him gently back into the chair and bent to retrieve the blanket that had fallen to the ground, just as Joanna came running out of the house and Jack Smythe walked through the open alley door.

"I was making fresh lemonade," Joanna said, after everyone was sure that Mark hadn't been hurt. "Would you gentlemen care to join us?"

Standing behind Mark's chair, Carl could smell the pungent citrus that still clung to Joanna's hands as she moved them over Mark's face, head and body, as if to reassure herself that her child was, in fact, unharmed. He wasn't sure if it was the fragrance of lemon or the sight of those hands caressing Mark that stirred his senses so.

"We'd love to, but we have to get back to work," he said, stepping away from the chair. His eyes met Joanna's and his pulse quickened as he saw the look of naked desire in hers. Or was it wishful thinking? Confusion replaced the look he'd interpreted as desire and then those dark gold lashes lowered to shut out her expression.

"I'm Mark Keller," Mark said, holding out his hand and grinning. "And I owe you more than a glass of lemonade."

"Carl...Carl Martin," Carl mumbled, clasping Mark's hand. He cleared his throat and frowned a warning at Mark's mischievous smile. "You don't owe me anything. I'm just glad you're all right."

Jack was already walking toward the door in the wooden fence and Carl knew he was expected to follow. He cleared his throat and offered his hand to Joanna. "Nice to meet you, too, ma'am."

His hand was warm around hers and she could feel the newly raised calluses. She could also feel the surge of electricity that seemed to flow from his flesh to hers and she withdrew her hand quickly, frightened by her body's immediate response to his touch.

"Why don't you stop by tonight, Carl?" Mark urged in a low voice. "It'd be great to visit with you again."

"Coming Martin?" Jack called from the fence opening.

"Yeah. Right there, Jack," Carl called back.

"I don't think..." he started to whisper to Mark, while gazing steadily at Joanna.

"Please. Tell him, Mom," the boy begged.

"Yes. All right. Come over at around seven-thirty." Joanna turned away, flustered by the two pairs of eyes that seemed able to penetrate right to her soul.

"Good thing it wasn't serious," Jack commented as the two men strolled back to their building. "The boy looks like a good wind could break his bones."

"But he didn't have much weight behind his fall," Carl reminded sadly. "And there's enough grass out there to cushion him."

"Poor kid. I remember how active he was just a few years ago. He could scale that fence like it was nothing." He laughed out loud, remembering. "Many's the time we had to chase him off the dock, when he was little, lest he get hurt.''

JOANNA SPENT the rest of the afternoon doing light tasks around the house, determined not to allow herself to dwell on Carl's pending visit.

As she dusted, rearranged books, chopped vegetables for salad and soup, she planned and replanned her strategy. Finally she settled on the plan to make herself scarce during Carl's visit, making it clear that he was there only at Mark's request and for the sole purpose of visiting with the boy, not the mother.

Mark chattered happily all through the day, calling out to Joanna when she was busy in other parts of the house. Finally she couldn't tolerate any more of his cheeriness and threatened to cancel Carl's visit if Mark didn't take a nap. His late-afternoon medication helped and Mark slept from four-thirty until six, an hour and a half in which Joanna was left with a silence that only seemed to encourage the very thoughts she'd been trying to avoid all afternoon.

By seven o'clock, she had changed clothes three times, put cookies on a tray and then returned them to the canister, set out makings for coffee and moved the chairs around in Mark's room at least half a dozen times. She'd brushed her hair out, letting it fall in its natural curve around her face, woven it into a braid and then unplaited it, pinned it into a bun, low on the back of her head, and unpinned it, and finally brushed it and left it down.

"Mom, do you want to talk about it?"

Joanna looked up from the drawer she was rearranging unnecessarily. "About what?"

"Come sit with me," Mark ordered, patting the side of his bed.

"Why?" she asked almost defiantly. But she did join him on the bed.

Mark was silent a moment and she knew he was going to question her nervousness about Carl's visit.

Instead, he asked, "Mom, did you love Dad?"

"Why, Mark! How can you ask that? You know I did."

He shook his head. "I don't know, Mom, sometimes you act like you hate his memory, like you're always angry at him."

Joanna started to sputter a protest, but Mark raised his hand and pushed on. "You don't seem to want to talk about him, even to recall the good times we all had, and when I mention him you get that bitter look on your face."

She wasn't going to let threatening tears surface. She swallowed hard, blinked repeatedly, twisted her fingers together painfully and cleared her throat. "I...it's very...painful to talk about your dad."

"It shouldn't be," Mark said gently, taking her hand and caressing the back of it against his cheek. "Not after all this time." His smile was devilish. "Is that why you're avoiding Carl?"

She snatched her hand back and jumped off the bed. "I'm not avoiding anyone," she said huffily, returning to the dresser and the open drawer with its neatly lined stacks of underwear. She kept her back to her son and again moved the stacks needlessly.

"Carl Donay—or Martin—or whatever his name is— and I have nothing in common. Whatever he does for a living, he'll be gone from next door when the job is finished. And I've got my life here, where I've always had it."

"Don't you ever wonder what life is like *outside* this house, Mom?" Mark asked softly.

"Wh-what do you mean?" She was forced to turn around to respond to such a strange remark.

"Well, you know, most people don't live all their lives in one house, as you have. Most people go away to school, or their families move sometime during their lives, or they live somewhere else when they get married. Even widowhood often alters a person's living arrangements."

Why did this subject make her feel so defensive?

"Mark, you know that the house was an inheritance, handed down to Mother and I in natural succession because neither of us had any siblings, and that there was enough money to allow us to go on living here comfortably. Under those circumstances, why would we move? And as for school, why would I have gone away when there was a perfectly good university right here?" She sat in the rocker and started the motion with her foot without thinking about it. "If it hadn't been for that, I might never have met your father, after all."

Her eyes misted over as she remembered the day they'd met, right there on the quad in front of the physics building. She'd been running, late to class, and almost knocked him down. Books had spilled from both their arms and they'd knocked heads when they'd kneeled, simultaneously, to retrieve them. Sam had fallen backward onto the concrete walk, in a sitting position, and put his hands up in a gesture of surrender.

"Okay, lady, have your way with me but, please, don't hit me again."

She'd had to laugh at that and when he laughed with her, sunshine had spilled from his smile and turned a cloudy, routine day into a festival.

She was seventeen years old then, a freshman at the university. She never made it to her sophomore year; she and Sam were married three months later and Mark was born just a week short of their first anniversary.

It hadn't bothered her to learn Sam was a police officer, taking special courses in criminology at the university; she knew very little about police work or the people who did it. As far as she was concerned, police were people who helped kids across the street after school and directed traffic around the Civic Center after a concert or on the street in front of the fairgrounds every summer; police were fictitious characters on television who always got the bad guy and pretended to talk tough while hiding soft spots for their families and their partners.

She didn't learn about fear—about living with it on a daily basis—until they'd been married a couple of years. By then she had Mark to fill her days and she closed her mind to the reality of her husband's occupation.

In the old house, so sheltered from the mainstream of the city, it was easy to pretend they were a normal little family when Sam came home from work at night. With no neighbors to see, and none to see them, it was as if there were no world outside of theirs to lure Sam away, to threaten their happiness.

Even the people at Argylle were as unreal to Joanna as the characters on the daily soaps, disappearing when night fell, leaving the plant dark and silent.

Her rocking stopped with a jolt as she realized that Carl had brought a different kind of life to the plant next door. Now she was always aware of the place, carrying around with her a sense of his presence there even when she was in the house, away from the windows that overlooked the spice company.

"Let's play a game while we're waiting," she said, breaking her silence and moving with restless energy toward the bed.

"Changing the subject again," Mark muttered, shaking his head, but he drew himself up on his pillows and reached for the miniature backgammon set on the shelf over his headboard.

CARL WAS BEYOND WEIGHING the pros and cons of an involvement with the Kellers. He'd crossed that line when he'd held Mark Keller in his arms that afternoon and had felt his own trembling correlate with the boy's as each reacted to the trauma of Mark's fall. He might have been able to resist their lure, if it had been only the mother's unquestionable charms that beckoned him, or simply compassion for the boy that moved him; together, their effect on him was a siren's call he couldn't resist.

He wasn't yet ready to acknowledge that the bait they used to attract him was the illusion of *family* for he had been solitary too long to recognize the need, but he did sense that the house itself was part of it, giving him a feeling, almost forgotten, of home and warmth and ease.

He stopped at the boutique on the first floor of his building and bought gifts: flowers and candy for Joanna, a book and a Scrabble set for Mark.

The amber porch light gave the house a special glow and Carl sat in his car, across the street, and gazed at it for a few minutes. The two dark buildings on either side seemed like two giant sentinels shadowing the small, recessed property between them. There was a dim light in the front room and as Carl watched, he saw Joanna pass in front of the window, holding a book in her hands. He visualized her seating herself under that light, her long legs curling under her as she settled down to read, her silver hair sparkling under the glow of the lamp. But she'd apparently only returned the book to a table or shelf because a moment later she passed in front of the window again and out of his sight.

Finally, he left his car, walked up the path and rang the bell, taking deep breaths, willing his heartbeat to ease. In the time it took for Joanna to come to the door, his mind played with scenarios that defeated the breathing exercise. He saw himself dropping his packages to the floor and sweeping Joanna into his arms in a desperate embrace the instant the door opened, or bowing low and making a frivolous, gallant speech that would elicit her wonderful laughter and reveal her happiness at having him there.

She opened the door and stood back, saying a polite, "Come in." Her face, in shadow, seemed closed, offering no hint of reaction to his presence.

"I—these—for you," he stammered, tripping over the slightly raised threshold, and thrusting all the packages at her.

She moved back into the light to receive them, her eyes almost jade as they stared into his. And then she laughed, that deep, throaty sound that stirred his senses and filled his heart with pleasure.

"You didn't have to do this," she said, the laugh changing to a giggle as she held the bouquet of spring flowers to her face.

"I wanted to," he said, shoving his hands into his pockets. They itched to touch her.

"Well, thank you. I'll put these in water. You know the way to Mark's room." She moved toward the kitchen.

He stood for a moment, watching the graceful way she moved, and then went on to the boy's room.

"Hey, Carl," Mark sang out, his face an open display of pleasure. "Sit down, look at this, you might get some pointers." Mark gestured at the television set where a car chase scene was playing across the screen.

A few moments later Joanna stood outside the room, carrying the two packages for Mark, and listened to the laughter and bantering. Such a long time since she'd heard the harmony of sound made by the mingling of a man's and a boy's voice. It made the house come alive, filling it with warmth and a sense of family—feelings this sad house had too often had to forfeit. She hung back, loving the sound, wanting it to last forever, fearing that her very entry into the room would shatter the illusion and restore the empty reality.

But Mark called out to her, unaware that she was just beyond the door, "Mom, get in here, you're missing all the fun."

She blinked at the brightness of the well-lit room and focused on her son, propped against the pillows, his eyes gleaming with happiness, his cheeks flushed from excitement. Her heart lurched at the sight of him. Was all this excitement detrimental to his frail health? Or—just as scary—*did he need it to restore his health?*

She turned her gaze to Carl and felt her heart jump. There was no question of this man's health; he was pure brawn, total masculinity, from the broad expanse of chest under the off-white polo shirt to the solid thrust of thigh against the lightweight fabric of his brown slacks. His golden hair gleamed, as if freshly washed, and his dimpled grin displayed the two rows of large, even, white teeth. His long legs were stretched out before him and his arms were folded up behind his head. She had a sudden urge to go to him and curl up on his lap, bringing those masculine arms down around her to hold her close.

"Look what Carl brought you," she said, tearing her gaze from the man and smiling brightly at her son.

Joanna meant to leave the two of them alone, but they teased her into joining them by challenging her to a game of Scrabble. Before she knew it, they were a solid three-some, arguing over the validity of words, questioning Mark's addition on the score pad, jeering at Carl's dilemma of getting caught with a *Q* without the support of a *U* or blank letter tile.

Joanna made coffee, served cookies, passed the box of chocolates Carl had brought and laughed and blushed at the way Mark and Carl ganged up to tease her.

Carl ate enough cookies to compensate for the dinner he hadn't had any appetite for earlier and laughed heartily when Mark warned him that Joanna's cooking might be hazardous to his health.

Mark's sighs of happiness thrummed in his throat as he enjoyed the warm, companionable feeling that reverberated in his room. It seemed forever since he'd seen his mother so animated, so young and carefree and *beautiful*. His heart filled with affection for Carl Donay, the man who made his mother laugh uninhibitedly and blush like a schoolgirl.

And maybe Carl was the man to turn Joanna away from fear, away from sadness, and after Mark was gone, away from loneliness. He snuggled down in his pillows, his mind reeling with possibilities and plans. And the first one was to get Carl to take his mother out of this house once in a while, starting with tonight's walk.

CHAPTER FIVE

CARL TOOK THE TRAY from Joanna's hands and led the way to the kitchen. "Why don't I rinse these while you get Mark settled," he offered, turning on the faucet as he spoke. "Then we'll go for that walk."

"Carl, you don't have to wait, you know. I'm used to walking alone at night, and really, I feel quite safe in this neighborhood."

He turned to face her, the water running behind him. "I would have offered if Mark hadn't suggested it first, Joanna. And not because I'm concerned for your safety."

He spoke quietly but she could hear him over the rush of water. His expression was serious. Something in his look told her it would be pointless to argue and something inside her wouldn't allow her to protest. She wanted to prolong the evening with him, and more than that, she realized she also wanted to share another part of her life with him.

They left Mark sleeping, the kitchen spotless, and began their stroll, their arms at their sides, not touching each other. Neither could remember later, the exact moment their hands touched, held, and kept holding for the remainder of the walk.

They grinned at each other as they passed the bridge, each recalling their first meeting there.

"How about a glass of that brandy?" Carl suggested, nodding toward the café on the wharf.

"I'd like that."

They drank brandy and coffee and talked about Mark, Joanna's hand still clasped in Carl's on the Formica tabletop. Carl's thumb massaged the back of her hand gently and all of Joanna's senses seemed mesmerized by that single, small gesture. But the intimacy was disrupted by Carl's next question.

"I never see anyone going in or out of your house, Joanna. Don't you and Mark have friends who visit?"

Joanna pulled her hand from his and lifted it to her forehead, pushing her hair back as she did so. "We used to. Mark's friends from school came, at first, but after a while—" her sigh quivered across the booth "—you know how kids are, they haven't much patience with illness, nor much compassion over the long haul."

"What about your friends? You grew up in this city, didn't you? You must know a lot of people here."

Joanna thought about that and shook her head. "The truth is, most of the people I knew were either my mother's peers or my husband's. You see, Sam was much older than I. And then I lost touch with his coworkers after he...died."

Carl made mental note of Joanna's uneasiness at the mention of her husband's death but didn't comment. Instead he asked, "What about people your age, friends you grew up with, went to school with?"

She shrugged and moved her fingers over the rim of her coffee cup, her eyes downcast. "I have one close friend, my best friend, Claire Hanson. She owns a modeling agency in New York so we don't see her for years at a time. We went to university together. She's Mark's godmother."

"That's it? Just one friend?"

"You have to understand, our house was never part of a residential neighborhood when I was a child, so I never got close to the kids I went to school with—they lived too far from us, for one thing."

"And..." he coaxed.

"And my mother needed me around a lot," she blurted, lifting defiant gold-green eyes to his. "She was a widow, she had no sisters or brothers, no cousins or aunts and uncles. She was lonely...she needed me. I was all she had."

Carl recalled what Jack Smythe had told him and realized Joanna was describing her own condition as well as her mother's. Did she see Mark as her own savior from loneliness in the same role she had played for her own mother? And was that healthy? How would she survive after Mark was gone? His heart ached with compassion for mother and son. As if his feelings for Joanna weren't enough, now there was another hook—compassion—binding him to the two of them.

But lust was what had kept him safe from entanglements in the past. Lust was a temporary emotion, an easy one to walk away from once it had been satisfied. He knew he must concentrate on that if he was to survive this relationship. Lust should be easy enough with a woman as desirable as Joanna Keller. Walking away might be another story.

He took her hand in his again. "You're a very beautiful woman, Joanna, it's hard to believe you don't have a slew of men beating a path to your door." His grin gave her a chance to treat the subject lightly if she chose.

She chose. She returned his smile, adding a touch of flirtatiousness to hers, and said, "How do you know I don't? I could be doing that bridge-jumping thing every night, just as a ploy to attract handsome strangers."

His grin softened, a more serious glint darkening his eyes. "You think I'm handsome?"

She cocked her head and made a study of his face. "Cute," she said sassily, her own eyes twinkling at him. "I think you're cute."

He groaned and put his hands up to his face. "Ohhh, the kiss of death."

She giggled and pulled one hand from his face, exposing a leering gray eye. "Cute's not all that bad, Carl. What about Richard Gere, or Kevin Costner, or Michael Douglas."

She wouldn't add that those actors were also sexy and seductive as well as "cute."

Carl scratched his head, his expression bemused. "Old boyfriends of yours?"

She giggled. "Movie stars, Carl, where have you been?"

"I guess I haven't been to too many movies in the past few years. You probably think I lead a sheltered life."

She laughed. "No, I'm the one that's been leading the sheltered life, remember? You, obviously, have been too busy *living* life to spend time observing other people's fictional versions of it."

"Hey, that's pretty good." He patted her hand. "Very good. Very insightful."

They sipped brandy and smiled at each other.

Carl cleared his throat. "So, those guys...those actors, they're cute?"

"Very." *Gorgeous, actually, and so are you.*

"Hmm. Well, I can't say I'm crazy about your adjectives, but having played Scrabble with you, I'm not surprised."

"I refuse to dignify that slur with a rebuttal, since it was obvious you and Mark were cheating." She removed her hand from his and used both hands to lift her coffee cup to her mouth.

"Mea culpa," Carl intoned solemnly, pounding his chest with his fist. "Can you ever forgive me, sweet lady? I was absolutely wrong."

"Yes, you were," she sniffed. "But, yes, I'll forgive you, because I know you were under my son's bad influence." She sat back and grinned at him. "And if you're very, very nice to me, I might enhance your knowledge of film and rent a few videos for you to see."

It was an obvious admission that she wanted to keep on seeing him, wanted him to continue to come to the house. She couldn't withdraw the invitation now, and realized, as warmth flowed upward through her middle, that she didn't want to.

Her face did incredible things to his insides. When her expression was calm, she was elegant and mysterious-looking. But animated, as she was now, as she'd been most of the evening, her eyes flashed green fire and a pink flush high in her cheeks emphasized her unusual coloring and her flawless complexion.

With the sadness gone from her eyes, she looked like a girl, a happy, carefree girl. And though it had been the classy elegance that had first attracted him, he knew now he'd give his soul to keep the sadness, and the fear, from creeping back. The intensity of his feelings made him uncomfortable.

"Let's go," he said abruptly, rising and reaching into his pocket for a bill to leave the waitress.

He put his arm around her waist when they came out onto the wharf and she responded by placing her arm around his. Their footsteps matched, echoing companionably on the wooden planks.

"Going to be warm again tomorrow," he murmured, looking up at the sky.

"How do you know?" She looked upward, too, and saw the sky was clear and star-studded.

Her uplifted face was just inches from his. Carl swallowed with some difficulty and then, helpless to resist, pressed his mouth to hers and clasped her against his trembling body.

She felt the force of gravity take over as Carl's mouth clung to hers, and she wrapped her arms around his neck to keep from falling.

He was delicious, tasting of brandy and coffee and something she could only identify as sweetly masculine. She relished the taste of him, kissing him back with abandon. The feel of his arms around her was as wonderful as she'd suspected it would be and she snuggled closer to the solid length of him.

"You're so lovely, Joanna," he whispered, drawing away only enough to fit her more comfortably against his body. She whimpered a little at the momentary separation and then seemed to melt into his arms, succumbing to the adjustment as if it had been her own idea. His breath shuddered in his throat as he took her mouth again and felt her slender body move against his arousal.

She couldn't tell where his trembling ended and her own began. There was a sweet, familiar ache that ran the length of her legs, making her feel both weak and powerful at the same time. It had been so long—too long—since her body had known such pleasure, the feeling that her blood was humming through her limbs. Desire centered itself at the apex of her thighs, thrusting her forward against the hard demand of Carl's need.

They clung to each other, ravenous for this closeness that both had been deprived of for too long. They were hardly aware of their surroundings, of their vulnerability out in the open.

Joanna felt the vibration of footsteps on the planks before she actually heard them and jumped away from Carl, startled and embarrassed.

"I told you to check your pockets before we left," the voice of an elderly woman scolded. The sound of a purse clasp snapping shut echoed in the quiet night.

"How many times do I have to say I'm sorry?" a man's voice whined. "Jeez, Clara, it was only four dollars. I told you I'd pay you back."

"I know just where you left it, too," the woman said, ignoring her companion's lament. "I saw it on the dresser when you were shaving."

The elderly couple had rounded the corner, almost bumping into Joanna and Carl who had pushed back against the brick exterior of a warehouse building.

They were both short and plump, the man bald, the woman's gray hair topped by a pillbox hat with a tall feather.

"Sorry," the man muttered, brushing Joanna's arm as he and the woman passed. The smell of beer wafted behind the couple.

Joanna stifled a giggle and turned her face against Carl's shoulder. She could feel him shaking with silent laughter and punched his chest lightly to warn him to stop.

"I don't care what you say," the little woman's voice floated back. "You never listen to me and you always forget something when we go out. Remember when we were going to..."

Her voice faded away to an indistinguishable mumble and Joanna could only assume they'd gone around yet another corner.

"The sound of marriage," Carl said, laughing softly.

"Sometimes," Joanna admitted. "And sometimes a lot worse."

"Oh? How about your marriage? What were your sounds like?" He pushed away from the wall and took her hand, prepared to continue their walk.

By some unspoken agreement, they didn't attempt to resume their lovemaking, both sensing the momentum had diminished for the night, both a little relieved it had been interrupted.

"Pretty quiet, really," Joanna said, thinking back to the kind of communication she and Sam had had. "As I've already told you, Sam was a lot older than I."

"So, you didn't quarrel much?"

She shrugged, a little uncomfortable with this subject. "He was away from home a lot, working long hours on one case or another, and when he was home, we were both pretty preoccupied with Mark."

She chuckled softly, memories of Mark's toddler years replacing thoughts of her relationship with her late husband. "Oh, Carl, he was the most darling little boy you ever saw. So smart and so funny with it. He was always scolding Sam, making him take his feet off the couch, or telling him he had to eat all his vegetables—you know, imitating *me* scolding *him*."

An aborted sob caught at the back of her throat. Carl heard it and squeezed her hand. "He's quite a kid now, I can image he must have been a real character when he was small."

Their arms swung a little in rhythm with their stride and they were silent for a few minutes as they came to the end of the wharf walk and stood at the curb, waiting for the traffic light to change.

He looked over at her and she turned her head and smiled into his eyes. A warmth flooded up through his chest that he suddenly knew had nothing to do with sex or lust or anything even remotely physical. The sensation suddenly made him feel panicky and he looked away, afraid she'd read his thoughts.

Joanna thought she'd caught a glimpse of something strange, and *wonderful*, in Carl's glance but he'd turned away too quickly for her to be sure she'd read the look accurately. Suddenly she recalled the excitement of falling in love with Sam and a thrill escalated through her body and buzzed in her head.

But as she looked up, the Argylle Spice company loomed into view, and beyond it, her own little house. Her world. And where, she wondered, stealing a sidelong glance at Carl, would he fit in?

He wouldn't.

She knew that, and some part of her, accustomed by now to losing loved ones, made note of it and accepted the inevitable. Her history was proof of that; death had always lain in ambush, ready to pounce on anyone she'd ever dared love.

She knew that she had only enough strength to carry her through Mark's passing. After that, she'd never be able to put herself at such risk again, never be able to tolerate another day of living with such fear. And, with sudden clarity, she saw that she could have everything, every shimmering iota of happiness, as long as Mark lived. But not one minute longer.

And so she decided in that moment, as they moved across the street and closer to home, that she would let Carl be part of whatever was left of Mark's life and that she would be prepared, when the time came, to say good-bye to both of them. Maybe she couldn't alter time, or control it, but she could cheat it by cramming this last measured block of it with all the joy that life would allow.

Convoluted as it seemed, she thought that giving up Carl, when the time came, would dilute the agony of losing her child. By grieving for both of them, she would mourn the loss of each only half as much. She sensed there might be something amiss in her rationalization, but it was a straw to grab on to, and she needed that badly.

Meanwhile, it was clear that Carl was bringing something vital to both her's and Mark's lives, and the rightness of that outweighed any other consideration, she told herself. Their little house seemed brighter, filled with a vibrant energy whenever Carl was in it.

And Mark. There was definitely an improvement in Mark's health since Carl had come into their lives. *Wasn't there?* She was sure some of Carl's energy flowed into Mark, giving the boy more stamina than he'd had in months.

They kissed in the shadow of the porch; a tender, sweet kiss filled with promise that was not allowed to escalate beyond that for tonight. But as she entered the dimly lit foyer and turned to wave to him, he called out softly, "Hire someone to stay with Mark Saturday night, and we'll do something wonderful."

HE CAME TO VISIT the next night and the next, no longer making a pretense of coming just to see Mark.

The three of them watched movies on Mark's VCR and played board games and chattered endlessly about everything and anything. They argued a lot, especially after the ten o'clock newscast, any two of them ganging up against the third, depending on the issue at debate.

Through all the fun, the discussions and the game playing, Joanna found her eyes straying to catch surreptitious glimpses of Carl. His masculinity was emphasized by his every gesture, by every slant of light on his head, by every expression that crossed his face. When his face dimpled with laughter she had to clench her fists to keep from reaching out to touch him and when he shouted her down in an argument, she'd recall those moments on the wharf when she'd pressed herself against his raging need. Sometimes she wanted him so badly it made her insides quiver with longing.

The bonus to the promise of a relationship between them was her secret knowledge that it was only going to last for a few months. It made her that much more impatient, more excited, more vulnerable to his every glance, his slightest touch.

Because he stayed so late on those nights, Joanna skipped her nightly walks. Their good-night kisses were almost frenzied, exchanged in the little foyer with Mark calling out last-minute comments from the back bedroom.

She could hardly wait for Saturday.

She'd called an agency and asked for an RN for Saturday night. Mrs. Hughes turned out to be a middle-aged, maternal type with a whiplash sense of humor. Joanna left with Carl with the sound of Mark's laughter echoing happily in her ears.

"Where are we going?" she asked as he held the car door for her. "Am I dressed appropriately?"

He was wearing a light gray suit under the leather topcoat he'd worn the night she'd first met him and he looked so handsome she found herself quivering every time she looked at him.

As for herself, she'd finally settled on a jade, two-piece cotton dress that she hoped would be dressy enough for any place Carl might have in mind. The dress was wonderful for her coloring, complimenting the silvery-blond of her hair and bringing out the green lights in her eyes.

"You'd do me honor, whatever you wore," Carl said gallantly. "But that particular dress is sensational, and perfect for where we're going."

It was as much as he'd tell her, teasing her by letting her make countless guesses and agreeing with all of them.

"Just tell me this much," she asked, exasperated. "Are you going to feed me?"

His grin, accompanied by a raised eyebrow, was downright decadent. "Are you hungry?"

All of a sudden, as her stomach lurched with excitement, she wasn't.

She changed her mind when they arrived at his condo and she saw the table set for two on the small terrace beyond his living room. "You cooked?" she asked, astounded.

He picked up the phone. "I ordered dinner from the restaurant on the top floor." He held the receiver aloft. "Are you starving, should I have them send it down?"

"No, I want a tour first." She looked around with pleasure, as he set the phone back in place. It was the kind of place she'd only seen on television or in films; it was modern, spacious, airy.

She clasped her hands under her chin and tried to take it all in at once. "Did you decorate and furnish it yourself?"

He heard the approval in her tone and smiled shyly. "I didn't hang the wallpaper or paint the walls, if that's what you mean, but I picked out the furniture I thought would go with the colors that were here. And the art and ornaments are things I've picked up in my travels."

There was a kitchen to the right of the foyer. Joanna made no bones about her curiosity, opening cupboards, fridge and freezer doors, and even peeking inside the oven, which looked as though it had never been used. The microwave, on the other hand, was clearly a well-used appliance, a bit of cheese still clinging to its single rack.

Beyond the large living room was a small room that doubled as den and office with a TV set on one wall, book-lined shelves on another, and a desk near the windows on which stood a computer terminal. The room was furnished in brown leather-upholstered chairs with beige drapes at the windows and a handwoven Indian rug done in earth tones on the floor.

There was only one bedroom, but it easily accommodated the king-size bed, dresser and armoire, with room to spare. Here again Carl had used earth colors, mixing them with various shades of turquoise and blue and Joanna was free with her praise.

But it was the master bathroom that really impressed her. "This is...it's magnificent," she called out, spinning around to take in the black-and-white marble room with its huge, sunken tub, separate shower stall, and vanity-style double sinks. The room was filled with plants and it occurred to Joanna she hadn't seen any in the other rooms.

"I forget to water them," Carl admitted sheepishly, when she mentioned it, "and if they're in here, I just splash them when I bathe or shave."

The other thing she noticed was how spotless everything was, and when Carl told her the building offered maid service, she sighed with envy.

"I didn't realize people in real life lived this way," she said, falling onto his bed without thinking about it.

He hid his smile. She was really quite ingenuous, not given to coy posturings or artful ploys. She sat on the bed because it was there and she was near it. He couldn't very well read anything seductive into that.

"Let's go in the other room to wait for dinner, while I have the fortitude to resist my baser impulses," he said wryly.

Joanna followed him, ignoring his statement, still admiring the grandeur of the place.

"The restaurant on the top floor offers this service to tenants of the building, but if you'd rather go up to their dining room and—"

"Oh, no," Joanna interrupted. "This is much nicer." She went out to the terrace and leaned against the waist-high wall, enjoying the view of the city at night. "It's beautiful out here and I can see the river and look, that's my street, isn't it, way over there, across the river."

He couldn't remember when he'd had so much fun on a date. No one had ever enjoyed his apartment so much or been so impressed by the little amenities that condo living provided. It surprised him, too, given her usual poise, until he realized she'd lived in that same traditional, old-fashioned house all her life.

"This is very nice of you," she told the waiter who brought their dinner, as if he owned the restaurant and saw to it personally that the tenants were pampered in this way. And when he came to take the serving dishes back, she raved about the Steak Diane as if he'd prepared it himself. The waiter was so obviously taken with Joanna's beauty and charm, Carl was sure the man would have forfeited his tip without a qualm if one hadn't been offered.

After the waiter left, they sipped liqueurs and coffee, the windproof candle flickering gently between them, the fragrance of azalea plants mingling with the fresh night air.

"This is like another world from mine," Joanna said, with a happy sigh. "I'm so glad you brought me here."

"My intentions weren't entirely honorable," Carl said, his expression grave, his arms coming down to rest on the table as he leaned toward her.

Joanna's breath caught in midsigh, and the very air around her suddenly seemed to vibrate with emotion. How strange that she had been able to spend this hour with him here, alone for the most part, without giving a thought to the possibilities of intimacy. It had all been so...so friendly, despite the romantic ambience.

She said as much to Carl, adding, "I haven't felt the least threatened."

He laughed out loud, throwing his head back, clapping his hands together as he did so. "Sex isn't supposed to threaten you, woman," he said. "I wasn't talking about taking you against your will, you know."

She frowned, not sure she hadn't made a fool of herself. "Well, okay," she fumed. "But it wasn't that funny."

He looked at her gravely. "I'm not laughing at you, Joanna, I'm just feeling so damned good about everything—especially about having you here. I've loved the past few nights with you and Mark, but sometimes I've felt if I couldn't be alone with you soon, I was going to bust."

His speech was so painfully direct, its content so totally paralleling her own feelings that she couldn't resort to humor, or feign virginal shyness. "It's what I've wanted, too, Carl," she said softly, slipping her hand into his.

He stood up and drew her to her feet beside him, folding an arm around her waist and pulling her against him.

Their kiss began slowly, intoxication building gradually as their senses became heightened, their desire opening fully.

Breathing raggedly, Carl whispered, "Is there any reason for us to wait any longer?"

Joanna moaned softly and tightened her arms around his neck. "No, oh no, Carl, please, there's so little time as it is."

Carl's own passion had spun so far out of control that her words seemed oblique, translating themselves in his mind as merely words of encouragement. He moved his arm to her waist and carried her toward the bedroom.

CHAPTER SIX

CARL SET JOANNA on her feet beside the bed and undressed her and then himself, quickly and smoothly, his eyes never leaving hers, his heart racing with excitement.

Her eyes were large, luminous in the dim light, trusting. She made no coy gesture of modesty as she stood before him nude, nor did she make any effort to glance away from his body as piece by piece of his clothing fell to the floor beside hers at their feet. Her face clearly expressed her pleasure at the sight of him, her eyes darkening with desire, her lips parting hungrily.

This was the moment Carl had dreamed of—his fantasy was coming true. He took her hands and placed them on his chest. "Touch me, Joanna," he said, his gaze intent on her face.

Her hands felt like silk whispering across his body, caressing his skin, molding the shape of his muscles, redefining him so that he became molten beneath her touch. "Like this, Carl?" she asked, her voice oddly rough compared to the gentle quality of her touch.

"Yes, yes, like that. I've dreamed of your hands on me, love, dreamed of having you here." Her hands felt exactly as he'd known they would, gently drawing him to the edge of a passion so dangerous it made him flush with heat, shiver with desire.

He groaned as her fingertips made teasing circles around his nipples and then began to inch down the arrow of dark gold hair that led to his belly.

He reeled under her probing fingers, his legs giving way and causing him to stumble back against the edge of the bed.

She followed him down to the mattress, her hands still doing their magic, calling his blood to the surface of his flesh so that he tingled all over. Her hair fell forward, touching his face, his upper body, while her hands continued to raise havoc on his lower torso.

She looked down into his face, her smile triumphant, her eyes glowing with pleasure, and kissed his mouth, her moans mingling with his to tell him how much she was enjoying her exploration of his body.

He could stand no more of the painful ecstasy. Swiftly he moved, turning her onto her back, grasping her hands in one of his and lifting them above her head. "My turn," he growled.

"Yes," she cried out, her body lifting to meet his touch.

He began to do an exploration of his own with his lips and his one free hand. Her skin was as firm and smooth as that of a peach, exuding a delicate fragrance as fruity and fresh. His tongue laved her breasts, flicked her nipples that were already erect, while his hand rubbed across the mound of her stomach and across her thighs. When his mouth made a path that followed his hand she cried out in anguish and he moved back up her body to press his mouth to hers.

They clung to each other, dizzy with need, their kisses deepening until their bodies could stand no more of the stress of waiting and then Carl knelt above her, perspiration marking his forehead, his hands trembling as they moved down her body to test her readiness.

She cried out, a soft bleat of pleasure and pain as his probing fingers opened her wide and then her own hand closed around him and she led him into the warm haven of her body and closed herself around him so that he was one with her and the world outside of them no longer existed.

THE SMALL SUITE of offices in the federal building seemed to be teeming with agents, all in a celebratory mood. Chief Wisher was holding up a bottle of champagne and the men were all laughing and talking at once.

Carl stood in the doorway for a moment and then stepped inside.

"Hey, Jones, Willow, how ya doin'?" he called out, waving to two of the men he'd worked with in the past. He turned to Mary Carlson, in her usual place behind her desk, the switchboard headpiece in place. "What's going on?"

"We cracked the Fresco case," the young, freckled redhead chortled, holding up a paper cup filled with a beverage that was still fizzing.

"Geez . . . well. That's great! Just . . ." He swallowed, forcing back the lump that formed in his throat and raised his voice. "Hey, guys, great news. Congratulations."

His eyes moved to Harvey Wisher who shook his head slightly and then smiled consolingly at Carl.

The biggest case in this area, in the past decade, the Fresco case had been in the works for three years, and a dozen agents, most of them in this room now, had been assigned to it. One of those agents had been Carl himself, until he almost cost them their cover by being in the wrong place at the wrong time. He'd been trying to help a young girl who wanted to get out of the town of Fresco and away from the corruption that had contaminated almost the entire teenage population of the small, rural Minnesota community, but his heroic gesture had cut no ice with the chief; Carl had been immediately called in from the field and reassigned to other cases that came into the bureau.

Wisher's conciliatory smile told Carl that the chief knew he was feeling left out of the glory, a little cheated, but that he respected Carl for hiding his true feelings in front of the others.

Carl accepted the cup of champagne a fellow agent brought him and raised it to join in the toast Harvey Wisher was making to the team, while his mind reviewed the report he'd come in to make about his own case. He was going to have to enlighten the chief about his relationship with the Kellers and he dreaded the possibility that Wisher might see it as just one more complication that might foul up the case.

Memories of his night with Joanna flooded forward instantly, making him choke on the drink. God, she'd been so beautiful, so incredibly responsive and giving. She'd been worth it; worth the chief's disapproval if that happened, worth any sacrifice it cost him.

Despite the sacrifices he was willing to make, he wondered about what kind of future he could hope to have with a woman who had already lost one man to the dangers of police work and had such a fear of death that she could hardly say the word, even with her son's death imminent. All that aside, what about his own commitment to keeping his personal relationships superficial as long as he continued his career in the service?

"Donay, did you want to see me?" Wisher's voice penetrated Carl's musings. Carl blinked, looked around and saw that some of the men had left, leaving only a small group to finish off the last bottle of bubbly.

"Yeah, I do," he said, nodding, following Wisher into his office.

"And you admit you're actually involved in a relationship with this Keller woman?" Wisher asked, when Carl had made his confession. He was toying with the ubiquitous rosary, stopping every now and then to make a note on a pad on his desk.

Carl sighed. "Yes." His palms felt damp, his throat dry.

"Well, Carl, I appreciate your honesty," the chief said shaking his head. "But I don't really see that this concerns our case in any way unless you let the Kellers distract you from the job at hand. As you know, this assignment requires all your concentration." He chuckled. "You don't have any reason to connect the woman and boy to what's going down over at Argylle, do you?"

Carl shook his head, still sifting through the emotions that arose over the knowledge his relationship with Joanna wasn't a problem, as far as the chief was concerned.

But what if it would have made a difference? Wasn't this another example of how he followed his emotions first and then sorted out the results later? He looked at the kindly man across the desk and wondered if the chief had ever had any doubts about himself and his career choice.

"Look, Chief, I'll resign if you think it would be better," he blurted, hardly aware he'd intended to say that.

The older man looked startled and then his expression firmed as he looked Carl right in the eyes.

"You're certainly jumping the gun on this, aren't you? I just told you I don't see you breaking any rules. Unless..." He frowned and leaned forward. "Do you want out, Carl, is that it?"

Did he? Carl ran a hand across his forehead and through his hair. If he quit now it would change his relationship with Joanna altogether. As a private citizen, a lawyer, he'd be able to promise her security—a life free of risk.

But, no. Nobody could ever make such a reckless promise to another. Too many factors could come into play to skew the best intentions of any man. One was at risk every day of one's life. Just getting out of bed in the morning could prove hazardous to one's health, considering all the freak accidents reported in the newspapers.

And anyway, what kind of personal security would he have if he had this unfinished business hanging over his conscience the rest of his life, never knowing if he could have brought the case to a successful conclusion? Plagued by personal doubt, would he be a fit attorney for any client, a fit companion for a woman like Joanna? Despite her fears, Joanna was a much braver stronger person than she realized. Put to the test, he was sure she would always be a survivor. She deserved a man who was one, too.

"No, Chief, I don't want out. Not yet."

"Good. Good. Because I'll tell you something, Carl. I have a very strong feeling about this case and about your ability to resolve it. If I didn't, I wouldn't hesitate to replace you, because God knows this one is as important as the Fresco case, or any other we've had to deal with."

Their handshake was a firm commitment to the special, if peculiar, friendship that existed between them.

CARL ADJUSTED THE VOLUME on the portable radio strapped to the arm of Mark's chair and tucked the lightweight blanket around the boy's waist.

"Okay, now you're sure you'll be okay over here?" he asked for the third time, looking up again to make sure the tree afforded Mark enough shade.

"Go already," Mark said wryly, making a face at the older man. "You fuss worse than Mom."

"Okay, well, we'll stay right at this end of the pool, and you can call out if you need anything."

"Carl, this is my first time out in the world in almost a year, will you please let me enjoy it?"

Carl grinned sheepishly and nodded, walking backward away from Mark, waving as he went.

Mark chuckled and then laughed heartily as Carl, not looking behind him, stepped over the edge of the park pool into the water. Joanna's laughter joined with her son's as Carl's body sent a fountain of water splashing upward, spraying the concrete deck and their towels and clothing.

He came up sputtering and shoved water at her with the heel of his palm when he saw her amusement.

Mark sat in the shadow of the tree and watched his mother and her lover cavorting in the pool and his heart filled with gladness. He knew they were lovers though Joanna would never admit it to her son.

But Mark wasn't as naive as his mother hoped he was. The glow about her, the chemistry between her and Carl, were so obvious that any ten-year-old would be able to recognize the signs. He'd had sex education courses in school before he'd become bedridden, and a few dates that had given him an inkling, at least, of the mechanics of sex. If he'd missed anything, television and videos had filled in the gaps.

Whenever Joanne and Carl were elsewhere in the house together, he could hear scuffling and giggling and whispers. When they were in his presence they could hardly keep their eyes off each other and his mother had taken to blushing like the proverbial farmer's daughter.

Like now, for instance. He put his sunglasses on so they wouldn't be able to detect that he was watching them. Their antics in the water were innocent enough, maybe, but then he saw his mother's hand go up to caress Carl's head and Mark recognized the tender, loving gesture she so often used on him.

She loves him! It wasn't just sex, it was love. The thought both frightened and exhilarated him. If he was any judge of people, both Joanna and Carl were too sensitive, too caring, not to suffer from emotional pain when the relationship came to an end. And it would. Mark knew it would, knew his mother would go into a tailspin when he, Mark, died. Grief and guilt would make her deprive herself of the joys of love.

Mark had tried so hard to enlighten her, but she was stuck with the old teachings, the old messages that taught that everything had to be paid for, that it was selfish to be too happy. She believed in death even though he'd shared with her the many metaphysical theories that espoused there was no death just as there was no time. But because she clung to her belief in death, she also clung to the belief that she must suffer over it.

He sighed and shook his head, sadly. Carl wasn't much better. He clearly saw himself as set apart from the rest of the world, partaking of life's pleasures only momentarily, until the next assignment took him off to other places, other people. He probably didn't even know he loved Joanna, probably wouldn't be able to admit it to himself for fear he'd be committing to something he didn't feel he was entitled to.

"What a pair," he whispered, and sighed again.

"Bored, young man?"

Mark jumped, startled by the voice behind him, and turned to see an old man sitting on a bench just a few feet away. "No, sir," he said, chuckling wryly. "Hardly that."

"Got problems?" The man scooted to the end of the bench nearest Mark and peered at him over the top of his wire-rimmed spectacles.

"No, sir. Not problems. Just thinking about how people waste their time worrying about death instead of enjoying life."

"Ain't that the truth." The old man smiled toothlessly and nodded his head. "Just come from the mission. Now there's a place they do just what you said. Always preaching about life after death. I eat their soup and drink their coffee and wonder why they don't preach about life *before* death, when it might do a man some good."

"Exactly," Mark said excitedly. "That's right on, sir."

In the pool Joanna looked over Carl's shoulder and saw Mark talking animatedly to an old man seated on a bench near Mark's chair.

"He hardly looks sick," she murmured.

Carl turned to look at Mark. "I know. His color's better and he seems a lot stronger. You don't suppose the doctors could be wrong?" He squeezed water off the end of his nose and brushed his wet hair off his forehead.

Joanna shook her head, tiny droplets of water spraying around her and turning to crystal in the sunshine. "No. Dr. Michaels told me not to be misled by days of increased strength. It's one of the peculiarities of leukemia."

A soft breeze blew over her wet skin just as a cloud passed in front of the sun. She shivered and Carl immediately wrapped his arms around her. He turned her in the water so that his own back was to Mark, putting Joanna momentarily out of Mark's line of vision.

"Be grateful for the good days, Joanna," he whispered, brushing her lips with his own, for emphasis.

She kissed him back and nodded. "I am. Very grateful."

Funny that one minute she could feel such sadness and the next such dizzying excitement. She slid a hand up over the wide, hard expanse of Carl's chest and moved her torso closer to his, feeling the familiar ache of need that his body engendered in hers.

He smoothed her hair back with both hands and tilted her head slightly so that he could kiss her without moving their bodies. He could feel himself growing hard as her hips pushed against his and he thought again about how perfectly her height matched his.

"God, I want you," he gritted, slipping one hand down beneath the water to clutch her buttocks and pull her closer.

"I know," she said huskily, gasping as his arousal pressed at her loins. "We'd better swim," she said, her voice made hoarse by desire.

"Yes." Carl dived away from her, immersing himself in the cold water, swimming underwater toward the other end of the pool.

They'd come early because Joanna said no one ever used the pool the morning of Memorial Day. It was the day the pool opened for the summer and few people visited that part of the park before eleven o'clock. Most people were at the picnic sites, reserving spots early, before the crowds descended on the park.

But a swimming pool was a seductive place for two people who had just become lovers. Something about the combination of water, fresh air and little clothing had a decided influence on one's libido. The fact that they had the pool to themselves only made the temptations greater.

It had been Mark's idea that they take a swim. The original plan had been just to get Mark out to the park, maybe have a picnic. But Mark had remembered the pool and how much his mother loved to swim and he'd insisted the adults bring their suits and have some fun of their own.

Carl leaned against the concrete wall, panting from his sprint through the water, and watched Joanna swim lazily but steadily down the length of the pool. She moved through the water as she did on land—gracefully, smoothly, efficiently. He loved to watch her walk, the way she carried herself with no apology for her height and with the poise and self-assurance one usually associated with royalty.

When they'd first arrived at the park, Carl, seeing Joanna's eagerness to get in the water, had suggested she change and go in while he got Mark settled. She'd hesitated for a minute, considering her duty, but the call of the water had won out.

He remembered how his breath had faltered when he saw her walking from the changing house to the pool in her pink-and-yellow flowered bikini. She looked like a model from the swimsuit edition of *Sports Illustrated*. Her body was lithe and perfectly shaped, her skin smooth and lightly tanned. He was suddenly glad there wasn't a crowd there. He didn't want to share the sight of her with strangers.

Only a couple of days since they'd made love and he could hardly stand to be near her for fear he'd grab her and embarrass both of them, while at the same time he could hardly stand to be away from her for more than a few minutes. He could see now why newlyweds needed a honeymoon, time to be alone, to get the first flush of desire satisfied to the point where they could stand to be parted.

"You look very pensive," Joanna called out, stroking through the water toward him. She eased herself into a tread a few feet in front of him, grinning happily as she swept her hair back and took a couple of deep breaths.

"I was thinking about chicken and sandwiches," he lied, returning her grin.

She cocked her head and studied his face, her arms scissoring across the top of the water. "You're lying, Donay."

"Now how do you know that?"

She suddenly ducked under the water and in a moment Carl felt her hand at his groin, firmly cupping proof of his lie. She surfaced just inches from him, but kept her hand in place.

"Stop that," he whispered roughly.

"Then tell me what you were thinking about."

He cleared his throat. "Fried chicken."

Her hand tightened around him and he groaned.

"Now the truth."

"You," he grated, clutching her against him, "you, dammit."

She released her hold on him and smoothed her hand up over his flat, hard stomach to his chest, her lips nearly touching his. "Yes, and you're never going to lie to me again, right?" Her fingers teased over one of his nipples and brushed idly at the circle of golden hair around it.

He kissed her lightly and drew back to squint at her. "Two can play at this game, you know."

She was too fast for him, jumping backward and diving off to her right to swim away.

Carl laughed and then groaned again as the water swirled against the tension in his groin. "You're not going to get away with this," he called out.

She laughed over her shoulder. "What are you going to do about it?"

"You'll see."

"When?"

He swore under his breath and tugged his suit away to ease the strain. "As soon as I can get away from this damned wall."

Over on the grass Mark and the old gentleman grew silent, caught up in the frolicking and laughter that rang from the pool.

"Makes me wish I were young again," the old man muttered.

"Makes me wish I were going to live to be old," Mark said softly.

The man turned and stared at Mark.

"How long?" he asked finally, his expression merely curious.

Mark shook his head. "Not long, now, I think. Probably not past Christmas."

"Your people will miss you," the man remarked, the first hint of sadness crossing his face. "It's hardest on the ones left behind."

Yes, Mark thought, and it will be harder on those particular two people than most, and sighed again at the hopelessness of the situation. But then, he knew, they had to play out their life plans just as he had to play out his. Only they could change their thinking to free themselves to find their way back to each other, if they were meant to be together.

With sudden clarity he realized that his dying might very well be part of the scheme of things, the catalyst that would drive a wedge between them so they could learn from it, and grow, and come back together with a deeper understanding of love.

CHAPTER SEVEN

JOANNA BENT to kiss Mark's cheek as she retrieved her book from his nightstand. "I'll sit in the rocker and read for a while, just until you fall asleep, kiddo."

"Mom," he called softly, just as she'd adjusted the gooseneck lamp and settled in her chair, "thanks for today."

She smiled over at him and then frowned. "But we shouldn't have kept you out so long this first day. You're overtired."

"Yeah, I know I am." He shifted his body with effort so that he could see her better. "But it was worth it. I met this great old man in the park, got to watch the kids playing. And I got to see you having fun for a change."

She put her book down and strained forward, her legs folded tailor fashion on the seat of the rocker. "I always have fun with you, honey-bunch, you know that."

Mark sighed. "Yeah, but that's different. I mean with other people."

"No, you don't, Mark, you mean with Carl."

"Yeah." The word seemed to trail off and Joanna realized Mark's medication had kicked in. Only a moment more and he'd be asleep.

And then he said, very clearly, "Even though it was fun, Mom, I don't expect you to drag me along on all your dates."

Words of protest came immediately to mind, but she realized the boy wouldn't stay awake through half of them, and besides, she really didn't want to have to clarify her relationship with Carl. Especially not to Mark who had a talent for seeing through her motives as if he had emotional radar. "Go to sleep, Mark. We can talk later."

She picked up her book, making a show of ending the discussion. But it was hard to concentrate on the words. Last night, and again today, had been such a wondrous time, both satisfying and frightening, that she could think of little else.

She had only to think of Carl and the butterflies in her stomach would begin their fluttering dance, making her shaky and lightheaded. His lovemaking had been everything she could have hoped for, but there was so much more—the humor they shared, his compassion and respect for Mark, their similar tastes in so many things from food to music. And their debates. She loved them. They made her feel so alive, so filled with another kind of passion.

Had she had that kind of communication with Sam? She didn't need to think about that for long. She knew she hadn't. Oh, she might have wanted to initiate sex, or argue a point, or refuse his request, but she hadn't acted on any of those wants; she had merely bowed to what she had considered his older, wiser, male superiority.

She chuckled softly, glancing over at Mark. Asleep. She rocked a little in the chair and folded her arms in front of her to hug her waist. When had she stopped thinking in terms like "male superiority"? After Sam died? Much later? Maybe some of the books her son insisted she read had raised her consciousness, after all.

When they'd made love, she'd been—what had Carl called her? Oh, yes. His little volcano. *"You can be so quiet, so utterly composed, and one would think the fire's gone out for all time. And then, suddenly, you erupt and flame up and pour hot lava all over me."*

She'd been so moved by his description of her. She really had never thought of herself as having a unique persona, as having a sexual mystique. His insight had freed that last ounce of reserve she'd been hiding behind all these years, making her feel young, sure of herself, and incredibly desirable.

Determinedly she reopened her book. She'd sent Carl home when they'd returned from the park at twilight, because both she and Mark needed quiet time after the happy rigors of the day. She shouldn't be getting herself worked up with her musings.

The phone, turned low for the night, burbled softly. She snatched it up before it could penetrate Mark's medicated sleep.

"Are you settled for the night?" Carl asked, his voice low and compelling.

"More or less. Mark's had his meds and is sleeping for now. And I'm . . . reading."

His laugh was gently mocking. "What were you thinking about?"

"Chicken salad," she answered promptly, stifling a giggle.

"Hmm. Great minds think alike." His voice was a seductive purr in her ear. She clutched the phone with both hands, wishing he were here, or she was there.

"What have you been doing?" she asked softly. She could visualize every corner of his apartment now that she'd been there.

"Well, first I showered. Then I puttered around doing odd jobs. Then . . ."

"What jobs? Tell me."

He laughed. "Every move I've made?"

"Yes," she said, eagerly. "Every gory detail."

"Okay. First, I cleaned the filter on the microwave vent."

She settled back more comfortably in the rocker and took a deep, satisfied breath.

She could picture his kitchen; she could see him bent over the sink, scrubbing the filter, wearing only jeans, his upper body and feet bare, his hair and skin glistening damp from his shower. She could see the curve of his spine, the breadth of his shoulders, the rounded muscles of his upper arms bulging with every movement. His hair would fall forward over his forehead as he worked, and he'd have to brush it out of his way with his forearm since his hands were both busy.

"Then...let's see. Oh yeah. Then I grabbed a beer and went in to watch a bit of the news on cable."

She imagined him sprawling back on the lounger, one leg over the armrest, one arm behind his head. She could see the strong column of his throat as he tilted his head back to swig the beer.

Her hands remembered the feel of that neck as he'd arched above her, calling out her name. She swallowed to relieve the sudden dryness that burned her own throat, and willed her heart to slow down.

"Then what?" she urged, her voice reedy.

"Um, then I worked for a while, going over some files I've been neglecting."

The desk in his office was mahogany, she remembered. Large, old, slightly scratched, a secondhand buy he'd told her, with history he could only guess at. Did he wear glasses when he worked? She'd seen a pair on the desk top. They must be his. The image of him in those glasses, still half-undressed, made her heart feel as if it could overflow at any moment.

"Did you get a lot done?" she asked.

A heavy silence ended with a telling sigh. "It's hard to concentrate when my mind is filled with thoughts of you."

She liked his honesty, his directness and the fact that they shared the same dilemma. It made it easier for her to admit to her own feelings. And after all, with time so much a factor in their relationship, she didn't want to waste a second playing games.

"Maybe we should have arranged for someone to be with Mark again tonight," she said in a near whisper.

"Yeah. Or at least I could have stayed there with you. We could have found something quiet to do together while Mark slept."

The silence this time was hers, myriad images of ways to share quiet time with Carl buzzing through her mind. She decided it was time to change the subject.

"What are you going to do now?" she asked.

"Take a shower."

"Another one?"

His voice was a low growl. "Yeah, as many as it takes."

Picturing him in that exotic bathroom filled with plants, under the shower made her hand shake so badly she almost dropped the receiver.

"Do cold showers work for women?"

"I don't know but the thought of you in the shower is doing crazy things to my libido." His laugh was short and shaky.

"Maybe we'd better hang up now," Joanna said, though she hated to part with the sound of his voice.

"Right. But I'll see you tomorrow," he said.

She clutched the receiver to her chest for a few minutes after she hung up, feeling disoriented, shaken, excited.

Tomorrow. She'd be surprised if she'd be able to sleep at all with that promise ringing in her ears.

She shook her head, reminding herself she wasn't some starry-eyed teenager. It was time to check on Mark.

She leaned over the bed and pushed his hair off his face. He'd got a little sun today, giving his skin an unaccustomed glow. He looked almost healthy, almost like any normal, sleeping seventeen-year-old boy. His hand twitched slightly, against the sheet, and she looked down at it. He'd been a nailbiter, but somewhere along the way he'd given up the nervous habit and now his nails had to be clipped periodically. Long, thin, bony hands that she suddenly saw promised to be much like his father's had been. At rest, lying against the sheet, they seemed to have a life of their own.

These hands could grow into the hands of a surgeon or, with those long fingers, a pianist. She smiled and shook her head. Maybe not, he was a little old to start a career as a pianist, and a little tone-deaf, besides. She should have been one of those mothers who forced piano lessons on her kids when he was eight years old, then maybe he'd have a chance.

But these hands will never grow to be those of a man.

The thought struck her with sudden, brutal clarity, bringing home to her as nothing else had done, how brief a time remained for her child. She doubled over as pain spasmed in her solar plexus, leaving her momentarily breathless. She shut her eyes, concentrating hard on regaining her composure.

When she opened her eyes, the dim glow of the lamp seemed at first to brighten, then recede. How could she have been so blind, so stupid? She'd convinced herself she could cheat time when all the while she was simply cheating herself of what precious little time she had to spend with her son. Like a squirrel storing nuts for the long cold winter ahead, she thought, she should be storing every minute of Mark's life for that bleak time ahead when all she'd have would be the memories.

She had mental scrapbooks of all her loved ones. They were all she had and she'd learned to call them up, to browse through them when the pain of loneliness became too great to bear. But she'd had no warning with the others as she did with Mark. It was a great blessing that she was given this knowledge so that she could use every minute wisely. And here she'd been squandering it on an affair that could never be anything more than a temporary alliance.

She stood up and began pacing agitatedly, her thoughts spinning. Wasn't this the very thing she'd warned herself against when she first met Carl? How had she so quickly forgotten her resolve? She had worked so hard to spin a web of solitude around herself and Mark—to keep him with her as completely as possible. Yet in the blink of an eye she'd let her guard down. She'd let Carl into their world and let him take her out of it.

She went to the window, needing to see the night sky, to lift her face toward what she'd been taught to believe was the source of all power.

Dear God, her prayer began, but just at that moment she saw a light go on on the third floor of the Argylle building.

Seconds later a strange tableau played itself out in front of the window about ten feet from where Joanna was standing, as two men appeared from out of nowhere, seeming to be struggling with each other. Suddenly the arm of one man came up, striking at the other man. The second man seemed to crumple in slow motion and then fell from sight. Holding her breath Joanna watched as the attacker bent and then began a slow, jerky movement away from the window, as though he was dragging something heavy.

She let her breath out in a strangled gasp and took a faltering step backward. Had she just witnessed a murder? Her own vulnerability swooped down on her as she realized how visible she was if the murderer returned to the window and looked down to see her there. She moved quickly to turn off the floor lamp, heedless of the table she knocked over on the way, sending the phone careening to the floor.

"Mom... Mom, what is it?" Mark called out groggily from the bed.

She spun around and then hurried to his side. "Mark, there's someone up on the third floor next door... I think... oh, God, I think he killed him..."

"Mom?" Mark eased himself up against the headboard, shaking his head to clear it. "You saw something at Argylle?"

The hum of the phone that lay on the floor penetrated her consciousness. "Police. I should call the police." Quickly she set the table back up, returned the receiver to the phone and began to dial 911.

"No!" Mark cried out. "Mom, call Carl."

She held the receiver away, a puzzled frown on her face. "Carl?"

"Yes. This is probably something to do with the case he's on."

"The case?"

"Mom, you know he's no private detective...he's some kind of agent, I'll bet. And he should know what's going on over there. The police might just get in the way of what's really going down."

She had to look up Carl's number in the phone book, her fingers trembling and missing pages, her eyes blurring at the tiny print, the long columns of similar names. What if he wasn't listed? She searched the Dor's, swore softly when she realized she was looking under the wrong letters, recounted the alphabet under her breath and paged back to the Don's.

He answered the phone on the second ring. "Joanna, get away from that window," he ordered as soon as she'd described what she'd seen. "I'll be over there as fast as I can."

He hung up without another word.

She replaced the receiver, turned the lamp off again and hurried over to Mark's side. "He's coming," she said breathlessly.

She plunked down beside her son without ceremony and caught her breath. "What if the murderer leaves before Carl gets there?"

"Mom, you don't even know there's been a murder. And even if there has been, the guy will have left clues, they always do."

"But what if they're still there, and Carl gets h—"

Mark grabbed her arm and shook it. "Don't even think that way, Mom, just think positive thoughts."

She wanted to go back to the window, to see if she could detect anything else. But Carl had ordered her to stay away, and she knew she didn't want the man at Argylle to see her, to know she'd been a witness to his crime.

The minutes seemed to pass endlessly. Joanna and Mark spoke in low tones, stopping every now and then to listen, when one or the other thought they heard a sound from next door. Finally the waiting was too much.

Joanna got up and moved toward the door. "I'm going out to the back porch."

"No, Mom," Mark begged. "Someone might see you."

"I'll be careful," she promised over her shoulder. "You just stay here."

The screen door from the kitchen to the porch needed oiling. She stopped with a jerk as its rusty squeak echoed in the night; she held her breath, listening to hear if there was movement at the back of Argylle. Nothing. She let her breath out on a soft, tremulous sigh and eased around the door and onto the porch, creeping along the wall to the far end where shadows would hide her and where she would have the best vantage point of the Argylle loading area.

She'd lost track of time when she finally saw a figure, crouched low, come around the side of the building and up to the loading platform. He straightened and she saw it was Carl. She clenched her fist to her lips to suppress the urge to call out to him as he hoisted himself up onto the dock and crept over to the smaller entry beside the huge loading doors. In a moment he disappeared from sight and Joanna realized that this waiting was going to be almost unbearable. She crept to a wicker chair and settled into it, planning to stay there until Carl reappeared.

After a half hour had passed, with no sound or sign of human movement from next door, Joanna could wait no longer. What if Carl had been discovered by the murderer? What if he was hurt? What if the killer was still there, holding Carl prisoner?

And what could you do about it in any case? she jeered at herself.

"I could get out and call the police," she whispered aloud. The sound of her own voice in the otherwise silent night was all the impetus she needed. Moving stealthily, she made her way off the porch, down the path to the wooden door that opened onto the alley. She walked on tiptoe, her ears alert to any sound that would send her scurrying back to the safety of her own yard.

All was silent.

By the time she crept up the concrete steps to the loading platform, her heart had gone into overdrive. Her mind was telling her that the relentless silence could easily mean that Carl was dead.

And when she reached the door, it occurred to her that she'd given no thought to how she'd achieve entry into what would most likely be a locked building. Carl, in his position as receiving clerk, might have a key. If not, he certainly would have been trained to get past any barrier, key or no.

The door had been left open a scant inch, either by the fleeing murderer or by Carl in his haste to penetrate the building. She pushed it cautiously, and the redolence of exotic spice assailed her, causing her head to jerk reflexively.

The scent, wafting from the building out into the neighborhood, had always been distinctive, and mildly pleasant. Within the confines of the building, however, it was a harsh, caustic odor that clogged the back of her throat and burned her nostrils. An urge to sneeze conflicted with a desire to cough and she quickly covered her mouth and nose with one hand.

From her visits here as a child, she should have remembered the impact of that first assault to the olfactory senses.

What she did remember was the layout of the building. The room she was in had floor-to-ceiling bins along the wall to her right; the outline of the forklifts lined up in front of them was barely visible in the dark. To her left, and some distance down the room, she recalled, were the workbenches where the cases of processed and packaged spices and herbs were labeled for shipping.

She let her eyes become accustomed to the dark and then detected a faint glow coming from across the cavernous shipping/receiving area. As she headed toward the light she saw that it was coming from the corridor beyond, the door at the end of it wide open. She moved forward, certain the source of that light would help her find Carl.

The light, she found, came from a cold drinks vending machine, midway down the hall on her right. Doors she passed along the way were all closed. She hadn't the courage to try any of them, but moved steadily, slowly onward, listening for any sound that might indicate other life in the building.

It took her a long time to get to the third floor, using the stairway, lit only by recessed nightlights above the door at each landing; her movements were hampered by shaky stealth and a positive dread of what she might find.

The door from the stairwell to the third floor opened directly across from one of the two laboratories. Large expanses of window showed her that the lab was uninhabited, an eerie glow reflecting on stainless steel surfaces from the electronic eyes on various machines around the room. One of the labs, she knew, was a kind of research kitchen where the home economists experimented with alternative uses of herbs in new recipes.

Her father's office had been located on this floor, around the corner at the end of the hall. For a moment, as she stood against the wall, catching her breath, getting her bearings, she could almost pretend she was seven years old and hiding from her father's secretary who was supposed to be keeping an eye on her while her father was in a meeting with Mr. Argylle and the other executives.

There, in the dimly lit passage she almost giggled as she recalled the exasperated face of Miss Cavenaugh when the secretary finally located Joanna.

Joanna Banana. She could hear her father's voice booming down the corridor as he ran to scoop her up into his strong arms to swing her around. *We'll go have a Joanna Banana Split and won't Mom be surprised when we can't eat our dinner.*

Oh, she'd loved him so. He'd been so big and protective, so warm and funny. Everybody loved him. Mr. Argylle had told her that at the funeral, hugging her thin, preadolescent shoulders awkwardly, his eyes brimming with tears.

Joanna hadn't set foot inside this building after her father had died. Until tonight.

A faint sound penetrated her reverie, bringing her back to the present, to the threat of the danger that hovered around her.

It had come from her right, the direction of the executive offices. She tiptoed in that direction, holding the wall to control her steps.

She saw the light as soon as she rounded the corner. It was spilling out of the open door of the office that had once been her father's. At the same time she heard the low mumble of a man's voice.

Inch by inch she moved on, straining her hearing to make out the voice, the words.

"... sure ... no,   no   sign ... positive,   Chief ... whoever ... got away ..."

Carl! It was Carl's voice. Was he talking to the killer? Were they holding him at bay with a gun? She quickened her step as quietly as possible.

"It's definitely the saffron, chief," she heard Carl say as she made a fast, silent dash across the hall and crouched against the wall between a trash basket and the open door. "It must have come in after plant hours. It's sitting right inside the dock doors, plainly marked."

Joanna held her breath, waiting to hear the answering voice. But there was none. Only silence. And then Carl spoke again. "Yeah, Chief, I think that's our best bet. I'm positive Argylle himself is clean and he's the only one who can make sure the stuff doesn't get processed. Right now we have to clear up this other mystery."

Another pause. "Oh yeah, no doubt about it, this definitely implies an insider, though Joanna Keller didn't mention that she recognized either of the men."

He was speaking on the phone. And that meant he was alone in the building—except for her, of course—and that the other men had disappeared. She expelled her breath on a heavy sigh of relief and started to push away from the wall, using the trash basket for leverage. It fell over with a resounding clatter.

Joanna bent to pick up the basket just as a voice behind her yelled, "Freeze!"

She spun around and found she was staring into the barrel of a gun.

CHAPTER EIGHT

JOANNA'S CRY OF FRIGHT collided with Carl's shout of surprise and in the confusion of the moment the gun clattered to the floor and Joanna fell backward onto the trash basket.

"Joanna, are you hurt?" Carl caught her arms and pulled her forward, freeing her from her entanglement with the blasted metal container.

"Only my pride," she snapped, jerking her arm away so that she could rub her bruised bottom. "What the hell did you think you were doing with that...thing?" She gestured angrily at the gun. Even lying on the floor it looked lethal. Residual fear made her tremble.

"What the hell are you doing here, anyway?" Carl shouted back as they both stared, with distaste, at the weapon. God, what if his trigger finger had acted involuntarily? He'd heard that happened more than the authorities liked to admit.

Joanna glared at him, her heart still doing an erratic dance in her chest. "I came to make sure you were all right," she ground out through clenched teeth. Why was she still trembling, when the danger had passed?

"I told you to stay away!"

"Yes, but you didn't tell me what to do in the event that you were killed," she snapped. She leaned against the wall, rubbing her arms. God, it was so cold in here. Her gaze fell to the gun again and her teeth began to chatter.

Carl saw that she was suffering from shock and was instantly contrite. He drew her into his arms, holding her stiff, unresponsive body against his own, and rubbed her back. "I'm sorry. I didn't mean to frighten you like that," he whispered against her silken hair.

His breath on her sensitive scalp only chilled her more. She shivered and leaned into his strength. Muddled thoughts—conflicting and dismaying—made her feel out of touch with reality. Images appeared in her mind and then fragmented in tiny explosions like sentences breaking off midword.

Carl's hands on her back, large and comforting... Mark's hands... Carl's hands holding that gun... Mark's life dwindling away... Carl in a life-threatening, death-dealing job... Sam falling backward, a gaping bullet hole in his chest... a huge clock with the hands swinging around at breakneck speed... Daddy... Mother...

"My head feels like a popcorn machine," Joanna whimpered and slid down Carl's body in a dead faint.

She came to, blinking to adjust her eyes to the lamp on the table beside her and then looked down at herself and saw that she was lying on the couch in her own living room, a pillow under her head, her grandmother's afghan tucked in around her.

She started to sit up but Carl came dashing into the room. "Don't sit up too quickly, Joanna. Be careful."

He dropped the wet cloth he was carrying and helped her ease into a sitting position. "Better?"

"Yes." She looked around. "How... when?..."

"I brought you back over here when you fainted."

"Fainted? Don't be silly, I never fai—" She recalled everything then, the whole night, as if in slow motion.

She started to get up. "I have to see Mark."

Carl held her back, gently but firmly. "Mark's fine. I've just been with him and I've explained everything. He agreed that you'd just had a bad scare."

A bad scare? She stared at Carl as if seeing him for the first time. Big, handsome, gentle, loving, sexy Carl. Her friend, her lover.

And then her mind replayed the vision of his body looming over her. His legs were spread apart, his arms held stiffly before him, his hands clasped together around a large, ugly service revolver. His eyes were cold steel, his jaw set in murderous determination that drew his lips into a thin, cruel line.

She shook her head to clear the image and swallowed the bitter saliva that formed in her mouth. Her stomach lurched uneasily. She suddenly remembered the moments at Mark's bedside, just before she'd become distracted by the action over at Argylle; she remembered her conviction that her involvement with Carl had been a mistake, that she should be devoting every minute to her son.

"I'm feeling fine, now, Carl," she said coolly, "really. I'd like to go in and reassure my son that I'm all right."

Carl studied her face and admitted that she did look better. But there was something missing that he couldn't put a name to. He shrugged and stood up, holding out his hand to help her up.

She ignored his offer and moved past him without a second glance.

He realized then what was missing: that special look of warmth, of intimacy, that he'd come to expect when he looked into her face.

He sat down and slumped back against the cushions. The hollow feeling that started in the pit of his stomach moved to his legs. So, it was over. It had happened before and he should have become inured to it, but somehow this time he'd thought it would be different.

This time it was worse. This time he'd fallen in love.

The futility of that realization struck him a fresh blow of pain.

He gazed around the room. It was filled with Joanna's history. There was nothing of himself here, never would be. He'd come into her life briefly and would leave her life unchanged, when he was no longer a part of it.

He should go. There was no sense hanging around, prolonging the agony. Joanna didn't want him and the sooner he got out of her life the faster he'd begin to pick up the pieces to rebuild that wall around his heart.

But he couldn't seem to find the strength to lift himself off the couch. Like biting down on a sore tooth, he relived those moments up in the Argylle plant when he'd heard the sound out in the hall and rushed out, gun at the ready, to confront the enemy. He'd been prepared to shoot—to kill. His memory was quite clear about that.

He would never forget the horror in Joanna's eyes as he held the gun, poised to fire directly into her face. It was the sort of memory recurring nightmares were made of and, with a sinking heart, he realized that those nightmares were all he and Joanna would share in the future.

His mind cleared and suddenly he saw the purpose in the turn of events. It was all for the best. There was never going to be a future with Joanna, anymore than there'd been with the others. What had happened tonight had given him a chance to get out of the involvement before it became impossible to do so without complications. And what was better yet was that Joanna was the one who had withdrawn, allowing him to escape without first inflicting emotional pain. All clean and easy, like a surgeon's cut.

He stood up with renewed vigor. He could go now with a clear conscience. No use staying around to mess it up with empty phrases. He could spare Joanna, and himself, that much.

He let himself out without putting that final goodbye into words.

HARVEY WISHER THREW the pencil on the desk in a gesture of disgust and laid back in his swivel chair with a groan of fatigue. "It's just not there, boy," he said, referring to the computer printouts they'd been poring over for hours. "Nothing to tell us which of the Argylle people might be involved."

Carl lifted the smaller stack that contained less than half a dozen printouts. "We've got these possibles."

Wisher grunted and rubbed his eyes. "Doesn't seem like enough evidence to warrant putting any other men on the case."

"I disagree, Chief. I know it's here. It's right in front of our eyes and we're not seeing it because it's so simple, so obvious. We bring some fresh eyes in on this, they're going to see what we're missing. For one thing, how did this John Morton get his hands on the thirty thou we found in his savings account?

"And this one—" he slapped one of the printouts on the desk "—this Bill Harold. Mixed up with some pretty militant groups in college."

"With no record," Wisher pointed out.

"But exactly the type to get suckered into a cause."

The chief didn't look convinced. "If I had to pick one," he said, grudgingly, letting his chair return to an upright position and reaching over to poke through the slim pile, "I'd have to say this one."

Carl took the paper from his superior and glanced at the name at the top. Scott Levinson. His eyes moved down the page of dot matrix print. "Arrested at seventeen, driving a stolen car. One year at Chelton Reformatory. Picked up twice in the next couple of years, suspicion of armed robbery. No convictions. Busted in a bar fight two years ago. Found him holding weed—but not enough to pin a dealer rap on him. Looks clean the last couple of years—or careful. Sounds like a punk to me."

"Yeah. Just tainted enough to be our candidate," the chief said dryly. "Well, let's get photos on these people. All of them." He gestured toward the larger pile. "And have your Mrs. Keller see if she can identify any of 'em."

Not my Mrs. Keller. Not anymore.

"Um, couldn't we turn that part of it over to the guy you bring in to track down these possibles?"

Wisher squinted thoughtfully at Carl, who kept his head lowered. He shrugged tiredly, and reached for his source of comfort. The beads of the rosary slipped between his fingers with practiced ease. "Okay, we'll turn the paperwork over to Mick Johnson. Meanwhile, we'll contact Mr. Argylle, make sure the saffron isn't processed and let him know you're on the inside, keeping an eye on things."

He watched Carl leave, the agent's shoulders slumped in a gesture that bespoke more than just common fatigue. Wisher's mind played back what Carl had told him about the physical set-up of the operation.

Maybe it was time to check it out himself. If they were fortunate enough to gather enough information to make a bust on this end, he'd be better off knowing the layout of the place.

Tired as he was, and late as the hour, Wisher got his car out of the underground garage and pointed it in the direction of the small industrial area across the river.

JOANNA PUSHED the carpet sweeper back and forth across the worn Persian rug, with a vengeance unwarranted by the minimal amount of dust there. For a week she'd been trying to eliminate the hollow feeling within herself. She'd used a variety of strategies. Today it was heavy-duty housecleaning. Tuesday and Wednesday she'd gone on a food binge and only succeeded in proving to herself that her stomach would not tolerate a sustained onslaught of gluttony. Thursday and Friday she'd beleaguered Mark's bedroom until he'd begged for some privacy.

Last night he'd asked about Carl, forcing her to look him in the eyes as she admitted they'd stopped seeing each other by mutual, unspoken consent. For once Mark hadn't argued with her, or questioned her decision. He'd merely nodded, picked up his book and allowed her to take her pain back to the privacy of the kitchen.

She had purposely avoided the window in Mark's room, and the backyard, during the hours the Argylle plant was in operation.

She recalled that Tuesday, a man, introducing himself as Special Agent Michael Johnson and offering her his credentials, had appeared at her front door. He'd taken a stack of photos out of his briefcase and urged her to look them over carefully. None of them looked anything like the two men she'd seen in the window on Monday night, but then she'd only seen the one man briefly before the other had felled him, and only seen both of them in profile.

Johnson had asked if he could see the window from which she'd viewed the struggle and when she took him into Mark's room, he agreed it would have been difficult for her to give a really accurate description of the men. Her only sense of them had been that the assailant had been taller than his victim, and that both men had been dark-haired, though that could have been the effect of lighting behind them.

The agent had been friendly to Mark, answering the boy's questions with careful openness and cautioning them to keep the doors locked at night and to stay away from that window.

Joanna hadn't asked, nor had Mark, whether Carl was still on the case, and neither had encouraged the man to stay longer than the time he needed to analyze the events of the previous evening.

As he was leaving, Mick Johnson had turned back and asked if Joanna was willing to come down to the Federal Building and look at some mug shots.

"You think those men might have been known criminals?" she'd asked.

The young, husky man, who looked more like a truck driver than an FBI agent, had shrugged and smiled. "You never know. Terrorists, for example, sometimes move from cause to cause like soldiers of fortune, just going where the action is. We don't think these people are known to us, but we have to cover every possibility. If you agree to come downtown to examine the mug shots, we'd send someone out to stay with the boy, or pay for someone of your choice, of course."

She'd agreed she'd help in any way she could, and he'd said he'd let her know when she was needed.

Suddenly aware that she'd been sweeping the same area repeatedly for the last ten minutes, she jerked the sweeper up and carried it out to the kitchen.

Maybe it was pointless to expect her mind to relinquish thoughts of Carl as long as the mystery next door remained unsolved. Surely once that case was resolved she'd be able to get on with her normal life.

Even her dreams had been penetrated by Carl and the business at Argylle. Each nightmare ended with a vision of Carl pointing a gun at her head and the smell of spices acrid in her nostrils as the sound of Carl's voice yelling, "Freeze," startled her into wakefulness.

Lying wide-eyed in the dark waiting for her heart to stop racing, her thoughts would carry her back to those moments she'd lain in his arms at his condo, their bodies heavy with pleasure, their spirits lightened by joy.

How could hands that had so gently traced threads of ecstasy across her flesh have held that gun with such muscular determination? How could a voice so tenderly croon words of love one day, utter that single word of violence the next? And how could she, a woman whom death had robbed, love a man who dealt in it every day of his life?

For love him she did, despite the fact that he was completely wrong for her and regardless of the fact that she would never go back to him again.

Sleeping or awake, she couldn't escape the pain, and the void within her seemed to yawn wider with each passing day.

She jumped, startled, as the doorbell chimed, almost causing her to drop the sweeper she was still holding. She glanced at the wall clock. Three o'clock. The mailman? She hurried to the front door before the caller could ring again and disturb Mark's afternoon nap.

Harvey Wisher stared at the vision before him, his mouth agape. Even dressed in faded jeans and ragged-sleeved sweatshirt, her silver-blond hair carelessly pulled back, Joanna Keller was a beautiful woman. Her eyes gazed steadily into his own and he felt his heart lurch with misgiving. Pain in those eyes could not be disguised despite the impersonal, polite smile she gave him.

"Yes? May I help you?" Her voice was well-modulated, her manner gracious.

He cleared his throat. "I'm Harvey Wisher." He reached inside his jacket and withdrew his badge and identification. "I need to speak to you, Mrs. Keller, about this business over at Argylle."

He followed her into the house, his trained eye quickly assessing the quality of the furnishings, the warm feeling of continuity that the very walls seemed to reverberate.

She led the way into the front parlor, a room that seemed almost to be awaiting their arrival. Wisher chose a straight-backed chair beside a round, cherry wood table with cabriole legs.

Joanna sat in a bentwood rocker near the front window. Sunlight, peeking in between the panels of sheers, frosted her hair and gave her face an incandescent glow.

She gestured for him to begin.

"Apparently you know one of my men—Carl Donay."

She nodded, her face expressionless. Only a slight narrowing of her eyes betrayed the least hint of response to Carl's name.

"And you know we have a...situation next door."

"Yes." She sat perfectly still, not taking advantage of the rockers on her chair, her hands folded in her lap.

"Frankly, Mrs. Keller, I'm here because I need a favor."

She waited.

Wisher cleared his throat. His hands twitched as if he was wishing he'd brought his rosary with him. Instead, he reached into his pocket and felt around for loose coins, turning them over and over between his fingers as he pushed ahead.

"You see, the situation over at Argylle calls for an increase in surveillance at this point. It's not going to be enough for Carl to be there during work hours. Obviously those men you saw earlier in the week are involved in this case and have access to the building after hours."

She'd begun to move, just slightly, the chair rocking almost imperceptibly.

"Mrs. Keller, I need to have a man over here, at night, so that if anything goes down he'll be able to get over to Argylle instantly."

The rocking increased in tempo, and the facade she wore to hide her agitation slipped. He rushed on. "I could assign another man, but this is Donay's case, and I feel I owe it to him to have this chance to see it to its ultimate resolution."

She shook her head and squeezed her eyes shut tightly. *Carl here, in the house, all night, every night for God knows how long? No!*

"No," she said.

"I wish I could fill you in on all the details, Mrs. Keller, so you'd know just how important this is. Can't you just take my word that I wouldn't inflict this imposition on you if it wasn't in my best judgment, absolutely imperative? Well, Mrs. Keller?" He sat forward, his tone stern, his expression suggesting he would not accept refusal. "I could appeal to your sense of patriotism, but I think you know I wouldn't be here if it wasn't necessary, so I won't insult your intelligence with melodrama."

The set of her chin, the firm line of her jaw, betrayed her resistance.

He stood up and shook his head sadly. "I can't force this on you, of course. Fortunately, Agent Donay is still a young man, so I guess it won't kill him to live in his car for a few weeks, or so.''

He moved in for the kill when he saw the confusion of expressions that chased across her countenance. "You know, the government would reimburse you for the expense of having Agent Donay on the premises."

Joanna stood up abruptly, her hands clenched in fists at her sides. "It certainly never crossed my mind to ask for money, Mr. Wisher."

"Ah . . . I see. I'm sorry, Mrs. Keller, I didn't mean to insult you. But so many people will only help our cause when it means lining their own pockets." He smiled wryly. "Usually the same people who yell the loudest about how we don't do enough to protect their lives and their property."

She knew he was backing her into a corner, knew she'd regret ever having opened the door to him. Despair welled up in her, choking the words in her throat. "I . . . I suppose . . . if this is the only way? . . ."

He nodded and his face softened with sympathy. "The *only* way, Mrs. Keller."

"When . . . when would C . . . Agent Donay? . . ."

"This evening, if that's not too inconvenient. We've wasted a week already and we don't know how much more time we've got."

With a quiet dignity Joanna saw the man to the door. He had appealed to her sense of duty and she had seen no way out. Now she wondered whether the excitement might prove more than Mark's fragile health could tolerate. What was she going to tell him?

So preoccupied was she with that thought, that she barely heard her caller's final words of gratitude and farewell. The blood roared in her ears as she clung to the doorjamb and visualized Carl here in her house every night, his presence a constant reminder of all she most feared and, worse yet, all she most desired.

CHAPTER NINE

CARL MOVED IN at seven o'clock that evening, carrying a briefcase and a single pullman bag containing a week's change of clothing. Joanna led the way up the narrow staircase to the second floor and awkwardly gestured to the smaller of the two bedrooms. It had been Mark's until it had become more expedient to move him down to the bedroom on the first floor.

"The dresser is already empty," she said, from the doorway. She cleared her throat and avoided his eyes. "I only use the closet for seasonal storage—it's cedar-lined—but I'm sure there's room in there for whatever..."

Carl stood in the middle of the room, still holding his briefcase, and drank in the sight of the woman he loved, the woman who had turned from a warm, passionate, happy person to this withdrawn, polite, impersonal creature who wouldn't meet his look.

"I'm sorry about the inconvenience, Joanna," he said. "I wouldn't have accepted this arrangement if my boss hadn't been adamant."

"It's...it's all right." She started to turn away and then turned back, her eyes beseeching his. "Carl...please, I don't want Mark upset, or too excited. It might be too much for him to handle."

He couldn't stand the revulsion he saw in her face. Did she think he'd let any of the business from next door touch her or Mark? She would never have experienced what she had last week if she'd stayed over here in the first place.

"That won't happen, Joanna," he said curtly. He turned away, setting his briefcase beside the nightstand, prepared to unpack.

Joanna stared at his back, broad and muscular beneath the soft cotton striped shirt. He seemed to fill the small room, his vibrancy overpowering the quiet charm of old furnishings and country decor.

"Have . . . have you had dinner?" Her throat felt rusty, the words snagging on their way out.

Still bent over his luggage he turned his head toward her and grimaced. "You don't have to play the polite hostess with me, Joanna. I can get take-out for my meals."

This seemed the perfect moment to tell him—no, warn him—about the lie she'd told Mark. The necessary lie. She'd told Mark that she and Carl had decided to live together. If Mark knew the truth, he'd become obsessed with that window. He'd want to help and he would ply Carl with questions and endless speculations about what crime was going down next door. The constant excitement could only take its toll on him.

But the steel-gray hostility in Carl's eyes turned her blood cold, made the words stick in her throat. She needed time, a few moments to recover from the shock of his actual presence here in her home.

"There's no question of your eating take-out, Agent Donay," she snapped. "I have to cook anyway and besides, if you're going to be staying here, you might as well do your best to make it look as though you're part of the family."

Carl sat on the bed and listened to Joanna's footsteps descending the back stairs, his body in an attitude of despair, his hands clasped under his chin. Jesus, did the chief realize what he was doing when he'd suggested this arrangement? How could he be expected to concentrate on his job while living under the same roof with a woman he loved but who hated him?

To add insult to injury, her point about fitting in was a perfect example of how she was operating on cool reason while his thinking was muddled by emotion. He had to chill out, maintain a professional veneer. And maybe "acting as if" would help heal the wound that seemed to tear his insides apart.

In the kitchen, Joanna leaned her head against a cupboard and prayed for inner strength. How could she maintain a cool, impersonal facade if she was tempted to express her anger every time she got near Carl? Had he seen that that anger was fed by hurt and frustration? Oh, she was an utter fool to have agreed to have him stay here but she wasn't going to make the situation more volatile than it already was by allowing herself to be so vulnerable to his every word, his every gesture.

She straightened up, opened the cupboard and took down the canister of coffee. She had to pull herself together, for Mark's sake. He was particularly sensitive to tensions and, if he was to believe the lie she'd told him, she'd have to work out an agreement with Carl and act accordingly.

She filled the pot with water, centered the basket over the pot and sat down to wait for the coffee to filter through and for Carl to come down for dinner. She had to warn him about the cover story she'd invented for Mark to explain Carl's presence in the house.

She was just sipping the first cup of hot brew when she heard sounds from the front of the house that set her heart hammering. Carl had used the front stairs and had gone straight to Mark's room!

She dashed into the room just as Mark was saying, "Man, I'm so glad you and Mom worked out your differences and that you've decided to live together. To tell you the truth, Carl, I don't think I could have stood another day of Mom's moping around when you guys weren't seeing each other."

Carl's eyes had darkened to pewter as he glared at her across the room. Joanna's fingernails dug into the palms of her hands clenched in fists at her sides, and her breath seemed to come in painful gasps from her lungs. Mark's head turned from Carl to Joanna and his smile encompassed both of them.

"Mom, hi! I was just telling old Carl here, what a real little Nellie Sunshine you've been to live with this past week." His voice vibrated with happiness. "Thank God I've got someone here now to taste my food before I eat it. It's been a real hardship facing my possible demise at every meal."

His laughter turned to a cough and Joanna forgot everything else and rushed to the boy's side. Mark grabbed her arm, pulling her hand off the tank, and shook his head, the cough subsiding. "Noth—nothing to worry about, Mom," he choked out, settling back against his pillows. "Just a catch in my throat."

Relief weakened her knees, brought tears to her eyes. Joanna sank down on the edge of the bed and bent her face to her hands. "Dammit, Mark," she ground out. "Will you cut the nasty comments about my cooking or—" she lifted her head and forced a grin "—do I have to resort to the *Zucchini for Fun and Profit* cookbook?"

Mark clasped his chest and groaned, "Oh no, not the zucchini experiments again, anything but that!"

Carl stood, mouth agape, and stared at mother and son. In the blink of an eye they'd gone from the bombshell of Joanna's lie about the status of her relationship with Carl, to what seemed to be a fleeting panic about Mark's health, to the soft-shoe routine they did about her cooking. He sank onto the chair behind him and glared at them both. A guy could get a heart attack from those two. And here he was, forced to live with them for God knows how long, and expected to keep a professional distance on top of it.

They were laughing now, totally at ease with each other, ignoring him and acting as if nothing unusual had happened. And what about Joanna's lie? Did she expect him to move into her bedroom to convince Mark they were still romantically involved? Was he expected to touch her, kiss her, send her yearning looks as he'd done in the past, to keep Mark from finding out the truth about his stay here? He almost groaned aloud. No way could he pretend to be having an affair with Joanna, not without getting turned on every time they added a convincing little scene to the act.

Joanna stood up and looked over at Carl. "I've got fresh coffee in the kitchen, Carl. Would you care for some?"

Time to confront her, put an end to this nonsense right now. He stood also. "I'll help you get the cups, Joanna. It'll be a good start for getting settled in."

Mark's happiness was obvious. He felt around for the remote control for the television set as the two adults left his room.

Carl held his tongue in check until they were out of earshot of the bedroom but grabbed Joanna's arm just as they stepped through the doorway into the kitchen.

"What the hell was that all about, Joanna?" he demanded, turning her to face him. "That kid thinks I'm here as your lover, for God's sake!"

"Keep your voice down, Donay," Joanna said in a harsh whisper, reaching past him to shut the door into the hall. "And take your hand off me."

"Not until you tell me why you lied to Mark. What can you have been thinking of?"

She lurched out of his grip and backed away, her eyes flashing green and gold in her anger. "I was thinking of sparing him the stress of worrying about you, of becoming preoccupied with some kind of crime going on next door." Her bottom came to rest against the wooden kitchen table, trapping her as he took a long stride toward her.

"I...I didn't want him exciting himself with cops-and-robbers games. And he would. You know he would."

Carl halted midstride, the anger and confusion on his handsome face replaced by comprehension. Joanna took a deep breath, relieved that she'd been able to get through to him before he'd had the chance to touch her again. For just a moment, as he'd held her arm, her body had seemed to move with a will of its own closer to his.

Carl veered away from her and collapsed onto a chair at one end of the table, wearily running a hand through his hair. "My God, this is a mess, isn't it?" He wiped his mouth and looked up at her with a bleak stare. "Are we expected to act like . . . like we're . . ."

Joanna shrugged and rubbed her arm, still conscious of the feel of his grip there. "I thought it was the best way, that we could pull it off without a lot of deceptive . . . um, touching."

She lowered her eyes, afraid he'd read her real fear there. "After all, most couples reserve their affections for when they're in private."

Carl got up and helped himself to coffee, keeping his back to her, hoping she wouldn't know what a terrible task she'd set for him. A task far more demanding than any the agency had ever required of him. He drew a deep breath and put a stoic expression on his face before turning to her again.

"Of course. Shouldn't be too difficult. We're adults, we should be able to place the welfare of the boy before our own feelings," he said quietly.

"Yes." She eased past him and took her own cup over to the pot for a refill. When she sat down, a safe distance from him, she sipped her beverage in silence, wondering if he, like she, was remembering the last time they'd sat at a table sharing a cup of coffee.

"Joanna—" Carl cleared his throat and set his mug down "—we should talk about what happened last week."

He saw her go rigid at the mention of that terrible night and then her blond hair swirled in a silver wave around her face as she shook her head. "Nothing to talk about, Carl. I'm almost glad it happened, glad I had the chance to be reminded that this relationship was never going to be right for me. It brought me to my senses, and for that, I'm grateful." She stood up, bringing the discussion to a close before he could add to it with his own thoughts. "I have to get back to Mark now."

"I'll join you in a minute," Carl said as she opened the door.

"That would be nice—for Mark," she said quietly.

He found them deeply engrossed in a television program, both of them propped up against Mark's headboard, Joanna with her head resting against her son's shoulder. Joanna gestured toward the chair on the other side of the bed, where Carl could see the screen as well, but he opted for the rocker near the window, holding up some papers he needed to study.

Concentration was impossible. More and more his eyes were drawn to the two people on the bed. Now and then one of them would make a comment about the show they were watching, or a harmony of laughter would ring out indicating they had a common sense of humor.

Impossible not to remember Joanna in his own bed, less than a week ago. Her laughter, as silvery as her hair, had been of a different nature then, teasing, wanton, the sound of a woman sure of herself, sure of her man. He licked his dry lips and rustled the papers in his hands, determined to concentrate.

Joanna was finding it difficult to keep her attention on the program, her attention wandering to the chair beside the window, conscious of each creak of the rocker, each crackling of the papers in Carl's hands. The gooseneck floor lamp had been twisted so that the light fell behind Carl, creating an aureole of gold around his head as he bent over his work.

Her fingers, resting in her lap, twitched as she remembered the feel of that thick, luxurious hair as he had bent over her to nuzzle her neck. His mouth on her skin had been warm and soft, demanding and fulfilling, making her flesh ache for more. No man had ever so excited or so satiated her.

She shivered and snuggled closer to Mark.

Carl glanced out the window and then at his watch. Only nine o'clock. Nothing happening next door and he couldn't handle the strain in here much longer. If he went up to shower now, it would still be only nine-thirty when he finished. Too early for bed. What then? He supposed he could read for a while, kill some time that way.

But what would Mark think if he went up alone? How much did the kid know about sex and relationships anyway? He was seventeen already, and pretty hip. He probably knew more than Carl had at that age. He surely knew what "living together" entailed.

Carl cursed Harvey Wisher and Joanna silently and tried to force his attention back to his work.

Joanna wondered if she should suggest Carl might be more comfortable working in the study, but that might sound as if she was trying to get rid of him. And wasn't she? She wanted to keep her distance but she was beginning to feel as if there were an invisible thread spinning across the room, attached to each of them, pulling her in his direction no matter how determined she was to ignore his presence.

Besides, wasn't this part of the image of one big happy family that would keep Mark from guessing the real reason for Carl's presence there? She wriggled around, trying to get more comfortable and smiled apologetically at Mark when he turned his head to frown at her.

9:10. Carl sighed and glanced out at the Argylle building, a dark, silent shadow in the moonless night. Joanna and Mark were watching another program now, something about a couple of lady cops who were so caught up in their careers, they were having a hard time settling their domestic conflicts. The print on the pages in his lap was beginning to blur as he forced his eyes to stay focused there. He squeezed them shut and then rubbed them.

He had to get out of there.

He stood abruptly, saying, "I think I'll go up and shower." The papers fell to the floor and he bent to pick them up, nervously conscious of two pairs of hazel eyes trained on him.

"This early?" Joanna's voice seemed to have gone up an octave. She cleared her throat but it didn't help much. "Maybe we could play Scrabble."

"Well, I don't know . . . I have to be up early for work. And Mark seems to be enjoying his show." Carl was having trouble getting the papers back in order.

"No, that's all right," Mark said. "It's not all that interesting."

They'd played Scrabble before, all three on Mark's bed laughing over misspellings, arguing over the validity of words, challenging one another as if the game were a matter of life and death. Joanna and Carl had exchanged warm glances over Mark's head, bent in absorption over his rack of tiles, their message of growing fondness reverberating between them. He wouldn't be able to tolerate that kind of intimacy tonight.

"I still have more work to do," he said, "so I think I'll just have that shower and get back to it."

Joanna hid her face from Mark's puzzled frown, pretending to straighten the books on the table next to the bed, as Carl left the room. Thankfully Mark made no comment, returning his attention to the television set.

She lingered in Mark's room as long as she could, watching his strength diminish almost in perfect sync with the ticking clock. By ten-fifteen she could see she could put off his medication no longer and she administered it with shaking hands. He was asleep within ten minutes. She sat in the rocker and strained to hear sounds from upstairs, sure that Carl was still awake.

She wondered how she could relieve her tension. She couldn't go out for her nightly walk alone; Mark would find that too peculiar on Carl's first night in the house. He would ask too many questions and she'd be forced to lie again. The one lie that she and Carl were living together was becoming more of a burden than she could tolerate.

If she went upstairs this early with Carl still awake, would she be able to lie in the bedroom next to his and shut him out of her mind? Impossible. But if she stayed down here, puttering in the kitchen or curling up in the front parlor to read, wouldn't he think she was afraid to go up? Well, at least that would be a bit of truth in the midst of all the deception.

She'd take a bath. That would kill some time, and perhaps by the time she finished, Carl would be sound asleep.

The bathroom was still warm and steamy from Carl's shower, redolent of a masculine soap and after-shave. The soap, a fat, yellow bar was still in the dish, still damp to her touch. Dreamily she caressed the surface, visualizing its path over Carl's flesh, and then flushing with shame at her erotic fantasy, she snatched her fingers away.

Even with the door closed and locked, she found nudity strangely frightening with Carl only a room away and she hurriedly lowered herself into the tub, holding a washcloth against her throbbing breasts. The feel of silken bubbles and warm water against her skin only heightened her excitement, making it impossible for her to languish in the tub as was her custom.

A floor-length, long-sleeved, cotton nightgown seemed excessive in the warm house, but she pulled it on and added a chenille robe before leaving the bathroom, turning the lock as quietly as possible.

She tiptoed past Carl's room, cringing at the creak of a board beneath her bare feet, and then fled to the safety of her own room as if the hounds of hell were after her. She slumped against the door, turned the lock she hadn't used since she was a teenager and breathed an audible sigh of relief.

"Locking me in, or intruders out?" a voice asked behind her.

Joanna gasped and spun around. Carl sat on her bed, propped with apparent ease against her pillows, a book open in his hands, a smug smile on his face.

"What the hell are you doing in my room?" More than indignation heated her skin, set her blood thrumming wildly through her veins. She took a step forward, hands on hips, and became uncomfortably aware of her nudity beneath gown and robe.

What, indeed? What devilry had pierced the armor he wore to protect himself from her and sent him to her bedroom to lie in wait for her, knowing she'd jump to the wrong conclusion?

Perhaps it had been those moments he'd spent in her bathroom, smelling her soap, touching her washcloth folded on the rack, seeing a nearly transparent nightgown hanging from a hook on the back of the door. While in the shower he'd been so aware of her presence elsewhere in the house that he'd let his mind wander back to that dangerous memory of their lovemaking at his apartment and he'd had to punish himself with five minutes of ice-cold spray before he was fit to leave the confines of the bathroom.

He could feel his body stirring to life again as he gazed at Joanna, her cheeks flushed, eyes flashing gold anger, dressed in what were clearly her least seductive nightclothes.

"I needed to talk to you about this arrangement." He hoped she'd attribute the huskiness of his voice to the fact that he'd just showered.

"You needed to be in my bed to talk to me?" She could never control that schoolgirl squeal that came into her voice when she was overwrought. She hoped it didn't betray her vulnerability.

"The discussion I had in mind requires privacy—it was either my room or yours and I didn't think I could lure you into mine."

Lure? An odd choice of words, surely? he thought. He cleared his throat and hoped his expression didn't betray his momentary confusion.

Blindly Joanna felt her way to the chair beside her desk and lowered herself onto it carefully. *Lure?* Didn't that connote a seduction? She stared at him, bigger than life, sprawled on her bed wearing a navy, cotton robe that was open to the waist, exposing the gold hair on his chest and legs, proof that he wore little else beneath it.

Her mouth felt as if it had suddenly filled with sand and her heart beat wildly in her chest. "What... what do you want to... to talk about?"

He cleared his throat. "First of all, I need to set up a special voice-activated camera in a window that faces the windows on the east wall of Argylle. I know Mark's room is out of the question. I hoped you'd have another suggestion."

"A camera?" Something to do with his surveillance, his job, the reason he was here in her house. At least this was a concrete problem; reality was the best cold-shower treatment in the world. She forced herself to concentrate on a visual blueprint of the house.

On the first floor, the room next to Mark's was the study, a small library that had no windows, other than the two oval piano windows, inset with stained glass, on either side of the fireplace. All the rest of the wall space had been lined with floor-to-ceiling bookshelves. The next room, on that side of the house, was the kitchen, but those windows were set too far forward to allow any viewing angle of the windows at Argylle Carl would be interested in. The other rooms, back and front parlor and

Mark's bathroom were all across the hall, on the west side of the house.

That brought her to the second floor. Originally a long, narrow attic, it had been converted to two bedrooms divided by a linen closet, with the bathroom inconveniently located at the end of the row beside the room Carl was using. A very narrow width of hall ran the length of the second floor between the staircase and the four rooms.

She looked at Carl and blinked. "Other than Mark's, my room is the only one with windows that align with those at Argylle," she said with a sigh.

"What's the room between yours and mine?"

"It's a linen closet—no windows."

She held her breath as Carl nodded and gazed thoughtfully at the window across the room, the one that looked directly out onto the spice company. The shade had always been kept drawn there, even during the day, to insure privacy from anyone looking down from the third-floor windows at Argylle.

"So how would you feel about having the camera set up in here? It wouldn't take up much room."

"Would you have to be behind it?" she asked, her tone wry.

He grinned, unaware of the effect it had on her heart. "Only while I'm focusing it. And I'd have to check the tape every day."

She shrugged. "I don't see that that would be terribly inconvenient." She pulled her robe closed at the neck though none of her body was exposed and the room was uncommonly warm. "Was there anything else you wanted to discuss?"

"Well, I'll be placing an apparatus in a few key locations over at Argylle, so that if anyone shows up there after hours, I'll be able to hear them in my room. I'll try to keep the volume down so it doesn't disturb you, but of course it would have to magnify sound enough to wake me out of a sound sleep.''

Apparatus—a nice, polite way of saying "bug," she thought, controlling a shudder. "As long as it doesn't disturb Mark.''

God, she could be a regular ice maiden. Carl rubbed his chest unconsciously and returned her impenetrable gaze. "Another thing, Joanna—I don't see how we're going to pull this thing off with Mark. Frankly, I found tonight very uncomfortable.''

"That's because you aren't keeping your mind on your job, apparently, Agent Donay," she sniped, ignoring the inner voice that jeered at her duplicity. If anyone had had their mind on matters of a more intimate nature tonight, it had been she, not Carl.

Feeling protected by her dishonesty, she stood up, went to her dresser and realigned the framed pictures of her family, turning her back to the man on her bed. She wanted to demand that he pull his robe closed, covering the tempting display of masculine chest, but she knew that she dare not let him know she'd even noticed.

The smooth, cool feel of glass covering one of the portraits did nothing to erase the memory of the way that crisp chest hair had felt beneath her seeking fingers, nor the hard, warm flesh of his pectorals under her palms.

"I thought you'd made it part of my job to convince Mark that we were living together," Carl's voice taunted from behind her. "Given that, I don't quite know what's expected of me.''

She didn't know, either. "Just act natural," she snapped, turning around in a flurry of fabric that clung to her legs. "I don't have to write a script for you, do I?''

"Are you so angry because you've created a monster you don't think you can control?" he asked softly, swinging his legs over the side of the bed and rising.

"I can control it!" she insisted.

He ambled toward her, the fronts of his robe swinging perilously close to revealing more than she dared view. He came up short in front of her before she could take a deep breath. "Let's just check that out, shall we, love?" he asked in a near whisper. His breath fanned her face, a sweet seduction in itself.

Eyelids heavy, lips parted slightly, Joanna clung to the edge of the dresser as Carl's mouth descended to hers.

It was a delicate kiss, of such tenderness that it brought tears to her eyes. The gentle brush of his lips persisted but he made no move to touch her elsewhere, nor did he hold her in place. She could have moved away anytime she'd wanted.

She stayed where she was, her lips trembling against his, her body aching to close the space between them, and breathed in the heady scent of soap and warm masculine flesh.

Lost in the aching sweetness of the kiss, it took her a few moments to realize it had ended, that Carl had moved away from her. She opened her eyes. He was already at the door, had it open. His smile was grim, his eyes dark with controlled fury.

"Sure, you can handle it, Mrs. Keller," he said softly. "But that makes only one of us!"

The door closed behind him with a firm click.

CHAPTER TEN

THE TEMPERATURE TOOK an unexpected dive during the night, so that when Joanna, who hadn't slept anyway, got up to check on Mark, she had to go round closing all the windows. By morning it had begun to rain, turning the little house into a dark island, and Joanna went from room to room, turning on lamps.

She had already helped Mark use the bathroom and get dressed for the day, and was making breakfast when Carl came down the back stairs.

She had put the sleepless hours to good use, strengthening her resolve to maintain a safe distance from Carl from now on—admitting to herself that if she went anywhere near the flame, she was going to get burned. The danger, she recognized, was her own attraction to the man. She spent hours visualizing the two of them, living together in the house, dealing with any circumstances that might arise in a friendly, unemotional, circumspect manner. By morning she was convinced she had regained her emotional equilibrium and could carry it off.

Carl had dressed with respect to the change in weather. He wore a gray sweatsuit, which made him look cozy—warm enough for snuggling against. Joanna silently repeated the affirmation she'd chosen to help her get through and smiled brightly in his direction.

"Pancakes okay? It's one of the things we especially like on rainy days."

He appeared to have made a few resolutions of his own for he smiled impersonally, the way he might smile at any waitress in any café, and nodded. "Sounds good. Can I help?"

"No, thanks. It's all mixed and ready to pour on the griddle, and coffee's made. Help yourself."

He had to pass close to her to reach the pot on the counter but he managed the maneuver without touching her. Only the fresh scent of his morning ablutions caressed her in his wake, stirring the first little response in the pit of her stomach. She squelched the disturbing sensation quickly by chattering about the change in weather.

Carl listened to her as he sipped the good, hot coffee, and finally interrupted her to ask, "Are you always so cheery first thing in the morning?"

She blinked and stared at him, unable to resist asking, "Are you a morning grouch?"

He gave her a grave, level look out of unfathomable gray eyes. "Sometimes."

The natural next step in this dialogue was going to lead to a game of questions and answers she didn't want to play. She shrugged and turned back to the griddle.

"Is Mark up?" Carl asked.

"Yes. I left him in the back parlor, writing in his journal. There's a fire in there if you'd like to join him."

"Good idea."

The kitchen seemed darker after he'd gone, despite the fact that all the lights were on. She brushed that thought away and poured warmed syrup into a small pitcher.

Carl went into Mark's room first, to look out at the Argylle plant, closed for the weekend, before crossing the hall to the parlor where Mark was sitting at a game table, bent over a spiral notebook.

"Good morning, Carl," Mark called out cheerfully, looking up from his writing. "Come and toast your buns by the fire."

Carl groaned and threw himself down on the chintz-covered sofa. "God, two morning birds in one house. I'm not sure I can take it."

Mark laughed, a happy, full-bellied sound that made fun of Carl's irritation and only irritated him more.

"Mornings are beginnings, pal," Mark said, ignoring the older man's derisive expression. "Meant to be a celebration. Just think, every day you wake up, you realize you've been given one more day of life. Not such a small gift when you think about it."

"Did you make that up or are you quoting one of your metaphysical gurus?" Carl grouched, but he felt ashamed, knowing the boy had every reason to celebrate any morning that he woke up to.

Joanna came into the room, bearing a tray. "He serves up a mixed bag, that one, quoting and philosophizing all at the same time. Mark, move your stuff off the table."

Carl jumped up to take the tray but Joanna had already reached the table, set it down there. "You guys start while the food is hot, I'll just go get the coffee."

They ate quietly, enjoying the sound of rain pouring from the gutters outside the parlor window, the crackling of wood burning in the fireplace, the homey click of forks against china.

"You don't need man-made music on a morning like this," Joanna said softly when the log in the fireplace made a small explosion of sound.

Carl was beginning to feel better, the cozy warmth of the room softening the hard edges of his night of frustration. And it was impossible to be with Joanna and Mark for any length of time without being drawn into their easy camaraderie.

"I'm a little tired, Mom," Mark said, suddenly putting his fork down. Carl turned to the youth and saw he'd grown pale, his eyes looking larger than usual with a darkening of the skin beneath them.

"Do you want me to get the chair, hon?" Joanna asked calmly.

"I can walk it," Mark said. But as he got to his feet, Carl saw him stagger slightly and without hesitation he leaped to his feet, lifted the boy into his arms and carried him across the hall to Mark's bedroom.

Mark was wheezing when Carl pulled his quilt up over him and his face felt clammy to the touch. "Easy, kid," he whispered, and went to get Joanna, his heart hammering in his chest.

Joanna was sipping her coffee and staring dreamily at the fire. Carl stopped in the doorway and stared at her askance. "Joanna, aren't you going in to Mark?"

She looked up, her face serene. "Did he ask for me?"

Carl frowned. Was this the same woman who'd reached instinctively for the oxygen tank when the boy had coughed the night before? "No, but he's obviously not feeling well."

Joanna's smile was grim, her tone wry. "Well, of course he isn't, Carl, he has leukemia."

"Well, aren't you going to do anything?"

"He's had his morning medication. He'll sleep for a while now, and then wake up feeling good for a few hours." She started to stack their breakfast dishes. "What you've just seen is his response to too much excitement, more activity around the house than he's used to. Our lives have been quiet and sedentary for good reason."

Her eyes, the color of honey in the lamplight, measured his angry stance. "Just think what kind of effect it would have on him if he was aware of your real reason for being here."

"But last night you panicked when he started to cough and—"

"Carl," she interrupted, "don't you think I know which symptoms to panic over? Coughing is one of those signs that he's in trouble. Fatigue is a natural response to stress, the medication and of course the disease itself. And I try not to overreact to his illness when it really isn't necessary. He hates thinking of himself as sickly."

She'd finished clearing the table and was just about to remove the tray to the kitchen. This time Carl was alert and hurried across the room to take it from her, glad of a chance to cover his embarrassment, though he did mutter an apology as he turned away.

He was at the door when she stopped him, her hand on his arm.

"Carl, thank you for being so concerned about my son."

Her face, turned up to him, seemed to glow with the inner warmth he'd so reveled in during their good times together. "No problem, Joanna," he said in a near whisper. "He's a very special kid. You've done a great job raising him."

A sudden and unexpected burning behind his eyes made him turn quickly to continue his trip to the kitchen.

Joanna stared thoughtfully at the wall and wondered if she'd only imagined the sheen of tears in his eyes. She decided to give him a few minutes to collect himself, busying herself by adding a couple more logs to the fire and rechecking the damper.

When she went out to the kitchen he was gone. Just as well, she thought, these emotion-filled episodes were dangerous to two people determined to keep their relationship platonic. But God, if she were in the market for a man, and their lives weren't so adverse, Carl would certainly fit any woman's dream of a sensitive, caring man.

She filled the dishwasher, went back to check on Mark and, satisfied that he was sleeping comfortably, went up to the front parlor to read until it was time to unload the dishwasher and start thinking about lunch.

She was almost dozing over her book when the doorbell startled her. She grumbled as she went to answer it, thinking the bell had rung more often in the past two weeks than it had all year.

Carl stood on the porch, a large black leather case beside him.

She stared at him, confused. "I thought you were upstairs."

"I had to go and get the camera," he said, nodding at the case. He was wearing a plastic raincoat over his sweatsuit and his wet hair had begun to pull up into curls that fell over his forehead. His cheeks were wind-reddened, his eyes the color of the dark gray sky overhead.

"Oh."

"And I didn't have a key to let myself back in."

"Oh, my goodness. Yes. I'll have to give you one."

They stared at each other until rain from the porch eaves dripped onto Carl's neck, making him shiver. "May I come in?" he asked finally, his eyes crinkling at the corners.

She stepped back, flustered, and laughed nervously. "You might as well," she said, "since you're living here."

"Is it okay if I go into your room to set this up now?" he asked.

"Sure." She glanced from his hair to his rain-soaked sneakers. "But hadn't you better get out of those wet shoes and take a hot shower first? You could catch a bad cold."

His grin, somehow brighter than usual against the wet sheen of his face, made her stomach lurch unexpectedly.

"Are you going to go all maternal about me, now that I'm staying here, Joanna?" He swiped at the water that trickled down his face.

"I wasn't thinking about you, Donay," she snapped, turning away, "I just can't have Mark exposed to cold germs."

But while she was putting dishes away, she heard the water pipes rumble the way they did when someone turned on the shower, and she had to laugh to herself.

A thick hearty stew with homemade bread for dinner would be perfect in this weather, so she decided they could make do with a light lunch. Mark had eaten only half of one pancake and wouldn't eat much more than that for lunch, but Carl, she knew, had a man-size appetite. She mixed up a batch of dough for bread, set it to rise and began to prepare lunch, all the while listening to the sounds overhead.

She knew that Carl had spent about fifteen minutes in the shower because she could hear the pipes shudder again when he turned off the water. Then a few minutes later, she heard the sound of the bathroom door opening and then his bedroom door closing. She'd just finished kneading the dough when she heard his footsteps in the upstairs hall, heading toward her bedroom.

By the time she'd heated some soup and turned the cheese sandwiches on the griddle, Mark was awake and calling to her and Carl was descending the back stairs, asking if that good smell was lunch and did she need any help. It occurred to her in that moment, as she tried to answer both of them simultaneously, that it was really rather nice to have a man in the house again, even under these circumstances.

The rest of the weekend passed in much the same way. The weather kept the three of them indoors with most of their meals taken in the back parlor in front of the fire. Carl spent a lot of time, it seemed, checking the tape in the camera and going over papers he'd brought with him. Once or twice she heard him on the phone but good manners kept her from eavesdropping.

Saturday night they watched television with Mark. On Sunday night Carl and Mark played chess while Joanna shampooed her hair and then brushed it dry sitting in front of the fire.

Carl, passing through the hall to go to the bathroom, caught sight of Joanna, on her knees in front of the fireplace, her head bent forward as she brushed her platinum tresses. Her hair fairly crackled as it reflected the firelight in a halo of pink and gold. He held his breath and continued to gaze at the lovely sight of her slender body in fluid motion.

It was only Mark's voice, calling out, "Your move, Carl," that brought him back to his senses so that he was able to slip out of the doorway before Joanna discovered him watching her.

Joanna was thinking about how helpful it was to have another adult around the house.

Carl had carried logs up from the basement bin where she kept them stored, and filled the boxes in both parlors. He offered to help prepare meals but she refused, fearing the intimacy of shared chores in the kitchen. So

Carl spent the time with Mark, which was the best help of all. The boy obviously liked Carl and had begun to banter with him as he did with Joanna.

On Monday morning, Carl left the house about fifteen minutes before most of the Argylle employees started arriving for work, driving his car around the block to park it where he had before he moved into the Keller house.

Joanna found herself hovering at the window in Mark's room until she realized she was hoping to get a glimpse of Carl at the loading dock and then she made herself stay away from the window altogether.

She knew he wouldn't be home for lunch but would go to the café he usually lunched at, keeping his routine normal. The house seemed unnaturally quiet without his presence and she found herself glancing at the clock frequently as the day dragged on. Suddenly fixing the noon meal for just herself and Mark seemed almost pointless and she took special pains over the evening meal that the three of them would share.

CARL USED THE PHONE BOOTH on the street near the café to call the office. The chief came on the line immediately, his voice hearty with excitement.

"Carl, we've had a break. Interpol telexed pictures and dossiers on two of the islanders they know to be part of the group that dreamed up this nasty little bit of sabotage. They are sure these guys have slipped into the States. It's heating up, my boy, and, if Interpol is right, we may catch ourselves some prime fish any minute."

Wisher's excitement was catching; Carl felt his insides begin to rev up with that peculiar adrenaline that flooded the system when an agent knew he was on track.

"I want you to pick up this stuff and have Mrs. Keller look at the photos. If she recognizes either of them, we'll know the perps are already here and have begun to set the operation in motion.''

Carl agreed to pick up the dossiers after work. He hung up, popped another quarter into the coin slot and dialed the Keller house.

Joanna's voice was even softer, more compelling, on the phone. He cleared his throat and forced himself to concentrate on his reason for calling.

''I have to pick something up at the agency before I come home. Will that be a problem for you? About dinner, I mean.''

''No...no. Of course not.'' Did he only imagine she sounded disappointed?

''It'll only make me about forty-five minutes late—I'd have had to drive around for a while, until the last stragglers left Argylle, anyway.''

''Yes, of course. Don't worry about it. I was planning to roast a chicken—I'll just put it on later than I'd planned.''

''You could just go ahead without me,'' Carl offered, ''and I can eat leftovers. I don't mind, really. Or I could pick up something at a drive-in.''

''No, no. Honestly, it's no problem to wait. We don't usually eat much before seven anyway.'' There was a long pause and then she said, ''We'd rather wait for you.''

He was smiling when he hung up, enjoying the warm feeling the conversation had given him. Suddenly he envied the guys he worked with at Argylle who complained about the demands of being husbands and fathers. He'd never thought much about the little things, like the lunch pails most of the guys carried. Now he could imagine Joanna packing him a lunch, maybe even making his sandwiches with that good homemade bread of hers.

He rounded the corner and Argylle Spice loomed up in his view, reminding him that he wasn't like those guys. He wasn't an ordinary employee of Argylle and he didn't have a wife like Joanna. He could never have a domestic life for any sustained period of time.

As he approached the front door of Argylle, he couldn't help but glance over at the little house next door, nor could he control the overwhelming feeling of "home" that came over him at the sight. Inside that house was everything any man could ever hope for, all the things he had been denied all his life.

Or denied myself. His heart was heavy as he entered the building and walked down the hall toward the time clock. To be perfectly fair, though, he hadn't had the kind of childhood that would have inspired him to choose those things in the first place.

It had been only drizzling when he walked back from lunch. When he got to the rear of the building, where shipping and receiving was located, the rain had increased and was creating a silvery curtain beyond the open loading doors.

The trucks wouldn't come in in this kind of weather, but would pull over to the side of the road until the rain let up. Jack sent the crew back into the stacks to check inventory and move stock forward by date; busy work he saved for otherwise idle time.

The work kept Carl's mind occupied so that he wasn't able to dwell on the past, or on the terrible prospect of that day when this case would be concluded and his stay in the Keller home would come to an end.

He was grateful for the mind-absorbing work; otherwise, he'd be champing at the bit, anxious to see the stuff Wisher had for him, anxious to show the photos to Joanna. *Anxious to be with Joanna.*

HE WAITED UNTIL AFTER dinner, when Joanna was alone in the kitchen, stacking the dishwasher, to bring down the file Interpol had sent. She had the radio on a station that played romantic tunes from the fifties and she was humming along with the music as she worked.

Carl sat at the table and called her over.

Joanna dried her hands and looked over Carl's shoulder. "That one!" she cried, shaking the dishtowel at the top photo.

He looked up, surprised. "You're that sure? It's in black and white and a little grainy so—"

"No, no," she interrupted. "It's him, the one that hit the other one." The man's name was typed across the bottom: Jan Podanski.

Carl picked up the second photo, feeling the excitement build within him. "And is this the one that got hit?"

Joanna stared at it, leaning on Carl's shoulder without thinking about what she was doing. She frowned, squinted, tilted her head to the side and then said just as emphatically, "Uh-uh. This one I've never seen before."

She looked at Carl. "Maybe," she said softly, "the guy who got hit was the inside man at Argylle."

"Yes, I suppose that makes sense." He'd twisted his head to look up at her, and as their eyes met, she became aware of her arm on his hard, muscular shoulder. His eyes had warmed to pewter gray and she felt the shock of his desire right down in the deepest part of her body.

His voice seemed to come down a long tunnel when he said, "If Podanski killed him, there should be a missing employee at Argylle. I guess I'd better check it out."

CHAPTER ELEVEN

HE'D NEVER WANTED Joanna more, or any woman as much. He knew his face had betrayed his desire when her cheeks flushed and her eyes widened with shock. He might have made a move to touch her anyway, taking a chance that she wanted him, as well, despite her moral objections, but she had dropped a viable clue into his lap and his professional training had kicked in, taking his mind off his libido.

"That's great reasoning, Joanna," he enthused. "And why didn't I think of it?"

She was both grateful and disappointed that the moment had passed. Even as he spoke she was moving away from the compelling heat of his body, going over to wipe an already clean counter.

"Because you're too close to it? Because it's too simple? Because you're a man?"

Laughter felt good after the momentary sexual tension, clearing the air perfectly.

Carl turned around in his chair and gave her a menacing look. "Feminist cheap shots?"

She laughed again. "Hey, I didn't make the situation, I'm just calling 'em like I see 'em."

He wanted to bottle that laugh, to find a way to make her do it more often. He wanted to hear it last thing at night and first thing in the morning. Well, maybe not very first thing in the morning.

He stood up, moved his chair back and started toward her.

Joanna held her breath as he moved toward her, his eyes darkening with serious intent, his movement catlike. Was he going to embrace her, kiss her, make love to her? She thought of the way he'd kissed her that first night he'd moved in, and the hours of sleepless tossing and turning she'd experienced afterward.

She backed away, still clutching the dishtowel to her middle. "Don't Carl," she said, a warning note in her voice.

He stopped just a couple of feet from her and held his hand out. "Don't what, Joanna?" he asked softly, "Don't ask you to dance with me?"

"D-dance with you?" She'd barely noticed the radio playing while they'd been talking. She became aware of it now, aware of the sweet, lilting melody she remembered from her teens. "H-here? Now?"

He took the dishtowel out of her hand, tossed it on the counter and pulled her toward him. "Here, now. Dance with me, love," he urged gently. "This may be the only place and the only time we ever get to dance together."

He didn't know why he wanted it so much, but suddenly it seemed imperative that he have one more memory to store in his growing cache of memories of this beautiful woman.

When their bodies first touched, Carl had to take a moment to remind himself that this was only going to be a dance. He took a deep, steadying breath and moved his arm around her waist.

She danced, as she did everything else, with fluid grace, following his lead as though they'd danced together every night of their lives. She'd been that way in bed, he recalled, her body matching his stroke for stroke, thrust for thrust.

"I haven't danced in years," she murmured against his shoulder.

"It's like riding a bicycle," he whispered against her fragrant hair, "Or driving a stick shift."

She drew back a little, to look up at him. "When was the last time you danced?"

He cocked his head to the side, and thought about it. "February 8, 1984."

"You remember the exact date?" She giggled, missed her step and sighed when he tightened his arm to pull her in on the next beat.

"It was my birthday. I was in Beirut, on assignment. I'd made an error in judgment, so I was alone in my hotel room, feeling sorry for myself, when I remembered that it was my birthday."

The music had stopped, but neither of them noticed; they continued moving, the next tune catching up with them as he continued his story.

"So, I decided to give myself a birthday party. I went to a club where a belly dancer zeroed in on me and made me dance with her."

"A belly dance?" She laughed heartily.

"Sure. What's so surprising about that?"

"Just a little hard to picture, is all."

He looked down at her and pretended to frown. "Come on, Joanna, use a little imagination. What do you think lovemaking is if it isn't just a belly dance done horizontally?"

She snuggled in closer, hiding her face against his chest, not wanting him to see that she could remember all too well just what lovemaking was like and how well he moved.

He knew what she was thinking. She could tell in the way his breath hissed against her hair, the way his arm tightened at her waist, his palm heated against hers.

"Wrong subject," he muttered.

"Yes," she whispered.

They kept dancing.

After a few moments she drew back again. "What did you mean when you said you'd made an error in judgment? How?"

He looked sheepish, an expression she hadn't seen on his face before. It was rather endearing.

His eyes looked off in the distance, over her head, as he recalled the events.

"We were working with Interpol. I was supposed to be following a guy who would presumably lead us to the ringleader of a terrorist group whose members had been slipping in and out of the country bombing foreign embassies. The guy made a detour—went into a house where a woman was apparently waiting for him. I saw, through a window, that they were about to make love. I figured they deserved privacy. I went across the road, sat down to wait him out and fell asleep. When I woke up, he'd gone."

She knew she shouldn't laugh, but the whole episode just begged for levity, despite the look of chagrin on Carl's face, the tone of regret in his voice.

"You think that's funny?" he said wryly.

"Actually, I don't believe you," she answered.

"It's true."

Her grin faded, replaced with a look of surprise. "I can't imagine you ever making a wrong move."

"Imagine it. It does happen."

She removed her hand from his and placed both arms around his neck, facilitating their discussion without ending the dance.

"Why do you do it then?"

"Make mistakes, you mean?"

"No. Why do you stay at that job?"

"Well," he said, turning her in a wide arc, "I guess it's because I love the business—or maybe it's because it's all I've done since I graduated from law school. Or maybe I just can't quit a loser."

Hard to imagine Carl a loser. She laid her head against his shoulder and pondered the thought. He was such a caring person, the kind of man who made a woman feel he could take care of anything. And then she had a flashback to the night over at Argylle when he'd crouched in front of her, pointing that gun. His face had been as steely and ferocious as the weapon itself. Not the face of a weakling.

She shook her head. Suddenly she felt tired. She stopped dancing and pulled out of his arms. "I've had enough dancing, Donay. I'm dead on my feet."

His arms felt cold, empty without her. But she was right to end the dance; he knew that if it went on, eventually it would lead to further intimacy. His body was already humming with excitement, his loins aching to resume the movement of her body against his.

"I should call my boss, anyway. Fill him in on your identification of that guy and pass along your idea that the other guy might show up on the records at Argylle as an absentee."

"Yes, and I should go in and see if Mark needs anything."

They were at least three feet apart now. They stood in place and stared at each other, Carl holding the file folder, Joanna with the dishtowel mysteriously returned to her hand.

"So...um...I'll catch up with you later."

"Yes." She cleared her throat. "Would you like to join us for a game or some TV, later?"

He shrugged. "It all depends on what old Harv wants. He may want me to slip over to Argylle and check the records tonight."

"Is that safe?"

"The name of the game isn't 'safe', Joanna." There was that steel gleam in his eyes again. The man went from soft, sensitive, tender, to rock-hard macho. This aspect of his personality reminded her of everything that made him wrong for her.

She needed that reminder to restore her sanity, to point out their biggest conflict. "No, I guess it isn't. And thank you for reminding me that this pretense at a friendship is only temporary, that once this case is solved, you'll go your way and I'll . . . go mine."

He nodded, his eyes suddenly bleak. "Yeah. Easy to forget sometimes." He turned and left the room.

Joanna turned off the radio with a vehement twist of the knob, telling herself she wouldn't cry, promising herself that she was going to be on her guard from now on, wishing she'd never uttered the words that had brought them back to reality.

Suddenly she had a picture of Carl in Beirut backing away from that window that revealed two people making love. Somehow that didn't fit her image of the average cop or agent. And with that thought, the tears came and she let them fall.

THERE WERE THREE employees who had been absent for the past week. One of them, Hayward Simpson, who worked in processing, was a black man, which automatically ruled him out as the man Joanna had seen struck down. Julio Venzuela was out on sick leave, reportedly having been hurt on a fall from his motorcycle. George Hoxton was just plain absent; his file indicated that his employment had been terminated when he didn't show up for work on Monday and hadn't called in sick. Both Venzuela and Hoxton were lab technicians.

"I'll have Mick check them out," Wisher told Carl when he called in his report. "Hoxton sounds like our man. Maybe Mick can get into the guy's house and find some photos Mrs. Keller can look at. Meanwhile, you stick close to the factory and make sure your equipment is working."

Carl returned to the house to find that Mark was already asleep, Joanna in her own room.

In his room, the screen of his monitor was snowy with rolling waves of black lines. The camera was voice-activated, turning itself on to record if voices were transmitted through the bugs he'd planted over at Argylle.

He backtracked the audio tape but found nothing had been recorded in his absence. He fiddled with the dials on the monitor and the lines disappeared. But the snow remained. That meant the problem was in the camera.

Which was in Joanna's room.

He looked at the monitor, at his watch, back at the monitor. No help for it, he'd have to go to her room.

He tapped gently at her door. "Joanna, it's me. I have to check that camera again."

"Come in," she called out.

She was sitting up in bed, reading, wearing a pink, cotton nightshirt with a matching robe. She looked rosy and damp, as if she'd just had a shower. She was also wearing glasses, which surprised him as he'd never seen them on her before. They did nothing to detract from her loveliness.

"I won't be a minute," he said. He made himself look away from her and went to the camera, where he made some adjustments to it.

She looked up from her book when he went to the door. "Finished already?"

It was his undoing to look back at her. She looked adorable. Her long, smooth legs were curled under her, her hair piled in a loose cluster of curls on top of her head and her glasses had slid partway down her elegant nose.

He leaned against the door frame, hands jammed in his pockets, and nodded. "Just a little glitch in the monitor. I think it'll be fine now."

"I went in to vacuum your room today and I couldn't help but notice that...receiver, is it?" She pushed the glasses back up on her nose with one rose-tipped finger. The lenses made her eyes look even bigger, giving her face a little-girl look.

"Yes." Carl coughed to cover the hoarseness in his voice.

"It's very impressive-looking equipment. It looks as though it would be complicated to master."

"Actually, what makes it so impressive is the simplicity of its design and how easy it is to run." Was she making conversation just to detain him? What would she do if he made a rush for her bed and began making love to her?

"I'm not very good with equipment, so of course it all looks complicated to me."

"I could teach you, if you're really interested." *There's no end to the things I'd like to teach you.*

She laughed shyly. "No, I don't think I'll ever have use for the knowledge."

"No, I guess not. Well..." He backed out of the doorway, drinking in one last heart-stirring sight of her.

"Good night," she called out softly.

"Good night." He closed the door, wiped the dampness from his forehead with his shirtsleeve and headed back to his room.

Joanna got off the bed, went to one of the windows on the west wall and peered out, past the edge of the coat outlet building next door, to the street beyond. It had rained again earlier that evening. A street lamp cast a glow on the wet street, giving it an iridescent sheen.

She remembered stories her mother had told. About when Katherine Harton had been a small child, playing in that street with no fear of traffic, and then how the construction gangs had come, filling the street with bulldozers and trucks and men in hard hats and the little Harton girl had been imprisoned behind the black wrought-iron fence her father had had installed around the house. Joanna had always loved hearing about her mother's childhood, making her own seem less lonely. It was as if the little girl she was had a companion in the little girl her mother had been.

The street in front of the house was always quiet at night now, reminding her of how isolated her life had been, so sparsely peopled, so seldom shared. Marrying had done little to change that, at least until Mark was born, for Sam had been a homicide detective who was gone from home far more than he was in it.

In those first years, she'd thought she wanted to fill the house with children, but she wanted to give Mark a few years of her undivided attention first. By the time she was ready to have another child, Sam was hardly ever home to make love with and when he was, he was usually too tired. The years had just slipped away from them and then suddenly Sam was gone and having more children was no longer a possibility.

Little Mark had been a robust, humorous child who'd filled the house with wonderful noise and brought the rooms alive with his vibrant personality. She'd often wondered if any other children she might have had would have been as lively as Mark.

She sighed heavily and turned away from the window. Carl brought life into the house, too. His presence, large and masculine, seemed to vibrate in the walls. She was always aware of him, even when he was a building away, working on the loading dock. When he was in the house, she'd know exactly which room he was in and what he was doing and her heart would lift expectantly whenever she heard his voice or his step.

She paced the length of the room, her hands pushed into the pockets of the short, cotton robe. It was amazing how much she'd learned about Carl in just the briefest exchange of conversation. Tonight, for instance, she'd learned that he didn't see himself as a first-class agent. It was a side of him she'd been unaware of. To her he'd always seemed a very take-charge kind of man.

She went to the camera he'd anchored in place and touched it gingerly, with one finger. He'd made it sound as if the fancy equipment was no mystery, took no special talent. He'd been just as modest when he'd fixed the intercom that connected her room to Mark's when it went all statical on Sunday afternoon, and just yesterday he'd shown Mark how to work out a difficult program on the laptop computer.

She paced again, too restless to read or sleep. She stopped at the door, opened it and listened for sounds in the house. All quiet. And then she detected the sound of running water. She looked down the hall and saw the bathroom door was closed. Carl must be taking a shower.

She stood there, staring at that closed door, her hands clasped behind her on the doorjamb. Almost as if she'd transported herself through that door, she could see Carl clearly, his arms stretched behind his head, the water beating down on his tall, hard, muscular frame. She could see his wet face, his eyes squinting to keep out the spray, the steam curling his hair.

I've never felt so totally absorbed by a woman before, Joanna. It was what he'd said, his face pressed to her bare shoulder, that night after they'd made love. She hadn't admitted it then, but she'd felt the same. Sex with him had been more than just an overwhelming physical tangling of their two bodies; it had been a sweet communication of whispered words, intense gazing into each other's eyes, hands clasping, minds meeting, souls searching. She closed her eyes and let the memory wash over her. She knew now what she'd never known when her husband was alive, the difference between the act of having sex and the act of making love.

So engrossed was she in her sweet musings, she didn't hear the door open at the end of the hall.

Carl put one bare foot into the hall and stopped, his breath catching in his throat, his eyes widening at the sight before him. Joanna was standing against her door frame, her hands behind her, her head back, her eyes closed. The light from the room behind her highlighted her. Her robe was open and he could see the thrust of her breasts against the flimsy fabric of her nightshirt. Her face seemed to glow with joy, as if her thoughts were providing her intense pleasure.

He took another step, barely making a sound.

But she heard him. Or rather, she sensed his presence. She opened her eyes, slowly, and looked down the length of the dimly lighted hall.

Carl was there, naked except for a towel around his torso, his bare flesh gleaming damply, his strong, well-shaped legs below the terry skirt drawing her eyes helplessly. There was another towel draped around his neck and he lifted one end of it to dab at a trickle of water that fell from his hair to his face.

Inconsequentially the thought came that this explained the drastic increase in towels in the laundry.

And then all thought, rational or otherwise, was gone as Carl flung the towel at his neck to the floor and the two of them raced the too-long distance to fall into each other's embrace, mouth meeting mouth savagely, bodies straining for that closeness that had never been far from their thoughts.

They fell to their knees as one, Carl yanking the robe down her arms and then her gown over her head, Joanna groping to pull away the towel tied at his waist. Naked, they kissed, caressed, suckled, their breaths mingling in short, sweet gasps of desire, their bodies squirming in aching need to come together into one perfect unit.

He lifted her onto the saddle of his lap and fit her into place over the hard thrusting organ of his manhood. His lips sought the sweet, pebbled peak of her breast and her hands wound around his neck to hold him against her.

She slid onto his flesh with perfect ease, her own body open to him in total readiness and gasped aloud as his mouth closed around her aching breast.

"There's no stopping now, Joanna," Carl whispered,

moving his hands to cup her face and looking into her eyes earnestly.

"No, no, Carl, I don't want to stop," she urged, pulling his hands off her face and placing them on her hips. "I want this, too. I want you."

Their kiss was deep and moving, sealing the commitment neither had the right to make.

CHAPTER TWELVE

"I THINK I have floor burns," Joanna murmured huskily against Carl's chest as they lay holding each other in the aftermath of their lovemaking.

"My knees can sympathize," Carl said, laughing shakily. "How about we adjourn to the nearest bed?"

She lifted her head and smiled down at him. "Only if you can carry me. I don't think my legs are up to the task."

He did just that, pretending to grunt with the effort. She pushed her face against his shoulder to stifle her giggles.

They grew sober as they faced each other on Carl's bed, Joanna tracing the outline of his sensuous mouth with her finger, Carl caressing Joanna's silken hair with his work-roughened palm.

"I want you again," Carl whispered.

"Yes, please," Joanna whispered back.

They were gentle with each other, each conscious of the other's need for tenderness. And somehow the gentleness was more sensuous than their runaway passion had been, so that when they peaked together it was more powerful than anything either of them had ever experienced.

SOMETIME DURING THE NIGHT Joanna had slipped out of Carl's arms and gone down to check on Mark. Then she returned to her own room and fell into a deep, contented sleep.

She awakened to the first morning of sunshine in a week and was startled to discover that it was after eight o'clock. She hadn't slept this late in over a year.

But when she hurried down to Mark, she found him dressed and already busy at his computer, with the TV on and an empty breakfast tray beside his bed.

"Carl fixed our breakfast and helped me get up before he left for work. Said you deserved to sleep in for once," Mark explained, his eyes going from the TV screen to the computer monitor on his lap.

She found herself humming as she showered and dressed, and smiling to herself in a way she was glad nobody was there to see.

She pulled half a dozen things from her closet and rejected them all, then settled on an outfit of pleated khaki slacks with a mauve, silk shirt that was both tailored and feminine and very flattering to her figure.

Midmorning she went into Mark's room to announce she was going to make a quick run over to the supermarket.

He was dozing, oblivious to the game show on TV, the cursor blinking on the computer screen. She took the computer off his lap and put it on his table, and used his remote to turn off the TV.

She scribbled a note and left it on top of the computer.

The air was fresh and sweet after the days of fog and rain. Joanna took deep, happy gulps of it and walked the few blocks to the market with a brisk stride.

She felt beautiful this morning, smiling smugly as a worker whistled at her as she passed a construction site a block from the river. She felt too good to grouse inwardly, as she normally did, about the way the downtown congestion was spilling over into her neighborhood. Lately there'd been items in the papers and on the news about plans for a big wharf renewal program that would turn the warehouse and wharf area along the river into a tourist mecca; usually Joanna responded to those ideas with grim distaste.

Though it was out of her way by two blocks, she returned home from the market by way of the bridge, stopping midway to look out over the river, sparkling silver and green in the sunlight, and thought romantically of her first meeting here with Carl.

The weight of the groceries reminded her that she didn't have time to dawdle. Mark had already been alone more than half an hour.

She quickened her step and hurried back to the house. She could hear the sound of his TV the minute she stepped into the house.

She dumped the grocery bags on the counter and called out to Mark. "I'm home, honey-bunch."

"Thank you for sharing that with me, Mom," the boy called back.

"Brat," Joanna muttered, laughing. She hurriedly stuck the perishables in the refrigerator, grabbed an orange and went back to Mark's room. He was sitting up in bed, fiddling with his computer.

"I brought you a treat," she trilled, holding up the fruit.

"What ever happened to real treats, like Ho-Ho's and chocolate bars?" he grumbled.

"Spare me the junk-food blues, kid, it's an orange or nothing." She tossed him the orange and ambled over to the window, trying to appear casual.

There was Carl, bent over to lift a barrel onto a dolly. The sleeves of his work shirt were rolled up almost to his

shoulders and his sinewy arms rippled with each movement. His exertion, under the penetrating rays of the sun,
had caused him to perspire and made his shirt cling to his
back, outlining the broad masculine shoulders that narrowed to his waist enticingly.

God, he's so gorgeous. She'd thought so the first time
she ever saw him and he'd grown more handsome as the
days went by.

Her insides seemed to quiver with excitement as she
watched him. There was something so sexy about watching her man at work, when he didn't know she was
watching.

Her man. She knew she was courting disaster to allow
herself to think of him that way—to think of him in terms
of forever. As she turned away, he looked up and spotted
her. His grin told her his thoughts were very much like her
own, remembering their wild, exciting night of love, the
promise of being together again tonight. She smiled back
and then fled from the window before she could make a
real fool of herself.

The phone rang just as she was setting Mark's lunch
tray down on the table beside him. She thought it would
be Carl and she answered it just a little breathlessly.

"So," a feminine voice drawled. "I can tell from the
tone of your voice that you've finally got a man in your
life."

Joanna gasped and almost fell onto Mark's bed in surprise. "Claire? Claire, is that you? Where are you? Are
you in town? When can I see you, what are you—"

"Hey, slow down, Joanna," Claire Hanson interrupted. "Give me a chance to answer."

"Oh, gosh, I'm sorry. I'm just so excited to hear your
voice." She beamed at Mark. "It's Aunt Claire," she said
excitedly.

"I got that, Mom," Mark said wryly. "Say hi for me."

"Your godson says hi, Claire," she said turning back to her conversation with Claire.

"Hi back to him. Listen, Jo, I was asked to consult on this designer fashion show for Dayton's at the last minute. No time to let you know I was coming before I had to leave for the airport. Want me to stay with you?"

"Oh yes, of course. You didn't even need to ask. Where are you? Come right over."

Claire laughed. "They picked me up at the airport with a limo; I had to come right over here for a meeting. But I'll be through around four and then I'll cab over."

"I can't wait to see you," Joanna said, winding the cord around her hand over and over. "I'll have the coffee on and the martinis chilling."

"Amen to that, sister. I'll need the latter, especially, after these yuppie-type execs get through with me."

It wasn't until they'd hung up that Joanna realized her best friend's presence in the house was going to put her lovemaking with Carl on the back burner for that week. She wondered how Carl would feel about that. Then the thought of seeing Claire again took precedence over everything else. She hoped Carl would like Claire.

"The inn is filling up fast," Mark said, grinning happily.

"Yes," she said, smiling back. She picked up the orange Mark hadn't touched and began to peel it. "God, we haven't seen Claire in three years. Where does the time go?"

"I wonder what color her hair will be this time?" Mark commented.

Joanna laughed. "Did I ever tell you about the time she tried bleaching it so it would be as light as mine, and it came out green?"

"Green? Come on, Mom, this is another one of your stories, right?"

"Uh-uh. It was really green." She frowned and grew pensive. "Wouldn't you think Claire would have married by now? When we were at the university together, guys would fall all over her. It seemed so unlikely that I'd be the one to marry and that she'd be the one to end up a spinster."

Mark hooted. "Spinster? Aunt Claire? Give me a break! She's an incredibly glamourous, successful woman."

Her smile was sheepish. "Well, you know what I mean." She finished peeling Mark's orange, took a section for herself and handed him the rest. "You know, she was a political science major in school. She only modeled to pay her way through university. Who'd have ever thought she'd end up owning and operating one of the country's leading modeling agencies and that big-name designers would be asking her to consult on their fashion shows."

Mark ate one section of the fruit and put the rest on his nightstand. Joanna frowned but decided there wasn't any point in nagging him to eat. Maybe he'd finish it later.

"Want to sit in the parlor for a while, or come out to the kitchen to watch me create one of my specialties?"

Mark lay back against his pillow, his eyelids drifting shut. "No, thanks, Mom. Maybe I'll just rest a little. Save my energy for Claire's visit."

Had he looked so pale this morning? Joanna brushed his hair off his forehead and bent to kiss his cheek. Warm. Warm enough to warrant taking his temperature? But he was already almost asleep. Maybe she shouldn't disturb him, maybe all he really needed was the rest.

He hadn't even made one of his smart remarks about her cooking.

She decided to stay near him for a while. She stood up and looked over at the rocker near the window. No, not there. The temptation to just sit and gawk at Carl would be too compelling.

She slipped her feet out of her loafers, eased down onto the bed and curled up beside her son. His breathing was soft and even now, his delicate eyelids twitching just slightly. Oh, he was so beautiful, this boy of hers. And even in the last stages of his illness, so bright and funny and loving and lovable. She didn't know if she'd be as generous of heart as he was if she knew *her* life was going to be snatched away from her before she'd had a chance to become a woman.

Thinking of herself at Mark's age made her recall her months at the university. She'd met Claire Hanson the first day of her freshman year, both of them stuck at the end of a long line of students trying to make last-minute changes in their class registration.

Claire had been as dark as Joanna was blond. The extremes of their coloring had appealed to Claire's sense of humor. She'd decided on the spot that they'd make a highly visible duo around campus and had immediately taken charge of the friendship. Joanna, always a loner, had resisted at first, but Claire would have none of it, insisting Joanna meet her for lunches at the student's union, dragging her to the boutiques in Dinkytown, even arranging double dates, in short overriding every one of Joanna's protests.

Joanna had let Claire be the leader because Claire's personality was stronger than hers. But once the friendship had taken shape she allowed her own personality to shine through. She'd come to love Claire. Claire had been

Joanna's only bridesmaid and, later, became baby Mark's godmother.

When Claire had moved to New York to accept a modeling contract, Joanna had thought she'd die from missing her. Of course she hadn't. She'd adjusted to that loss as she had to all the others. And at least Claire kept in touch, with funny greeting cards, a letter now and then and unexpected phone calls or impromptu visits when she could get away from her demanding career.

She'd been there for all the important events in Joanna's adult life, and had stayed with Joanna and Mark for a month after Sam's funeral, helping them to adjust.

What would she tell Claire about Carl? Not the truth. But the lie she'd told Mark had become truth, so maybe she could let Claire think that Carl was just there as her live-in lover. But then, wouldn't the fact that he had his own room make Claire suspicious? And what about the camera at the window in her room? How would she explain that?

Her eyes popped open and she looked around, feeling sudden panic. If Claire finished her meeting at four, as she expected to, she'd get to the house before Carl came home from work; there'd be no time to consult with Carl about how to cover his real reason for living in her house.

Her anxious gaze fell to the telephone. But no, whoever answered the phone might want to know who she was. And that would involve having to tell another lie.

Normally she'd have shared the problem with Mark but this time Mark was part of the problem.

She slid off the bed and tiptoed out of the room, needing to move around, to keep herself busy.

She went to the kitchen and set up a pot of coffee, so all she'd have to do was turn it on when Claire arrived. *I'll*

tell her he's my live-in friend, that it's purely platonic.
And would Claire believe that? *In a pig's eye.*

She groped in the freezer, tossing out packages until she
came across a fairly large standing-rib roast. A good
choice for a celebration dinner. *Claire, this is Carl Donay.
We needed a little extra money so Carl takes room and
board with us.* She gave a short, self-derisive laugh. If
Claire fell for that, she'd start sending them money on one
pretense or another. Anyway, how would Joanna explain
needing money when there was the trust from her grand-
father's will, and Sam's pension and insurance monies,
not to mention the lease payment from the buildings on
either side that came quarterly, as regular as clockwork?

She groaned aloud and slumped onto one chair, prop-
ping her feet onto one another. How could she stop Claire
from seeing the camera in Joanna's room? A brilliant
thought came to her and she sat upright. She could just
move all of Carl's stuff into her room and give Claire the
spare bedroom. *And keep Claire out of your room for a
whole week?*

"Besides," she muttered aloud, shaking her head,
"how would I move his equipment without screwing it
up?"

The idea came to her out of the blue, but she didn't
have time to stand around gloating about her mental
prowess; what she had to do had to be done in a hurry.

She tore up the stairs and rushed back and forth, ex-
changing her clothes in the closet and dresser with Carl's
and vice-versa. She couldn't move Carl's monitoring system by herself but she figured she could keep Claire
downstairs until Carl got home. She'd get him alone, tell
him the plan, and he could run up and move the equipment before Claire could know Joanna and Carl had
switched rooms.

Having come up with a reasonable solution, Claire went back to the kitchen to prepare side dishes to accompany the meat.

Claire's cab arrived at four thirty-five. The first fifteen minutes were taken up with greetings and hugs and everyone talking and laughing at once.

"I've got to get my things hung soon, or they'll be wrinkled as hell," Claire said, when there was a break in the excitement of her arrival.

"Oh, but the coffee's ready now and I've a pitcher of martinis chilling in the refrigerator. Come on, Hanson, unpacking can wait." Joanna pushed Claire back down on Mark's bed, ignoring the strange look her son shot her. "You just keep visiting with Mark and I'll get the goodies."

"So, Marky Baby, how's tricks?" Claire asked distractedly, turning from watching Joanna leave the room.

"Sixes and sevens, Auntie Baby," Mark retorted, falling into their old game easily.

She gave him her full attention. "So who's the guy?"

"What guy?"

"The guy your ma's all flustered about."

Mark grinned. "She told you about Carl?"

Claire's responding grin was tinged with triumph. "So I was right, there is someone. There's a special note in a woman's voice if, when she answers the phone, she's expecting a man to be on the other end."

She grabbed Mark's hand, wincing at its unexpected frailty and quickly covered the wince with a ferocious scowl. "Tell all, comrade, or your vife and zix kiddies go to Ziberia," she said in her best Greta Garbo voice.

Mark put his hands behind his head and lay back, his smile fixed happily in place. "No, no, not that," he said, by rote, in a monotone. "Anything but that."

Claire laughed. "As an actor you make a great Scrabble player, kid. Now come on. Tell all."

"Won't Mom want to tell you herself when the two of you get tanked up and start all that silly girl talk?"

"Yeah, but first I want to hear the unadorned facts. You know what women in love are like, they tend to exaggerate."

"Well, she met him when he thought she was trying to jump off a bridge. He saved her and it turned out he worked next door at Argylle and the next thing you know they're in love and he's living here."

Claire stared at her godson, her mouth agape. Her laugh was a short burst of surprise.

"You really know how to *un*adorn, fella."

Mark giggled and then coughed. And coughed again. And then the smile fell from his face and the coughing wouldn't stop.

Joanna was back in the room before Claire could get to her feet to go after her. "Move," she told her friend as she grabbed the face mask off the tank with one hand and spun the dial with the other.

In only a few minutes Mark was resting quietly again, pale but at ease. Joanna went across the hall to the bathroom, wet a washcloth, wrung it out and came back to wash Mark's face.

Claire was standing across the room, tears streaming down her face. Joanna glanced at Mark, saw that his eyes were closed and went over to Claire, an impatient scowl on her face.

"Stop that," she whispered harshly.

Claire blinked, surprised at her friend's tone. She put a shaky hand to her face and swiped at the tears.

"Go into the kitchen. He'll be fine now. I'll join you in a minute."

Claire's head was bent to her arms, at the table, and she was sobbing quietly when Joanna came into the room a few minutes later. Joanna went to her and held her, whispering soothing words, rocking her against her body.

"I h-had no id-idea," Claire stammered. "I'm s-so sorry, Joanna."

"Shh, I know, Claire, I know." She handed her friend some tissues from a box on the counter and left her to get the drinks out of the refrigerator.

She filled a chilled martini glass and handed it to Claire. "Here, drink up. It'll take the scare off."

Claire nodded. With a beautifully manicured hand she grasped the cocktail glass and gulped the icy beverage. "Aren't you joining me?"

"I'll wait a little—make sure Mark's stable again."

Claire's dark brown eyes were still glossy with tears but she held them back. "When did it get so bad?"

"About seven months ago," Joanna said tonelessly. "No more remissions, the doctor said, but no firm time for how long he'll last. Apparently he's doing better than they expected."

Claire finished her drink in three swallows and held up the glass for a refill, a thoughtful look on her face. She nodded. "I'll have to go back to clean up some details and arrange for my assistant to take over, but then I'll be back," she announced, matter-of-factly.

"You're crazy! Why in the world would you want to do that?" Joanna demanded, almost spilling the liquid she was pouring for Claire's second drink.

Claire's eyes fastened on her friend's and her expression was stoic. "I'm not letting you guys go through this alone. You need me and I'm going to be here."

"Claire," Joanna said softly, sitting down and taking her friend's hand, "we're not alone. We have each other.

And as much as we love you, we don't really need you to be here."

"Dammit!" Claire pounded her fist on the table.

"Listen, Claire, aside from everything else, the stress factor has to be considered. Mark's a smart and sensible young man—nearly an adult—he'd know you were sacrificing your career for him and he'd feel guilty as hell. And guilt makes for stress, especially in a sick person."

"I know you're right," Claire admitted with a sigh, "but it's going to be hell to leave you next week, knowing what you'll be going through. Knowing," she added on a sob, "I might never see Mark again."

"If there's time—some kind of warning—I'll call you and you can be here in just a few hours by plane, to...to say goodbye," Joanna promised. "Okay?"

Claire nodded. "I'm going to sit with him," she said, abruptly pushing back from the table, leaving her drink untouched.

Joanna groaned and laughed at the look on her friend's face. "You're not going to sit over him like a mother hen all week, are you? He'd see right through that and he'd hate it."

Claire's expression wavered between mutinous determination and doubt. Finally, seeing Joanna's own calm determination, she sat back down.

Joanna got another glass from the refrigerator and made a big show of filling it. "I'll even join you for a drink now," she bargained. "See?" She took a tiny sip and made a face. "Ugh. This is wicked enough to make me forget my own name. Let's slow it down with coffee."

An hour later they were deep in conversation, their reminiscences punctuated with martini-induced giggles. Claire was just about to pour the last of the pitcher into their glasses when she looked up to see an incredible apparition in the doorway.

She gazed in frank awe at the gorgeous man standing there, looking like a wonderful fantasy.

"This is a raid," the man said in a deep, thrilling voice, "Mrs. Keller, do you have a license to operate this saloon?"

Joanna spun around at the sound of Carl's voice, almost falling off her chair.

Carl took two long steps forward and caught the chair before it could topple over. He was laughing when he glanced over at Joanna's friend. The woman was frankly ogling him. He ogled back. She was as dark as Joanna was fair, midnight to Joanna's morning, with chocolate-brown eyes, hair the color of cocoa, and skin tanned to the hue of an acorn.

She held her hands up and he could see she had those very long, polished nails that always made him wonder how the women who had them could possibly manage anything as simple as dialing a phone or unlocking a door.

"I'll go quietly, Officer," the woman said, grinning.

"Go ahead, take her," Joanna said, laughing up at Carl. "She's not in town a day and already she's led me down the garden path to deg . . . degen . . . to trouble."

"I'm Claire Hanson," the woman said, leaving one hand out for a formal handshake.

"Carl . . . Martin," he said, taking the proffered hand and holding it very briefly in his.

Joanna stared at him, eyes wide with disbelief.

"Joanna, could we talk for a minute? Alone," he added sternly, when he saw she was gesturing toward another chair.

They excused themselves to Claire and went to the front parlor. Carl shut the door and turned to face Joanna.

Joanna asked, "Why did you use your cover name with Claire? She's my best friend."

Carl ignored her question and asked one of his own. "How could you invite her here, knowing my presence in the house was supposed to remain a secret?" he demanded.

"You mean how could I invite my own best friend into my own house?" she snapped, sobering instantly. "Easy. She asked, I said yes."

Sensing his barely controlled anger, she moved away from him.

"She hasn't even been cleared for security. For all we know, she could be anyone. She could even be a direct link to the gang we're after."

"Claire? She's my best friend, Carl, Mark's godmother. She runs a modeling agency. She's here to orchestrate a designer fashion show for Dayton's. I hardly think she'd qualify as public enemy of the year."

Carl refused to be daunted by the note of scorn in Joanna's voice. He had a job to do and this was part of it, the part most civilians couldn't seem to accept.

"You don't know that, Joanna," he said quietly. "She lives across the country, she could be involved with people you know nothing about. We're too close to solving this case to take any chances now. She has to be cleared if she's going to stay here."

Joanna glared at him. "If you do a check on my best friend I'll never speak to you again. That's an invasion of privacy!" She almost screeched the words.

He tried to reason with her. "Joanna, there were three other companies around the country that were possible targets for this operation. It could be more than coincidence that Argylle Spice is right next door to where Claire Hanson's best friend lives."

Fury made her vision blur, her hands shake. "You're a typical, paranoid *cop,* aren't you Donay?" she spat.

The way she'd said the word *cop* told him of years of unspoken bitterness and rage, and stressed, beyond words, how much she hated his job.

"I'm not a cop," he offered weakly.

"No?" The look she gave him was scathing. "Funny, I could have sworn I recognized the scent of blood on your hands!"

She flung open the door and ran out of the room before he could stop her.

"I'll help you take your things up now, Claire," she was saying. "You'll be bunking in with me."

It wasn't until she arrived back in the kitchen that she realized she hadn't told Carl about the room switch. But later when she went up to call him to dinner, she found that he'd seen the changes she'd made, understood what her intentions were and moved the monitor after all.

The camera and all of the other equipment were now in one room with Carl. Everything in its place.

Except her.

And later, when Claire asked when she'd moved out of the master bedroom, it was easy to add another lie by saying, "I didn't like to be reminded of Sam, so I moved back here to my old room."

CHAPTER THIRTEEN

CLAIRE TILTED HER HEAD to the side, looked the board over carefully and moved her bishop to capture Mark's pawn.

Mark chuckled. "You're a natural victim, Auntie Baby." Her move had freed his castle, just as he'd planned, and he captured her bishop.

"You're a barracuda, kiddo. Where did you learn the killer tactics?"

"I read a lot," he said smugly.

They laughed together and returned their attention to the board.

"So tell me," Claire asked casually, "is the kind of deep-freeze silence we've had at dinner the last couple of nights a common occurrence around here?"

Mark shook his head, frowning. "It's been like a roller coaster with those two. Mom is either moping or flying high. Carl is either mooning after her or on top of the world. I've never seen them so deadly quiet before, though. Never seen them really angry with each other. Did Mom tell you what she's so angry about?"

"No." Claire looked thoughtful. "Maybe Carl resents my being here. You know, men can be pretty possessive about their women when they're in the first throes of love."

"Carl? No way. Carl is—well, there aren't too many guys like Carl around. He's got the biggest heart of anyone I've ever known and if anything, he'd like you just because you're our friend."

"He's very nice to me," Claire admitted, "and not at all as if he's just being polite."

"Right. Carl isn't the type to fake anything. He's real."

Claire grinned and tousled the boy's head. "You really approve of him for your mom, don't you?"

Mark ducked his head and frowned at her. "Quit that."

"Hey, it beats pinching your cheek, doesn't it?"

"Yeah, I remember when you used to do that, too."

"I never!"

"You did!"

"What are you two fighting about?" Joanna asked, coming into the room with an armload of folded clothes.

"He's accusing me falsely," Claire said.

"You're doing laundry at this hour?" Mark asked, distractedly watching his mother place things in his dresser drawers. That was a bad sign. She did things like laundry at night when she couldn't vent her feelings any other way. He remembered that she'd stay up almost all night washing walls, scrubbing floors, for a long time after his dad died.

Claire must have remembered that, too, for she said, "Joanna, wouldn't it be healthier either to fight it out or talk it out?"

"Nothing to talk about," Joanna said, keeping her back to them, "and obviously we've already fought."

"Well, if you're through doing laundry, do you want to go for a walk?"

Joanna's eyes were bleak but her tone eager when she turned around. "That would be great. I've missed my night walks, lately. We can go after Mark has his medicine and is settled for the night."

"You can go now, Mom," Mark said, pushing the wheeled table with the chess board away.

"No, I'm not leaving you alone when you're up and active."

"Isn't Carl here?"

"I...I don't want to impose on Carl."

"Mom, *I* haven't had a fight with him, he's still *my* friend and I know he won't mind."

Joanna put the last stack of shirts into place and shut the drawer. "I don't like to ask him," she admitted.

"I'll just go up, knock on his door and tell him we're going for a walk," Claire announced, settling the matter. "I have to get a jacket anyway. Does this place ever decide what the season is?" she grumbled as she left the room.

At Claire's rap, Carl came to the door, opening it just a few inches. "Carl, would you go down and visit with Mark while Joanna and I go for a walk?" she asked.

"Sure. Be glad to. I'll be right down."

She tried to peer past him into the room. He seemed very anxious to keep her from seeing beyond him. Was he one of those messy types? He acted as if he had something to hide—something more serious than a messy room. "Okay, thanks. Well, we'll be leaving in a couple of minutes."

"I'll be right down," he repeated and shut the door in her face.

"How long have you known Carl?" she asked Joanna, a few minutes later as they started on their stroll toward the river.

"Not long."

"Days? Weeks? Months?" Claire persisted.

"Weeks, I guess," Joanna sighed. "And I don't want to talk about it."

"*I* want to talk about it," Claire said. "And you know what a bulldozer I can be when I want something."

Joanna laughed, in spite of herself, and linked her arm through Claire's. "Yeah, I know."

"So, give. I'm not asking what you argued about. That, I admit, is none of my business. I just want to hear the juicy stuff. Like how you met and got together; things like that. If you tell me, I'll tell you about the hairdresser I've been playing footsie with the past couple of months."

"A hairdresser? You?" Joanna stopped walking and gaped at her friend. "I thought construction workers and wrestlers were more your cup of tea."

"There's no cup of tea like a hairdresser," Claire quipped.

"Exactly," Joanna said, laughing. "So what's the attraction?"

"Uh-uh. Not until you tell me about you and Carl."

They resumed walking. It was hard to tell about Carl while keeping in mind that she couldn't reveal his real occupation. It was only patriotism that kept her from telling Claire the truth, not loyalty to Carl, she told herself.

Claire giggled when Joanna told about their meeting on the bridge and looked properly astonished when she said it turned out that Carl worked right next door at Argylle.

"That's some coincidence," she interjected.

"Not really. Not when you think about the fact that we met right here in the neighborhood."

"Oh. Then Carl lives—er, lived—close by, too."

"Well, no. Not exactly."

They'd reached the foot of the street leading to the bridge. Joanna sighed, exasperated. There was no way to tell just one lie, she was learning. One lie necessitated other lies until it was hard to keep track of them all. One more reason to resent Carl's job, she thought, and his presence in her life. She couldn't remember telling a handful of lies in her entire life and now here she was telling them on a daily basis and to people she loved, people who trusted her.

"Where did he live then?"

"Downtown."

"Downtown? But there's nothing but hotels and condos downtown anymore."

"Er... near downtown."

"I see. Then, maybe he's only been at Argylle a short time?" Claire prodded. It was clear Joanna was uncomfortable talking about Carl, but that made Claire all the more curious about the man. After all, despite having been married, Joanna was a real babe in the woods about men. She might need Claire's more experienced, sophisticated insight. And nice as Carl appeared to be, he definitely seemed to have something to hide and had obviously conned Joanna into helping him hide it.

"Yes, that's right," Joanna said quickly. "He's only worked there a short time." She spotted the café, relieved to have an excuse to change the subject. "Look, there's Mandy's. Let's go have a drink."

Once they'd entered the shabby café, Claire looked around with a raised eyebrow. "Come here often?" she drawled.

Joanna laughed shortly. "More often than you'd believe. This is the place where Carl and I came that first night. And we've been here a couple of times since."

"Returning to the scene of the crime?" Claire's wry tone matched the expression on her face as she checked the seat on the booth before sitting down.

"Come on, Claire, it's old but it's really quite clean."

Claire looked doubtful but settled into place and looked over at the woman behind the counter, expectantly.

Mandy was talking with two couples seated at the counter, but excused herself and walked over to where Claire and Joanna were sitting.

Mandy considered anyone who came into her place a second time, a regular. Joanna had been here three times and was now considered a charter member. The older woman lingered at the table, asking Joanna about her health and her handsome boyfriend.

"He's... busy tonight. It's just us girls," Joanna said, keeping her face carefully cheerful. "We'd like brandy and coffee, please, Mandy."

Claire looked around, impatiently waiting for Mandy to finish visiting with Joanna so they could get on with their own visit. When the older woman had gone to get their order, she asked, "Is this a café or a bar?"

"Both. Apparently Mandy inherited the license from the guy who owned the bar next door. She knocked out the wall between the two places, boarded up the entrance to the original bar and now you have to walk through the café to get to the bar."

"Weird. But legal, I suppose."

"It's the only place down on this side of the river that sells liquor so nobody would complain, even if it wasn't legal. This is no longer a residential area, you know."

Claire nodded and held her next question in check until Mandy had set their drinks before them.

"I always wondered why you stayed on here—after your mother died, I mean. Why not sell the place and move to a traditional neighborhood? You're so isolated here, especially at night."

Joanna sighed heavily. "I love the house, for one thing—it has my whole family's history within its walls. It's hard to walk away from the only home you've ever known." Her eyes gazed off in the distance for a moment, as if she were seeing all the years pass by. She shook her head, blinked, came back to the present. "Of course I've thought about moving, off and on over the years. When Mark was in grade school, and then again when he was in high school. I remembered how cut off I'd felt as a kid. But Mark was a different kind of child—he managed to have friends and socialize outside of the neighborhood. You remember, when he was well, how the house was always full of kids coming and going, and the phone was always ringing."

Claire looked surprised. "That's right! What happened to those kids?"

Joanna shrugged, an eloquent gesture that opened Claire's imagination so that she could guess what happened without words. "Kids don't mean to be cruel," she said softly, squeezing Joanna's hand.

"I know. And Mark understands, too. Sometimes he calls one or another of his buddies and they talk on the phone. He seems okay with that."

They drank in silence for a few minutes, each lost in her own thoughts.

"Mark is crazy about Carl," Claire said, breaking the silence.

"Yes. They've become good friends. So, Claire—" she cleared her throat "—how's it going at Dayton's?"

"On a scale of one to ten? About four. But that's not unusual for this stage of the planning. We'll be kicking ideas around, and disagreeing, until the last minute. And then, when the designer himself shows up, it'll all suddenly fall into place and he'll think we've been in total agreement the whole time. After that, it's his show and the rest of us just have to be on call twenty-six hours a day to pander to his ego."

Joanna laughed. "Sounds teddibly thrilling, dahling," she quipped. "You do lead such a glamourous life."

"Yeah, well, we can't all be lucky enough to steep ourselves in laundry detergent and Mr. Clean," she retorted, grinning at her own one-upmanship.

"Ah, but I can sleep until noon, if I want," Joanna teased.

"Yes, but at noon, I get to have lunch at places like 21."

"Yeah, but I get to eat real food for lunch, and not just a leaf of lettuce and a sliced carrot," she said, looking pointedly at Claire's size five figure.

"Dirty pool, Keller," Claire moaned. "That was really hitting below the belt."

Joanna enjoyed her victory for a moment and then sobered to ask, "Don't you ever get lonely, Claire? I don't mean from being alone—obviously you're surrounded by people all the time." She looked into her cup, searching for the right words. "I mean that hard-core lonely that wakes you up at night and makes you lie there wondering how you got here and what's the use of going on."

"I guess you've really learned about lonely the hard way, Jo," Claire said softly. "That the truth is, we die alone. That's hard for the living to learn and you, more than anyone I know, have learned it in spades."

"You mean the loneliness comes from that knowledge?"

"Yes. People who go through life without ever experiencing that gut-wrenching feeling are probably people who've never faced the truth about the death of a loved one. It proves you can never really hold on to another person—ultimately, people come into the world alone and go out alone. Ergo, they belong only to themselves."

Joanna shivered and gulped her brandy for warmth. "So in the meantime, we live an illusion when we think we're sharing our lives." She raised tear-sparkling eyes to her friend and laughed self-consciously. "Tell me about your hairdresser, Claire. I need a good dose of someone else's illusion for a change."

"He's an ex-trucker who just liked fooling with women's hair and turned it into a vocation," Claire said, straight-faced.

Their combined laughter worked to dispel the serious mood that their conversation had engendered. They ordered another drink, talked frivolously about men, clothes and movies. Two hours passed before they returned home, their friendship reinstated to its normal easiness.

The house was quiet. Claire tiptoed up the stairs to get ready for bed and Joanna went down the hall to Mark's room.

Mark was asleep. The dim base light on his lamp illuminated his bed. Joanna glanced across the room and saw that Carl was sitting in the shadows in the rocker next to the window.

He stood up. "He asked for his medication, knew how much he was supposed to have, so I gave it to him," he whispered.

"Thank you."

"Um, Joanna." He held his hand out, as if to detain her. "I thought you'd want to know, Claire checked out all right."

"I knew she would," she whispered back harshly. "And I didn't need to do a security check on her to find out."

"Joanna, it's my job, I didn't have any choice."

"We all have choices, Carl," she said, fighting to keep her voice to a whisper. "And mine is to let you finish whatever your job is and then to get you out of my life, once and for all.''

He moved too quickly for her to anticipate him, backing her up to the dresser so she couldn't escape, knowing she was trapped into silence by her sleeping son just a room's length away. His arms were steel bands around her slim body.

"What about this?" he growled low against her mouth. Her retort was aborted by his kiss, softening her lips, weakening her limbs, obliterating all thought from her mind. She opened under his demanding tongue, letting him taste her own hunger for him.

It was his chuckle of satisfaction, uttered as he drew back to change the slant of his mouth against hers, that wrenched her back to reality. His arms had eased from imprisoning to embracing when she'd responded to his kiss; she took advantage of that with a shove that caught him off guard and allowed her to move out of his reach.

"You do that again and I'll report you to your superior, Special Agent Donay," she threatened, her voice heavy with controlled anger despite the fact that she spoke in a whisper. She turned and left the room.

Carl stayed where he was, helplessly cursing the day he'd met Joanna, cursing Claire's untimely arrival, cursing the man who'd first recruited him for a career in the agency. And then he went over to look down at the sleeping boy, adjusted the covers under Mark's chin and went up to his own, lonely bed.

NOT MORE THAN a few blocks away, in a building soon to be condemned by the city, two men met in the shadows of the ground-level rear hall, embracing briefly before going to a room that had once been the home of the building's caretaker. The caretaker was dead, his body decaying somewhere in the bowels of a new building construction, killed by these men as a simple expediency.

"So, Jan, it goes well?" the older of the two men asked, when they'd closed the door and turned on the single, dim, overhead light. He was a tall man, nearly six-four, with a bald head, piercing blue eyes, and a hawklike nose that was too big even for his large face.

Jan Podanski, a smaller, bullish, dark, pinch-faced man, shrugged and averted his eyes. "Our inside man won't talk if that's what you mean. Not now that he has seen what happens to people who get in our way."

They spoke in their native language though both were competent in English.

The older man nodded. "When you asked me to meet with you, you indicated the shipment had arrived. That is so?"

Jan nodded, his long, dark, straight hair falling forward. He pushed it back impatiently and smiled at his superior. "Yah, Augustus, it is here."

"And they are processing it?"

Jan frowned, shrugging his overdeveloped shoulders. "Not yet. It seems the boss, Argylle, has put a priority on a large shipment of cumin and put the saffron processing on hold."

"We are fast approaching our deadline," Augustus warned. "You know we agreed that the poison must do its work exactly six weeks before the elections on Greenwich Island in order for the domino effect to occur and the present administration to crumble. We selected Minnesota for our target because it's in the hinterlands of the country, a place where fewer of their good agents would be assigned."

"Yah, yah, I know. But we risk everything if we move too fast, try to force the situation."

Augustus's mouth was a grim line, his eyes implacable steel. "If the saffron processing isn't begun in the next two weeks, you will, as you say, force the situation. Is that clear?"

"Yah, Augustus, sure. You're the boss." Jan laughed weakly, backing away from the cold threat of violence in the other man's voice and manner.

"Good, I knew you were the man for this job, Jan. It's the reason I particularly asked you to be assigned to this end of the operation. I know you would never let scruples get in the way of doing whatever must be done." It was a genuinely fond smile he bestowed on his young compatriot. "Much like myself."

He went to the door. "I must go now, Jan. My boat will only wait until midnight."

"You're going back?" Jan's voice reflected his surprise, his fear.

"Yah." He chuckled. "I am to be cook aboard a barge going from Lake Superior into Canada. There I will be met by another boat to take me home. I shall think of you when I spice the food the crew eats aboard the barge." His short, raucous laugh echoed in the empty hallway.

"What if I need you?" Jan asked.

"The time for needing was over when you accepted your assignment," Augustus warned. "You will be expected to follow through to its end—or meet your own."

The shaking began when the door closed behind the older man. Jan went to the sagging bed, lay back on it and stared up at the ceiling. He was alone now, with only the American contact to help him pull off the job. The American had resisted, at first, suddenly deciding the large amount of money wouldn't compensate for the risk. True, Jan had efficiently put an end to the man's pathetic mewling, but now he also couldn't rely on the man to keep up his end of the bargain.

He closed his eyes and allowed his mind to conjure up the image of Augustus Mueller as he had been when he first recruited Jan to the group. Augustus had stood at the front of the room, addressing the group, and his voice, rich and powerful, resounded with the passion of his dedication.

"We live alone, we die alone! Do not look to one another to give meaning to your lives. Look to yourselves. You alone are responsible for your commitment to this cause. We are not a brotherhood, a fraternity. We are each, singly, a unit of power nurturing this cause. This cause that will free us from the tyranny of communism, socialism and democracy, those philosophies that make us responsible for our brother's freedoms and rob us of our own!"

Jan shivered and curled into a fetal curve on the bare mattress. He'd been abandoned as a child and betrayed over and over as a man. Augustus's words had empowered him with a sense of purpose, of renewal, giving him the first reason for living that he'd had in years. He must never lose sight of that, or he would be less than a man, with nothing left to mark his life.

He straightened his limbs, opened his eyes, swung himself off the bed. He had two weeks left. He looked around the shabby room with its water-stained walls, its concrete floor that was cracking beneath his feet. Augustus was gone, there would be nobody now to expect to find him here. He had plenty of American dollars and more than enough time to explore some of the pleasures this poor misguided country boasted.

He dragged his duffel bag out from under the bed, crammed a stray shirt and his seaman's cap into it and went to the door. He looked around for a last time, making sure he'd left nothing of himself behind. For two weeks he would live as the hero he thought he was, with all the rewards due such a man. He turned off the light and left the room.

HARVEY WISHER SIGNALED to the waiter for a second round of drinks and returned his attention to his companion.

"Now then, Mick, you're sure about your source?" he asked in a low voice, audible only within the confines of their booth.

The younger agent squinted around the smoke from the cigarette that hung from his lips and nodded. "Used him once before, on that Dutch narcotics job. Seems he belongs to a club where most of the foreign seamen go when they're in town. He said the two men from Greenwich Island were with a crew from one of the tugs." Mick stubbed out the cigarette and took a swallow of his beer.

"Not only that, he insists our guys disappeared into the city and didn't go back out on the tanker they came in on."

"No names?"

Mick shook his head. "He says none of them use their real names anyway. Most of 'em are on the run from somewhere abroad and a lot of them are real paranoid when they come here."

"So we have one name—Jan Podanski, based on the I.D. Joanna Keller made. And we know enough about him to know he's dangerous."

"And loose somewhere in the city," Mick pointed out.

Wisher sighed. "Yes. Quite. And we can't put out an a.p.b. to help track him down without blowing the lid off."

The two men sat in contemplative silence for a few minutes. Mick lit another cigarette, Wisher played with his rosary.

"How did they get this far? Interpol has been on the job since the first rumor of the plot leaked through."

"Maybe they're Interpol-connected."

"What?" Wisher dropped the beads, startled.

Mick's eyes were shrewd, his smile saccharine as he watched his boss's reaction. "Is that so farfetched, after all, Chief? We use double agents all the time. It's naive to think other countries don't do the same. And remember, this isn't an international scam, this is one little fanatic group of anarchists who think what they're doing is all for the higher good."

Harvey Wisher shuddered and snatched up his rosary. "The longer I'm in this business, the more I wonder how we've managed not to become extinct as a race."

Mick ran a hand through his hair and shook his head. "That kind of thinking only gets in the way of getting the job done. One job at a time, isn't that what you preach?"

Wisher laughed self-consciously. "I am a pompous bastard at times."

The younger man grinned. "Yeah, but we all overlook that. So," he asked, changing the subject. "How's Carl doing? That's a pretty creamy assignment he's got, living with that gorgeous Keller broad."

Harvey thought back to his visit with Joanna Keller and shook his head. "No broad, that one, a real class act."

"Yeah, I guess that's true," Mick said. "But still a temptation for any man and we all know Carl is easy prey when it comes to the charms of a beautiful or needy woman."

"And Joanna Keller is both," the chief admitted. "But I always got the impression it was the women who fell all over Carl, and not the other way round."

Mick thought about it, his deceptively boyish face wrinkled bemusedly. "True. Women get serious crushes on the guy, but he never hangs around long enough to test the relationship."

"Unlike yourself?" Harvey asked, sarcasm tingeing his voice.

"Hey! I'm no ladies' man, Chief. I take it where I can get it, true, but I'm always looking for someone I can settle down with. I want something to look forward to in my old age besides a pension and a nursing home for over-the-hill agents." He took another swig of beer and wiped foam off his mouth with the back of his hand.

"You know, a couple of times I really thought Donay had something good going for him with some dame, and then for no apparent reason at all, he'd up and chuck 'em. Poof! History."

It wasn't going to be like that this time, Harvey thought. Whatever went down between Carl Donay and Joanna Keller, it wasn't going to end with a "poof!" They might end up together, they might break up—either way, it was going to leave its mark on them for life.

Mick made circles on the table with the bottom of his wet glass and then looked at his superior. "You realize, don't you, Chief, that our only probability of finding these guys is if and when they show up again at Argylle?"

Harvey nodded.

"And that will probably be when the thing is actually going down. They must be planning to be on the spot—not leaving it to chance—otherwise there would have been no need to send any of their people over here once the shipment had gone out."

Harvey twisted in his seat and snapped, "What's your point, Mick?"

Mick waited a moment, shrewdly studying Wisher's face, understanding his boss's defensiveness. He jumped in anyway, needing to say what was on his mind. "My point is, you're taking a big chance having only one man on it—and particularly Carl Donay."

"Carl's as capable as the next man," Harvey said, letting his glance just miss Mick's probing gaze, focusing on a spot just behind Mick's head.

"No one's challenging his capability," Mick said softly. "It's his penchant for getting sidetracked that worries me."

The rosary beads clicked tellingly against the Formica tabletop. Harvey met Mick's questioning brown eyes and shook his head. "I have a feeling Carl Donay is on the verge of resigning. If that's true, I'd like to see him finish with a success story." The beads lay silent across his hand, as if they'd become a burden. "He's doing fine so far. He's in good with his superior over there, gets along well with the other employees, sticks close to the site. I can't fault him at this stage."

Neither man wanted to belabor the point; Carl Donay was not the enemy.

"I think I've got a lead on Hoxton. I'll be following it up tomorrow," Mick said.

"Good." Harvey slipped the rosary into his pocket, stood up and took his fedora off the rack beside the booth. "I've got reports to go over tonight. I'll talk to you tomorrow."

CHAPTER FOURTEEN

THE PHONE RANG in the middle of the night. Joanna snatched it up and answered in a sleepy voice.

"This is Harvey Wisher, Mrs. Keller. I know it's late, I'm sorry to wake you, but it's urgent I speak with Agent Donay."

"Sure," Joanna mumbled. "Just a minute."

"Wha's that?" Claire asked from the other side of the bed, lifting her head from her pillow.

"Nothing. Go back to sleep," Joanna whispered, feeling around for her robe at the end of the bed.

She stumbled on her way to the door in the dark, and swore softly under her breath.

Carl was a light sleeper. He woke at her first light tap. "Right there," he called out, his voice muffled.

He came to the door in a state of dishevelment: jeans pulled on hastily over his briefs, the snap at the waist left open, his chest and feet bare, his hair falling across his forehead in front and standing up in a cowlick at the crown. Joanna forgot her errand for a moment.

"What's wrong?" Carl asked. He grabbed her hand. "Mark?"

She pulled her hand back, as though stung.

"Mr. Wisher on the phone for you," she said in a low voice. "You'll have to take it downstairs."

She watched as he descended the stairs, waited until she heard him pick up the phone and returned to her own room to hang up the phone there.

She heard his voice say, "Chief," and replaced the receiver carefully. She sat on the edge of her bed, hugging herself for warmth.

"Kind of late for a phone call, isn't it?" Claire asked quietly from behind her.

Joanna jumped, startled at the sound of her friend's voice and the sudden assault of light as Claire turned on the lamp at her side of the bed.

"I thought you were asleep," she snapped, feeling foolish.

"No trouble with his family, is there?" Claire asked, rubbing her eyes.

"Family?" She tried to remember what Carl had told her about his family. "No. I don't think he has any."

"Oh. But surely he wouldn't be called from his job at this hour. They don't work nights over there now, do they?" Claire persisted.

"His job." Joanna shook her head, as much to clear it as to indicate a negative response. "No, not his job."

"Hmm." Claire turned on her side, propped her elbow on the bed, her chin on her palm. "Phone calls at this hour usually mean someone's in trouble." Her face, free of makeup, looked both younger and somehow shrewder in the lamplight.

"I don't know what the call's about and I don't care," Joanna said sharply. "I just want to get back to sleep."

She shrugged out of her robe and got under the covers, turning her back to Claire.

Claire waited a moment and then turned and put out the light.

"If he were my man, I'd sure be curious. You're a lot more trusting and understanding than I am, dear friend."

As a final statement it begged no response but left Joanna with no doubt as to what her friend was thinking.

She squeezed her eyes shut and gripped her hands into fists. Claire was leaving tomorrow. Surely Joanna could make it through one more day of tension and subterfuge. She hated the idea that her friend's leaving would come as a relief, but in the circumstances that feeling couldn't be helped. Claire was too perceptive, asked too many questions, her presence added to the confusion that Joanna had hoped to avoid in these last months of Mark's life.

She forced herself to relax, doing the breathing exercises she and Mark had learned together. They didn't help. She realized that she was very aware of Claire's presence on the other side of the bed, that she was listening for Carl's return to his room. She also realized that she *was* curious, not about the nature of his phone call, she knew that, but about what had happened that would make Mr. Wisher call in the middle of the night.

God, Claire would die if she knew the truth. She smiled bitterly as she thought about Claire's last comment. Obviously Claire thought the call was from another woman. Maybe she even believed that was the reason Joanna and Carl were on the outs. Wouldn't that be a lot easier to deal with?

But then her mind did an instant replay of the picture Carl had made standing in his doorway, his virility emphasized by his disheveled state, and she knew she would never have been able to handle the idea of him with some other woman. Okay, she knew he'd had other women before her, but she didn't have to know about them.

And would have others after he left here.

She punched her pillow and readjusted her body on the suddenly hard mattress. All these thoughts about Carl Donay were counterproductive. His personal life wasn't now, and never would be any concern of hers. So why play these silly little mind games with herself?

From now on she'd only think about what life would be like *after* the case he was working on was solved and he'd moved on. It would be as if she'd never met him.

And she could go back to what Claire referred to as her "love affair with Mr. Clean."

She couldn't wait for the day she could sit down and write a long letter to Claire, explaining the complications that she couldn't explain now. She turned her head into her pillow to stifle the laugh that almost choked her as she visualized Claire's response. That would teach her to make fun of Joanna's dull, domestic life.

CARL HUNG UP THE PHONE but stayed on the deacon's bench in the hall, lost in thought. George Hoxton's body had been found washed up on the bank of the river. The autopsy had just been completed. Mick Johnson had stayed at the morgue, waiting for a firsthand report and then had called it in to the chief only minutes before Wisher called Carl.

Hoxton had been murdered, killed by a single blow to the larynx. The coroner reported the blow had probably been dealt by a man's fist. Mick had found snapshots in the dead man's apartment that they wanted Joanna to look at. The chief was convinced the man she'd seen struck down had been Hoxton.

Carl thrust his long legs out before him and put his hands behind his head, resting his body against the bench back, trying to work out what all of this meant in terms of his own end of the job.

Had Hoxton been the inside man? If so, and if they had killed him, how did they expect to pull it off with no contact inside the plant? Of course if Hoxton had a key, it would be nothing to take it from him once he was dead. But that would mean the perps would be planning to process the saffron themselves. Didn't that take some special knowledge? At least about the workings of the company. He thought about his own limited knowledge, even after working at Argylle for the past few weeks.

He played it over in his mind. Would he be able to go in, process some of the stuff, package it and get it down to shipping through regular channels, all in the dark of night without detection? Even if he got that far, would shipping accept it without the routine paperwork? He shook his head. He knew something about that end of the procedure. Jack Smythe was a tiger about procedure; nothing, but nothing, went out of his department without the stamped and initialed papers that accompanied every shipment. The FDA would come down on them like a herd of buffalo if any of their products hadn't been inspected and approved before leaving the processing plant.

And it was imperative to the criminals' plan that the saffron be shipped from the Argylle company; that was the whole key to their operation, their whole cover.

So, did that mean with Hoxton gone there was no way for them to actually have a hand in the operation? Or could they, at this late date, recruit another Argylle employee? They could even really just sit back and let the saffron go through processing through normal channels. Eventually the contaminated stuff would go out into the markets and then into kitchens and then, *Zap!* He shuddered. Nice people, these political hit men.

Some movement of shadow, or whisper of sound caught his attention and Carl peered down the hall. Did it come from Mark's room? He got up and tread softly to the end of the hall.

Mark was awake, his face pale against the pillows, his eyes still glazed from sleep and medication. He turned his head to look at Carl. "What's wrong?" he asked hoarsely.

Carl went to the bed, settled himself on the edge of it and felt the boy's forehead. "Nothing. What are you doing up? You're not in pain, are you?"

"Uh-uh. I thought I heard the phone ring. I guess I was dreaming."

"Do you need anything?" Carl chose to ignore the comment about the phone rather than lie to Mark.

"Would you sit with me for a while? It gets boring at night when I'm the only one awake."

Carl was surprised. "Are you usually awake during the night?"

"Most nights. I guess the drugs make me sleep so deeply that when I wake up I've slept myself out for a while."

"Why don't you turn on the TV. There's stuff on cable all night long."

Mark pointed to the intercom on his nightstand. "Even though I turn that off, I'm afraid Mom would hear something like the TV and come tearing down here. She needs her rest, needs to keep to a routine."

"That's very—" Carl cleared his throat "—very thoughtful of you."

Mark shrugged. "Usually I use the time to meditate, or just to think or read. Sometimes that helps me fall back asleep. But you know Mom, she'd feel guilty if she knew I was awake and she wasn't keeping me company or fussing over me." A sly grin crossed his face. "Sometimes, when I'm feeling really strong, I slip across the hall to the parlor where I can make a little noise without her detecting it."

Carl had a sudden flash of insight, recalling the way he had taken care of his mother when he was just Mark's age, trying his best to keep their home life as close to normal as he could despite the drinking and the poverty. His heart ached with empathy for Mark. It wasn't that their mothers had anything in common, God knew, but that the boy he had been had so much in common with the boy Mark was.

"Life is a series of repeating cycles," he said, and was surprised he'd said it aloud.

Mark nodded. "Yeah." He gestured at one of the stack of books beside his bed. "That's what I'm learning."

They sat in silence for a few minutes, thinking about that reality.

Carl had almost drifted into that comfortable place between consciousness and a light doze when Mark broke the silence. "Carl, I thought you and Mom had resolved your differences when you moved in here. Now you seem to have more problems. Do you think things will ever be smooth between you?"

Carl stared at the boy, caught off guard by the blunt, unanswerable question. He decided to honor the boy's maturity and be direct with him. "I don't know, kid, that's a tough one. You see—" he settled himself more comfortably on the bed, crossing one leg over the other, leaning back against the footboard "—you hit the nail on the head when you said 'differences', because that's what our real problem is."

"But you really l...dig each other," Mark said, faltering on the word "love."

"Yes. I guess we do. I mean, I know I love Joanna, and I think she loves me, too. You know, Mark, all my life I thought that love meant total commitment to someone, and I avoided it like the plague. But life's more complicated than that, things aren't always pat, don't always fall into place the way you think they will. Now that I really love someone, I'm discovering that love doesn't necessarily mean forever—not if the two people involved have different needs, or different life-styles. Sometimes love can't surmount, or survive, those differences."

"So what happens to it?"

"To love?"

The boy nodded.

Carl shrugged. "I think it must just stay somewhere inside of you, making you feel all sorts of emotions when you think about the person. I guess you chalk it up as one of life's better experiences and hope if it ever comes your way again, it'll be with someone you have more in common with."

Fat chance, Carl thought.

"Seems a shame," Mark said, his head lowered, tracing the pattern of his quilt with his fingers, "that you can't find some way to compromise. About your differences, I mean." He looked up, his expression guileless. "But you must think there's some chance, or you wouldn't still be here. Don't people usually move out when a relationship ends?"

The moment of truth! Carl bit on the end of his thumb and wondered what fancy verbal footwork Joanna would come up with to jump over this hurdle. But Joanna wasn't here, and the problem was dumped at his feet.

So, did he honor the kid with the truth or honor Joanna's wishes with another lie? Was she right, would the truth be too stressful for the kid? He *seemed* strong enough to handle it; why most of the time, to look at him,

you'd think he was perfectly healthy. Maybe a little ane-
mic. Pale. And too thin, of course. Carl frowned.

"We haven't thrown in the towel yet, kid," he said,
rising quickly and running his hands through his hair as
if to hand-comb it into some order. "I gotta get back to
bed—morning comes early, as they say, and I've got work
tomorrow."

He waited until the boy had eased down on the pillow,
and then adjusted his covers and patted his head. Mark's
hazel eyes, so like Joanna's, stared up into his with absolute trust.

"Carl, whatever happens between you and Mom...I
just want you to know how much I..."

It was as if he could read Mark's mind and heart. His
own heart filled with love for the boy and his throat suddenly ached with unshed tears.

"I know, Mark, I know," he whispered, smoothing the
boy's hair off his forehead. This could have been his son
if things had been different. If he and Joanna had met
under other circumstances, or if his life had taken a different turn when he was in college or if...*If, if, if!*

He felt a sudden awareness of the fragility of which
time, and their lives, were fabricated. He wanted to say "I
love you, son" to the boy. Instead he said, "We'll always
be friends, pal, no question of that."

He went quietly and swiftly through the house and up
the back stairs to his room. All his life he'd told himself
that you don't miss what you've never had and, there-
fore, he'd never missed having a nurturing family. He'd
grown up relying only on himself, always searching within
himself for the counsel a mother or father might have
given him, often rewarding himself with silent praise for
jobs well done and scolding himself for his mistakes. He'd

thought of himself as a whole man, mother, father, boy, all wrapped up in one self-sufficient package.

He entered his room and, instead of going back to bed, veered to the easy chair beside a window. This room was at the front of the house, facing the street. With the shade up, the street lamp illuminated the room with a soft, diffused light. He sat in the chair and stared out at the silent, empty night.

Why was he so uncertain of himself in this relationship with Joanna? Was it because this was the first time in his life that his emotions had been tested, his most deeply hidden desires allowed to surface?

The irony was, Harvey Wisher had always accused him of acting on his emotions, rather than remaining objective and impassive. But those were times he'd acted on behalf of someone else's needs, someone else's well-being.

It was as though he'd gone through life only as a caretaker, never needing care himself. Was that why, when faced with real threat, true danger, he could become cold, unfeeling steel?

He thought of the way Joanna nurtured her son. And all the ways she'd nurtured Carl. That kind of unqualified love was what had been missing in his life.

A sigh quivered in his throat and expelled itself as a gasp of despair. *You can't miss what you've never had.* But now he'd had a taste of it, how was he going to face the rest of his life without it?

A tiny flame of hope flared up in his heart; Claire was leaving tomorrow, it would be just the three of them again, with Mark confined to the first floor. He'd have another shot at talking with Joanna. Maybe this time he could make her see reason. There had to be some way to convince her that what they had was a rare chemistry that shouldn't be dismissed lightly.

He uttered a short, bleak laugh. A few weeks ago he might have been able to use their chemistry as an argument. That was before he'd become as addicted to her sense of humor, the depth of her caring for the people she loved, her every gesture, the sounds of her voice speaking and laughing, as he'd become to her sensuality.

He stood up, grunting irritably at his self-indulgent musings. He had no business wallowing in remorse over the relationship, not when all his attention should be turned to his job. He should be resting, reserving his strength, so that he'd be alert to any sign of anything unusual going down at Argylle.

Tomorrow he'd get those photos from Mick, show them to Joanna. If Hoxton was the man she'd seen being beaten up, it would give them a definite lead to pursue.

JOANNA DID NOT RECOGNIZE the man in the photos.

Both Mick Johnson and Carl had suggested she go through them again. She did so, and then shook her head, adamantly insisting she'd never seen this man before.

Mick shoved the pictures and driver's license back into the file folder and slumped back on the kitchen chair. "Dead lead."

"Coincidence?" Carl asked. "An Argylle employee comes up missing the night after Joanna sees two strange men struggling in a window at Argylle, and then shows up dead, murdered. Unrelated to our case? Give me a break!"

Mick shook his head. "I can't find a tie-in, can you?"

"No," Carl admitted, looking morose. "Do you get the feeling that every time we take a step forward on this case, we fall between the cracks?"

The two men exchanged helpless glances while Joanna drummed her fingers on the side of her coffee cup, lost in thought.

"The chief is going to love this," Mick lamented. "Especially when we have to turn this over to the local cops."

Carl glanced at Joanna, something in her manner catching his attention.

"Joanna," he called softly, breaking into her reverie.

"Yes." She blinked and looked from one man to the other, her face wearing a bemused expression.

"There was another man," she said, her voice low with surprise.

"Obviously," Mick said wryly. "Now all we have to do is find out who."

"No. I mean, that night—a third man. I just realized what I really saw."

The two men were instantly alert, straining to hear her every word.

"I saw two men struggling. One of them, that Jan Pod...Podanski?...hit the other. The one fell. Jan bent down so they were both gone from my view for a few seconds. Then I saw a man bent over, sidling away from the window as if he was dragging something heavy. I didn't see his face. I only assumed it was the same man I'd seen strike the blow. I just now realized he was wearing a sweatshirt and jeans."

Carl blinked and shook his head. Mick caught on at once, his voice raised by his excitement. "What had Jan been wearing, Joanna?"

"A suit and tie," she announced triumphantly.

"You're sure?"

"Positive. A dark suit, and a dark shirt. And definitely a tie. It swung out when he hit the man."

"The third man from the Island?" Mick suggested to Carl.

Carl nodded. "Or another inside man at Argylle."

Adrenaline seemed to whiz through his system as Carl pondered the possible ramifications of this new information. His feeling that there was still an operative working inside was stronger than ever and he could hardly wait to get back to his files to look for that elusive clue that would point toward the identity of the man.

To a civilian, the endless study of data might make the job seem boring, but Carl accepted the fact that it was a major part of the job, accounting for as much as ninety percent of their work, knowing that most of the time the answers were found somewhere in the miles of printed pages the computers spewed forth. It was not unlike working a jigsaw puzzle. The excitement began when the puzzle began to come together as a recognizable picture, even before all the pieces had been put in place. And sometimes, like now, it might take only the one right piece to help make sense of all the rest.

Mick, too, was eager to get back to the legwork. He stood up and carried his coffee mug to the sink. "I'll get back to the river. I've an idea that there's more to be learned from my man down on the wharf." He turned to Joanna. "Mrs. Keller, thank you for the coffee and for this latest bit of information. You've been a great witness and a big help."

Joanna smiled at the man, thinking again how much he reminded her of a young accountant or bank teller, and stood up to show him out. "I'm glad I could help, Mr. Johnson," she said, moving past him to lead the way through the hall to the front door. She lowered her voice in case Mark had awakened, "I'm so relieved that I remembered what I'd actually seen. I don't even know what triggered the memory, or why it didn't come to me sooner.''

Mick paused at the door and gave her the full benefit of his boyish grin. ''You'd be surprised how rare it is for us to get a true picture of events from eyewitnesses,'' he said with a short laugh. ''Usually, memories are so scrambled that the information we do get is practically useless.''

She was thinking about that when she returned to the kitchen, feeling good about the part she'd played in helping the men.

Carl was standing at the sink, looking out of the window at the side yard.

''Your roses are budding,'' he said, as she reentered the room.

''Those are the early roses,'' she said, going to his side to look out with him. ''They're tea roses, long-stemmed with small blooms. The big, fragrant, gaudy ones won't come into flower until the middle of summer.''

They stood, side by side, gazing down into the thorny bushes where tiny, tightly furled, pastel buds pointed upward as if seeking the last vestiges of sunshine before the sun set for the day. ''You're a helluva gardener, Joanna,'' Carl murmured.

He couldn't believe he was babbling small talk, and stringing it out so endlessly.

''It gets me outdoors, keeps me busy,'' she responded, hardly breathing for fear her emotions would surface and make her show her true feelings.

Carl cleared his throat. ''You do everything well.''

''Not everything. But thank you, anyway.''

The few inches of space between them seemed to pulse with excitement; it made Joanna's breath catch in her throat, made Carl take a step backward as if he was afraid it would somehow ensnare him.

"I should get back to my files," he said hoarsely, shoving his hands into his pockets before he could succumb to the need to reach out and touch her.

"Mark will be up soon, I should start dinner," she said, putting her hand out to the window frame for support.

"Claire got off all right?"

"Yes. A Dayton's executive took her to the airport by limo."

"Listen, Joanna, about Claire, you know there was nothing personal in my running a check on her, don't you? It was purely routine if she was going to be in the house." Desperately he searched for something he could say that would get through to her. "It was as much for your safety as for anything else."

"I *told* you she was not involved. You refused to believe me."

He rubbed his chin, frustrated. "Why do you refuse to understand that I couldn't just take your word for that? Don't you know how many people live with other people for years and don't know these people are leading double lives? Bigamists, counterfeiters, embezzlers, yes, even murderers, are usually very average-looking people. They don't usually wear signs around their necks that say Deviant. And there's always some neighbor or friend or family member who insists there was no sign that the guilty party was involved—or even capable—of perpetrating the crime."

Joanna went to the table and sank down on her chair. She knew, intellectually, that everything he was telling her was true, that he'd only done what any good agent would do. But that had been at the crux of their problems all along: the fact that he was involved in work that brought him into constant contact with criminals and that the methods he used to bring them to their knees were not so different from those used by the criminals themselves.

"You're right," she admitted to Carl. "But that doesn't make it any more palatable."

He sensed a letting up in her anger, an easing of the tension that had vibrated between them all week. He joined her at the table. "I know this has been difficult for you, Joanna," he said, his voice low, soothing. "And Claire's showing up in the midst of it, could only have made it worse. But I need you to know that I've always tried to keep from letting the work make me cynical." He gave a short bark of a laugh. "You'd be surprised how much that's got me into trouble on my job."

It was true, he really wasn't a cynical man, not the way she suspected Mick Johnson was under that bland, boyish exterior. There was something hard-edged about Johnson that was missing in Carl. Or was that wishful thinking?

"I have to start dinner," she repeated, pushing back from the table.

He looked up at her, his eyes beseeching. "Does that mean you forgive me?"

She shrugged. "It means if I don't start dinner soon, we'll have to resort to canned stuff," she said coolly. "I don't know that it means anything else."

"But you'll think about what I said?"

"Yes."

He had to be content with that, for now. It was clear Joanna needed time to sort through things.

CHAPTER FIFTEEN

DINNER WAS A QUIET AFFAIR with Claire gone. Mark pushed his food around on his plate listlessly, and seemed more tired than usual. Joanna bit her tongue to keep from prodding him to eat, and tried to make light, bright conversation. Carl ate as heartily as usual but seemed lost in thought, keeping his head bent over his plate for most of the meal.

When Mark asked to go back to bed, before dessert, Carl got up without a word and carried the boy back to his room. Joanna sat at the table in the back parlor and told herself there was no change in Mark's condition, that he was just reacting to the week's stress. Now that Claire was gone, the house would return to its normal, quiet state and Mark would spend more time resting. She and Carl could switch rooms again.

But something inside of her told her she was deceiving herself. Fear rose up from her stomach to her throat, filling her mouth with the bitter taste of bile. She shuddered and reached for her water glass, telling herself she was overreacting.

She was almost grateful for Carl's return to the table, glad not to have to be alone with her thoughts.

"I'll carry the dishes back to the kitchen," Carl said, starting to stack them, "and you can go in and sit with Mark."

"Don't you want dessert?"

"No, thanks. I talked to Mick Johnson just before dinner. Something's come up and I'm going to have to go out for a while."

She was surprised, and showed it; he hadn't left the house at night since he'd moved in. "What about your surveillance?"

"I don't think I'll be gone long. It's not likely there'd be any activity over there until much later at night."

He paused in the doorway. "Joanna, can we talk a little more when I get back?"

She considered saying no. But, although she wasn't ready to resume an intimate relationship with him, she definitely wasn't comfortable with the tension that vibrated between them, and she feared that some of Mark's stress might be a reaction to that.

"I should be back in a couple of hours," Carl added for incentive.

"All right, we'll talk," she agreed, hoping she wouldn't regret it.

She moved mechanically through the evening's chores, torturing herself with the pros and cons of resuming her relationship with Carl.

He wasn't home by ten. Mark had asked for his medication a little earlier than usual and was sound asleep within a few minutes of taking it. She showered, washed her hair, buffed her fingernails.

At eleven she decided to curl up on her bed with a book. When she found herself rereading the same page over and over, and listening for Carl's footsteps on the porch, she turned the book over and closed her eyes, falling asleep almost instantly.

She awakened to the sound of static, muted and distant, but clearly audible in the otherwise silent house. She eased quietly off her bed, crept out of her room and out to the hall, following the sound.

It was coming from Carl's room. She hesitated outside the door, listening to the strange sound. If he was home, why hadn't he knocked at her door?

Perhaps he had, and she'd been too deep in sleep to hear him.

She rapped gently. "Carl?" When there was no answer, she knuckled the door harder.

He still didn't answer and she turned the knob and peeked around the door. Carl wasn't there. His bed was still made, the only light coming from the monitor of his receiver. The screen was blank except for a snarl of jagged lines that obscured vision. Now that she was in the room, she could hear the sounds of people moving around and voices above the static.

Someone was over at Argylle! She stood in front of the receiver and stared at the assortment of dials. Would one of them clear the screen or reduce the static, so she could determine who was over there?

She moved over to the window. Yes. There were lights on at Argylle, but nobody appeared near the window. Frustration and panic swamped her. She bit on her thumbnail, wondering what she should do, wondering why Carl wasn't here tonight of all nights.

But he wasn't there, and something was going on next door that might be important. Dare she fiddle with any of those dials, try to get a clear frequency?

She studied the receiver. What would be the worst thing that could happen if she just reached out and turned that dial there, just a little? "You could lose the picture and sound altogether, dummy," she muttered, taking an involuntary step backward.

The receiver squawked and she heard a voice say, "Over there—", before more static chewed up the rest of the sentence. It sounded like a man's voice, but she couldn't be sure, and behind the voice she'd heard thumping and bumping sounds as if things were being moved.

Putting some distance between herself and the temptation to fiddle with the mysterious dials, she went over to the bed and sat down, straining to hear more audible words through the sputtering.

Where could Carl be this late? And where had he gone in the first place? What was it he'd said? Oh yes, that he had to go out for a while. Something had come up with Mick Johnson. Some FBI business.

A scenario played through her mind. He'd finished his business with Johnson and then gone to his condo to get some things, or to do his laundry. He'd lain on his bed, maybe to make a phone call, and the comfort of his own bed had lulled him to sleep.

She reached for the phone. Of course. He was probably just at his own home, sound asleep. She had to look up the number again, and then she misdialed in her panic and had to start over, taking deep breaths to steady herself.

She let the phone ring twelve times before she gave up. She sat, holding the phone on her lap. Could he be at the office—his real office at the agency? She wondered how one found the number for the FBI. But when she opened the phone book she found it easily, right there in the blue pages headed, Government Listings. She was even more surprised to find the CIA listed, just as accessible as any of Dayton's department stores.

There was no answer at the agency's offices, either, but after the fourth ring, a tape came on to announce their normal hours and to say that this tape was monitored regularly and the caller was invited to leave a message if his business pertained to something of vital importance.

She was so surprised to find herself listening to a recorded message that she missed the first sound of the beep. She dialed again, waited through the message and then said in a breathless voice, "This is Joanna Keller. It's imperative that I get hold of Carl—I mean Special Agent Donay—right away. Something is happening over at Arg..." She hesitated, wondering how much it was prudent to put on a tape that anyone might listen to, and then said, "next door. He'll know what I mean."

She hung up and then sat there feeling foolish. The tape had taken the wind out of her sails, somehow reducing the importance of the business next door.

She went downstairs, prepared to ignore the scratchy transmission on the receiver. She'd done all that could be expected of her in the circumstances. Nevertheless, she went to the front door, opened it and looked up and down the street to see if Carl might be coming into view. His car, a nondescript gray, midsize sedan wasn't parked across the street, either, so she was sure that it wasn't him prowling around over at Argylle.

She went back to her son's room. Mark was asleep, his breathing shallow, his face pale in the dim light. She crept to the window and peered out. The light was still on, but again she didn't see any people.

She pulled the rocker back into the shadows and sat in it, keeping her eyes on the window. What if the very thing Carl had been waiting for was going down now? How long would it take for Carl to get the message from the tape?

She rubbed her eyes, realizing she was straining them in her efforts to keep them trained on that window without blinking. Maybe the men Carl and Mick were trying to

identify were over at Argylle right now. What if they did
whatever it was they were planning to do over there and
then left, leaving no clues behind for the agents to follow?

She glanced over at the bed. Mark didn't show any signs
of waking anytime soon. The lighted window on the third
floor of Argylle seemed to beckon her with wicked per-
sistence.

What if she went over there, as she'd done once before, and just got a good look at whoever was there? At
least then she'd be able to positively identify the men for
Carl. And maybe she'd even be lucky enough to hear them
talk about where they were going when they left Argylle.
The idea unnerved and excited her. Did she have the
courage to try it? She'd been clumsy last time, bringing
herself to Carl's attention by her carelessness. She'd have
to be deadly careful this time.

The night was warm when she left the safety of her back
porch and crept down the path to the door in the wooden
fence, but as she unseated the metal latch she found herself shivering. She leaned against the fence on the alley
side and fought to control her heightened breathing.
Could she go through with this?

She decided to take it one step at a time, not committing herself to anything. She'd go as far as the loading
dock and maybe no farther.

At the concrete platform she told herself she was only
going to test the door, see if it had been left unlocked
again. She held her breath, more than half hoping it
would be locked.

She almost fell backward in surprise at the ease with
which the door opened, realizing then how desperately
she'd wanted it to be locked.

She didn't have to go in, she told herself.

She peered out into the darkness beyond the spill of light from the floodlight over the loading door. Still no sign of Carl.

A ray of hope illuminated her mind. She could just sit out in her yard and wait until the men came out and then follow them.

How? On foot? She choked back a groan. She didn't have a car—hadn't replaced her old one when the transmission went out six months ago. She hardly went anywhere beyond walking distance from her home these days and, when she did, she used cabs.

No, if she was going to get the goods on the bad guys, she was going to have to get up the nerve to go inside.

I'll just go as far as the shipping room, she promised herself. *If I can't hear anything from there, I'll just give up.*

In that fashion she worked her way from the alley door to the shipping room, and from there to the stairwells leading up to the third floor. Outside the door that opened onto the third floor, she rested against the wall, forcing her breathing to slow down, dabbing at perspiration on her face and neck with a tissue she found in her jeans pocket.

She was being an idiot. A reckless, suicidal idiot! How many times had she sat beside Mark, watching horror or mystery movies and insisting no woman in her right mind would go alone to check the noise in the basement, or single-handedly try to take on a murderer?

But she had no intention of confronting these people; she merely intended to observe them and, if possible, find out from what they said to one another who they were and where they were going. She wasn't going to let them know she was in the building.

She heard voices the minute she eased the door open and was startled into almost letting the door handle slip out of her hand. She tightened her grasp on the knob and peered through the narrow opening.

The lab across from the exit was in darkness. But the one beyond it, farther down the hall, was lit up. She let the door close quietly and pondered her next move. She tried to recall the layout of the two labs. They were adjoining. Was there a door between them? She simply couldn't remember.

She slumped against the stair rail, thumped her forehead with her fist. *Think, Joanna!*

Her mind unfolded an image of herself as a child, sitting on a high stool in a lab, her father's secretary waving at her, a cherry-red lollipop in her hand. Joanna had almost fallen, trying to scramble down off that high stool.

She'd seen the secretary through a glass window that separated the two labs!

That meant that if she could get into the lab across the hall undetected, she could crouch down behind some equipment and observe what was happening in the adjoining room.

But if the first lab was dark, that meant the light from the other room wasn't spilling into it. So either the window had been taken out or there were some kind of blinds or drapes that were drawn across it. The good news was she'd be able to get into the lab unseen by anyone in the other room; the bad news was that if the blinds were drawn on the other side, she wouldn't be able to see a thing.

You'll never know until you get in there, she reminded herself.

The four feet of floor space between the exit door and the door of the lab seemed to stretch for miles. She had to cross that distance as silently as a rose opening and still do it fast enough to get into the lab before anybody came out of the other room into the hall and caught her.

It wasn't until she had her hand on the knob of the lab door that it occurred to her the room might be locked. Sheer panic swamped her, dampening her palm with perspiration so that it slipped on the knob. The sound of men's voices was louder in the hall though she couldn't make out the words over the roaring of her own blood in her ears. It seemed to take forever to wipe her palm on the seat of her pants and get the door open.

The lab was dark except for the tiny monitor lights on the machines, and blessedly cool. She rested against the door until her shaky legs felt strong enough to bear her weight and her eyes adjusted to the darkness.

She almost gasped aloud in relief when she saw that the blinds, drawn across the window that divided the two labs, were drawn on her side. Light from the other room made a glow around the frame of the window, indicating that there was enough space there for her to peek through without moving the blinds. She made out the outline of a desk beside that window and crept to it, carefully feeling her way around two workbenches and a computer stand.

MICK JOHNSON threw up his hands and let his chair legs rock back to the floor with an angry thud. "I give up! This guy isn't going to talk. Let's ship him to Washington and let them try to break him."

Carl studied the elderly man across the table and shook his head sadly. "Since I've spent a whole evening with you, Augustus, I'd hate to have someone else get the last dance." He leaned forward and lowered his voice, "And you wouldn't like the kind of people we'd be turning you over to, their tactics are a little ... er ... crude."

Nothing. The man Interpol had identified as Augustus Mueller seemed unfazed by the hours of grilling. Unlike his two interrogators, he remained as neatly dressed as he'd been when Mick Johnson had come into the galley of the tug and placed him under arrest. During the interrogation, the two American agents had stripped off their jackets and rolled up their shirtsleeves. Mick Johnson's tie was pulled askew.

Mueller wanted a cigarette, badly, but the two men had denied him that satisfaction, hoping that as an irritant it would work to loosen his tongue. It hadn't. A man who was willing to die for his cause would certainly forgo minor addictions for it.

"We know you didn't come into the States alone, Mueller," Mick snapped. "We even know the guy with you was Podanski. So what do you think you'll gain by clamming up now? We've got you—we'll get him. You may as well consider the game over." He banged his fists on the table, almost spitting the words into Mueller's face, "We want the name of the guy you've got inside Argylle!"

Carl glanced at his watch and rubbed his eyes. "Christ, I've left my post for six hours, and for what? Listen, Mick, you're going to have to take over here, I've got to get back."

Mick nodded. "Yeah. The chief will be down shortly. Meanwhile, Mr. Elegant here, and I, will have another go at it. Listen, Carl, thanks for meeting me here. I appreciate your help. Nobody else was available on such short notice."

"For all the good I did," Carl said wryly, taking up his jacket and casting one last regretful glance at Mueller before leaving.

Carl passed through the outer office, buttoning his cuffs, his jacket under his arm. Fatigue had dulled his senses, making his eyes gritty, his head ache. He'd been up since six that morning, put in his eight hours at Argylle, passed an hour with Mark and Joanna before dinner, and then spent another six over here on interrogation detail after Mick had called to say he'd found Augustus and was bringing him down for questioning.

He almost missed the blinking light on the switchboard. It caught his peripheral vision on his way to the door, just as he was skirting the receptionist's desk.

BACK AT THE PLANT Joanna could hardly hear anything the two men were saying. Apparently the two labs were almost soundproof, and except for a single word or two, she couldn't follow their conversation.

But she could see them clearly through the minuscule space between the blind and the glass, and she could see what they were doing.

The man she recognized as Jan Podanski was lifting the tops off three aligned cardboard barrels, with a short crowbar. In the intense fluorescent light, the contents appeared a garish yellow color. It looked like saffron—one of the most formidably priced ingredients called for in her gourmet recipes. She hadn't bothered to replace her supply when she'd used up the small amount she'd purchased the first time, since Mark said he didn't like "yellow meat."

What she couldn't figure out was what they were going to do with it and what it had to do with the case Carl was working on.

The second man looked vaguely familiar. Maybe she'd seen his picture in one of the many stacks of photos Carl and Mick had shown her, though she couldn't recall that she'd heard his name. He was smaller than Podanski, and thin, with light brown skin and dark eyes and hair. Mexican, perhaps, or Puerto Rican.

They seemed to be arguing, though Podanski appeared to be overriding the other man's arguments for he continued to lift barrels onto the workbench, his mouth set in grim, determined lines.

If she couldn't hear them, how was she going to find out what their plan was? She crept away from the window and eased onto the swivel seat behind the desk. She needed to think. She put her head in her hands and closed her eyes. Nothing came to her. She'd put herself in a precarious position to try to help and she'd accomplished nothing. Now all she could do was either sit here until the two men had gone, a wait which might take up most of the night, or try to sneak out as she'd come in, taking a chance on being discovered.

It occurred to her then that she could hide in the stairwell, listening for their departure. From there she'd be able to hear if they talked about where they were going as they went through the hall. *But what if they used the stairwell themselves?* She had no idea if the elevator power was on during the night.

She opened her eyes and stared ahead bleakly. The phone on the desk caught her eye. It was one of those complicated affairs with rows of lighted buttons alongside the dial pad and a speaker for intercom exchanges. Maybe she should try the agency's office again, make her message more urgent. Given the soundproofing of the room, and if she kept her voice low, the men in the other lab wouldn't hear her.

She lifted the receiver very gingerly and listened for the dial tone. It was dead. She frowned and stared at the panel. Of course, she had to push one of the buttons to get an outside line. She fingered three of them and selected one, almost gasping with relief when she was rewarded with a dial tone.

She kept her voice to a decibel above a whisper as she begged the tape to get hold of Carl Donay or Mick Johnson as soon as possible and tell them that she was at the Argylle plant and that Jan Podanski and another man were doing something suspicious in the lab there.

She had barely finished leaving her message when the door sprang open and two men leaped forward to grab her.

CHAPTER SIXTEEN

"LISTEN, YOU CAN'T DO this," Joanna urged. She tried to keep her voice reasonable, tried not to display her fear, as she pulled uselessly at the rope that bound her hands to the water pipe that ran up the wall beside the very window she'd peeked into earlier. "I have a sick son at home, I must get back."

"Shoulda thoughta that before you come nosing over here, lady," Podanski growled. He had his back to her, his heavy shoulders hunched over the barrel he'd returned to after tying her up.

The other man, whom she'd heard Podanski call "Julio," kept sending her beseeching, worried looks, though he'd made no effort to help her nor to defy Podanski's orders. It had been Julio who had located the rope and had done the actual binding.

She slumped back against the wall, her legs curled under her, and fought back the tears of frustration and fear that welled in her throat and burned her eyes. How long had she been here, and how much longer would she be held captive, leaving Mark alone in the house?

And how could she not have taken this possibility into account when she'd left Mark alone? She couldn't see the wall clock from where she was imprisoned, but she knew she'd been gone a long time. Mark might be awake by now.

"You've got to forget about this now, Jan," Julio whined. "We'll never get away with it."

"We do it!" Jan snapped.

"Look, if this woman noticed the lights and came over, what's to stop anyone passing by from noticing?"

"Who?" Jan's head, too small for the broad breadth of his shoulder line, jerked up. "Who passes this way at night?"

When Julio didn't answer, Jan answered himself, "No one." He set the last barrel on the stainless steel table. "Now. You get started. We do something from six containers—that gives us a good chance it gets to enough people to do the job."

Joanna listened to the two men, her mouth agape with surprise. They were doing something to the saffron. Why? And why in the middle of the night in such a clandestine operation? She forgot her own fears for herself and Mark, her discomfort huddled against the water pipe, and gave the men her full attention.

"How am I going to get this past shipping?" Julio was arguing.

"You'll do it," the other man said, calmly. He looked up at Julio, a voracious smile on his face, "Or you die."

"The way George did," Julio rasped in a whisper.

"Yah. You saw what happened when Hoxton refused to cooperate."

"You didn't have to kill him," Julio snapped, his face gleaming with sweat under the bright lights.

"Yah, I did. If he was not with us, he was against us. And if he was against us, he was not to be trusted. He was executed for being a traitor."

The implacable calm of the man's tone made the words all the deadlier. Joanna shivered and hunched into herself. Such a man would not hesitate to kill anyone who got in his way. Did that include her? She swallowed a whimper and tried to make herself as small as possible.

Had Carl got her message yet? He couldn't have, or surely he'd be here by now. Where could he have gone? She bit her bottom lip to keep from crying out in frustration and watched, wide-eyed, as Julio brought a stoppered bottle to the work area, the skull and crossbones of the poison symbol clearly marked on its side.

Both men were absorbed in their evil task when Joanna became aware of a faint sound from somewhere outside the room. She thought at first she was only imagining the sound but then Jan lifted his head from his work, tilting it to the side in a listening gesture. Her heart sank. If whoever was out there had come to rescue her, he'd given himself away. And nobody she could think of would make a competent adversary for the cold-blooded Jan Podanski. Maybe she should scream, warn them.

As if he'd read her thoughts, Podanski came over to her and clamped a large, rough hand over Joanna's mouth. She tried to pull away from him but he was unbelievably strong and more than a little determined. His hand smothered her, cutting off her breathing; she was going to die there and then, from suffocation. She shut her eyes and prayed that she would die quickly and that Mark would be taken care of.

She felt herself beginning to sink into oblivion just as a crashing of the door resounded in the room and voices began shouting around her.

Podanski's hand flew off her mouth and gasping gratefully at the sudden freedom to breathe, she opened her eyes and saw Carl crouched in the doorway, Mick Johnson standing behind him. They were both pointing guns, holding them in two hands.

She watched as the scene unfolded in slow motion before her eyes, Julio throwing himself to the floor, Jan beside her, pulling a gun of his own from his jacket pocket, Carl taking one step forward, his face a grim, implacable mask. And then the terrifying explosion of sound followed by the weight of Jan Podanski as he fell back and slumped down on top of her.

The screams seemed to go on forever. She wanted to put her hands to her ears, to shut out the terrible sound, but her hands were tied and she couldn't move her arms under Podanski's weight.

And then he rolled off her and she was staring down into his sightless eyes, watching the trickle of dark red blood ooze out of his silent mouth, feeling the heaviness of his lifeless hand, thick-fingered and coarsely haired, resting on her knee.

The screams were her own; she realized it just as she was passing from the terrible light into blissful darkness.

THE HOSPITAL CORRIDORS were quiet, the lights reduced to a mere glow, at this hour of the night. Carl stood outside the door of Room 302 and spoke in hushed tones. "You're sure she's going to be all right, Doc?"

The doctor ran his hand over his face wearily and shook his head. "I told you, Mr...er...Donay, is it?"

Carl nodded.

"I told you she was suffering from shock. As far as I can tell, she suffered no other injuries. When the sedation wears off, she should be...better, depending on how badly she was traumatized. If necessary, we might have a psychiatrist look in on her before we release her."

"And the boy? Mark Keller?"

Dr. Stanton moved around Carl and used the wall for a backrest, plunging his hands into the pockets of his white coat, and closed his eyes for a moment.

"The boy is another matter." He sighed heavily and opened his eyes. "We called his own doctor, and as far as I know he's still with him. From what I've learned so far, the boy has been hanging on quite a bit longer than they expected and now he's had a relapse. No reason. It's the way the disease progresses. He could die during the night, or wake up in the morning good as new." He shook his head again, looked bemused. "No rhyme or reason," he said softly, sadly.

He cleared his throat. "And now, I've got to get some rest or I'll be joining my patients in one of these rooms."

Carl tiptoed into Joanna's room and pulled a chair up to the side of the bed. Joanna looked more dead than alive, her face pale, her body motionless. He could barely detect her breathing. He took her hand in his and kissed the palm. It smelled faintly of rubbing alcohol. She didn't stir.

"Joanna," he said softly, "I'm so sorry I got you into this, so sorry you had to see..." He couldn't go on. He cleared his throat. The lump didn't dislodge nor did the burning sensation go away.

"I love you, Joanna," he whispered, leaning forward.

He couldn't hold back the tears, they came suddenly, unexpectedly, bubbling in his throat, spilling from his eyes. His face was instantly wet with them. He used the edge of her top sheet to dab at his eyes.

He let the corner of the sheet fall back in place and stood up, going blindly, hurriedly from the room.

Joanna stirred, whimpered in her sleep, turned slightly on the bed. Her hand fell on a damp spot on the sheet and closed around it. She slept on.

Over the next two days, Carl haunted the hospital corridors, going from Joanna's room on the third floor to Mark's on the fifth. The nurses began to call him by name.

Mark's relapse had been brought under control by drugs, with intravenous feedings to compensate for his poor appetite. Almost overnight he seemed his old self, chatting up the nurses and teasing Carl about mooning around the place.

Joanna was another matter. Physically she seemed fine, if a little tired and a little pale under her tan. Carl told himself she'd look healthier, less wan, after she got back to her house and garden, back to her normal, uneventful life. But beneath her polite, even pleasant demeanor, there was a weighty reserve he'd never seen before. And with just the slightest gesture on her part, she'd made it clear she did not want to be touched.

That, the doctor told him, was the aftermath of trauma. In time she'd return to normal.

Carl believed Dr. Stanton. Because he needed to.

He was very busy now, cleaning up all the loose ends of the Greenwich Island/Argylle case. They were still interrogating Mueller who was no closer to breaking even after learning the mission had failed and Podanski was dead. Statements were being taken from Julio Venzuela, while the state department was checking back to see if Venzuela had made a legal immigration from San Juan into the United States, twenty years earlier.

Podanski's body would be shipped back to Greenwich Island for burial and in a few days someone would have to transport Venzuela and Mueller to Washington for further questioning and for a federal hearing. Carl supposed, since it was his case, he would be the one assigned to go, and most likely Mick Johnson would partner him on the trip.

Joanna brought Mark home from the hospital, gave a statement to two other agents and a secretary, who came to her home to take it, and caught up with her chores. Carl had removed his things from the spare bedroom while she was in the hospital; she went in to air and clean the room, keeping her mind blank as she erased every trace of his presence there.

Carl had sent flowers to the hospital, and brought another bouquet with him when he came over to see how mother and son were doing.

"Thank you," Joanna said politely, but Carl saw that her face was grave and that she didn't bury it in the flowers to enjoy their fragrance. She also didn't offer him refreshments and when he said this visit had to be short because he had to get back to the office, she didn't demur.

Mark's greeting was more enthusiastic and, for the half hour Carl spent with the boy, he could almost pretend that things were as they had been.

On the drive back to the office he questioned the wisdom of having moved his things out of Joanna's house during her absence. Maybe if he was still living on the premises, he could use those odd moments he was home to help speed up her healing process. Dr. Stanton had not been able to give him a definite time frame for how long that would take. And despite Mark's seemingly rapid recovery, there was something different about him that made Carl uneasy: an intensity in his eyes, a new hesitation in his movements as if his limbs had become too heavy to move freely.

As it was, Carl had moved out because his need to be at the house had ended once the plot to poison the saffron shipment had been aborted. Furthermore, he didn't want to take advantage of the fact that they had been lovers; if he was going to share a roof with her, he wanted it to be clearly at her request, and not because he was already living there under other pretenses.

Besides, the aftermath of a case often required more attention, was more time-consuming, than the field operation. He'd known he'd have to put his personal needs on the back burner until the case was marked closed.

Joanna worked with new dedication in her garden, pulling weeds almost violently, greeting new growth with a tenderness that exaggerated the plants' frailty. She took Mark out to the yard with her, refusing to be out of sight or sound of him for even short periods of time. When he protested, insisting he was too tired to go out, she gave up going herself and let the garden take itself over.

They returned to the life they'd shared before Carl had come into it. When Carl telephoned, Joanna was as polite to him as she would be to any stranger, answering his questions in as few words as possible, and offering nothing personal to encourage a more protracted conversation.

She slept very little, finding the nightmares sapped her strength more than the loss of sleep, and when she did sleep, it was usually on Mark's bed or in a chair beside it. Neither of them questioned this change in her behavior; Joanna was acting on instinct, Mark seemingly grateful for her vigilance.

He was too weary to protest, in any case. He wasn't going to make it to Christmas. He knew that now, though his doctor had pretended that Mark's resilience might surprise them all and give him another thirty or forty years. He was bone-tired, every movement costing him energy he couldn't seem to summon with the same confidence as before.

He'd given up reading and playing with his computer or board games, and he watched television with only half his attention. His meditations were lasting longer, he didn't seem to want to surface from them and when he did, he couldn't quite focus on the reality of his room, his house, his mother.

Joanna bit back the words of anger that raged in her mind and fought the tears that welled in her eyes. In silence the two of them began the journey that would bring them to the place in the road where they would part company. When she was alone, she prayed for the miracle that would make this relapse temporary and bless her child with one more remission. For those few moments, she could make herself believe it was possible.

When Carl called to say he was leaving for Washington the next morning, to transport Mueller and Venzuela there for a hearing, she felt nothing but relief. The farther away he was, the better.

Her aversion to Carl was growing in direct proportion to Mark's decline. Every time she heard from Carl she recalled, vividly, the sight of that lifeless body at her feet, a life taken by Carl with devastating speed and ease, and no sign of remorse whatsoever.

She knew, in some part of her mind, that he had probably saved her life by killing Podanski. She also knew that Podanski was a vicious killer. But the pieces didn't fit together to make her tolerant of Carl's part in the man's death; taking a life, *any life,* seemed horribly evil and immoral to her.

She didn't say any of these things to Carl; there didn't seem any point in giving him a chance to argue with her, to defend himself. She just wanted him out of her life, once and for all.

A week later Carl called to tell her he was being sent to Greenwich Island to help round up the rest of the organization responsible for the plan to contaminate the saffron.

For Joanna it was like hearing from an acquaintance from a distant past. She listened politely, made the proper responses and said goodbye with no regret.

Before hanging up, Carl asked, "How's Mark?"

"The same," Joanna lied.

"Listen, Joanna, I know this has been tough on you, and I don't know how long I'll have to be away, but when I get back..."

"Yes," Joanna said. "We'll see. Goodbye, Carl." She hung the phone up and went back to peeling carrots as if the call had never interrupted the chore.

THE PLANE WAS A SILVER bird with wide-spread wings, soaring against the autumn blue sky, before dipping and diving to ease onto the runway. Inside the cabin, Carl and Mick straightened their seats and checked to make sure their carry-on bags were firmly in place at their feet.

"I suppose you'll be going right to the Keller house," Mick commented, fastening his seat belt.

"Yeah," Carl said, not bothering to try to control the happy grin that lit up his face. "It's been hellish trying to get hold of her by phone. The Island must have the worst phone service in the world."

"Hmm." Mick glanced past Carl, looking out of the porthole at the airport terminal coming into view beyond the wing. "You're sure she was home all those times you called?"

"Even if she wasn't, Mark would have answered. Unless a miracle has happened in the past three weeks, and the kid is up and around like everyone else, they're pretty much housebound."

Mick kept his thoughts to himself. He'd seen Joanna after the business went down at Argylle; she'd been withdrawn, shown little interest in the kudos being pressed on her for her part in helping the agency, and even less in Carl Donay. Maybe it was the aftermath of shock, as Carl believed. Mick hoped so. If not, Carl was in for a real disappointment.

Mick cast a sideways glance at his friend and grimaced inwardly. If ever there was a guy who was setting himself up for a fall, it was his friend here. You'd think if a man waited until his mid-thirties to fall in love for the first time, that he'd do it with a little more reserve. But then, when had Carl Donay ever done things by the book, or like anyone else?

"Listen, Carl. Why don't I go over there with you?"

"You?" Carl looked surprised. What the hell did Mick think he could do to help if things went badly?

"Why would you want to go along, Johnson? You know you hate mushy love scenes."

He hated to see grown men cry, even more. Nevertheless, he persisted. "Yeah, well, actually, I was just thinking I'd like to get to know them a little better. After all, I am the closest thing you've got to a friend, or family, so I ought to be the one to sort of put the blessing on this whole thing."

He didn't blame Carl for laughing, it had sounded pretty hokey to himself, but what the hell was a guy supposed to say on the spur of the moment?

"So," he said, when Carl finally sobered. "You'll humor me?"

Carl studied Mick Johnson's face, looking for some glimmer of mischief there. Seeing none, he nodded and shrugged. "Sure, suit yourself, pal. You can keep Mark company while I give his mama a greeting worthy of a three-week absence. Ah, here we go."

People were standing, pouring into the aisles, eager to deplane and get to their destinations. Accustomed to air travel, the two agents remained seated, waiting till the aisles cleared before standing.

"You going to tell her about your decision to leave the service?" Mick asked.

"Yes, but maybe not right away. Joanna has some problems to work through, and blaming my job is just another smoke screen she throws up to keep from looking at the truth."

"Hea-ea-vy, man!"

Carl looked sheepish. "Okay, so that sounded like pompous pop psychology, but you know what I mean. I just think my job isn't our real problem."

"Maybe not, but you gotta remember, she already lost one old man to this business. That's bound to have an effect on her attitude toward our game."

"How many agents have we lost this year?"

Mick thought about it. "Maybe four?"

"And how many people were killed in car accidents, plane crashes, train wrecks? Not to mention, tornadoes, hurricanes, drownings and home accidents?"

"Yeah, yeah. I've heard it all before, buddy, but that doesn't change the fact that cops are out there asking for it. What's really amazing is that our incidence of fatality isn't higher."

"Exactly my point," Carl said, looking smug.

Mick clamped his lips around his teeth. It wasn't his place to play devil's advocate between Joanna Keller and

Carl. All he could do was be there for the guy if she dumped him, as Mick feared she would.

"You know, Wisher had a feeling you were going to retire. He mentioned it a few weeks ago, before you made it official."

Carl frowned. "I never discussed it with him. I don't think I really knew I was going to do it until we got to the Island and I realized I wanted to start a new kind of life with Joanna and Mark."

"New as in risk-free?" Mick asked with a chuckle.

"New as in debt-free," Carl said, ignoring his friend's humor. "It finally hit me that I was doing this job for all the wrong reasons and my real debt was in making a success of my life, not in my career choice."

"Do I know what you're talking about?" Mick asked. His face depicted sincere confusion.

"No. And you don't need to. I was just sort of doing a self-affirmation out loud."

The aisle cleared and they took up their bags and deplaned. Mick smiled coyly at the hostess as they passed her at the ramp. He'd carried on a flirtation with her for the entire trip and he knew he could score with her if he pressed his advantage. He didn't. It had been enough that she'd made the long flight a little more interesting, while Carl slept his way across the ocean and half the continent.

They'd driven to the airport in Carl's car. It was parked in long-term parking. They threw their bags in the back seat and buckled in for the ride into St. Paul.

"You come from a large family, don't you, Mick?" Carl asked as they swung into the line of traffic on the freeway.

"Oh, yeah! Eight of us kids, and two of my mom's sisters living with us when I grew up."

"I never knew that. How come they lived with you?"

"Dad brought 'em over from Ireland after my grandma died. My ma was so homesick for Ireland and Dad thought it would help to have her kid sisters with her."

Carl chuckled. "That must have been an interesting combination, an Irish mother and a Swedish father."

"You betcha. Food at our house was pure torture."

Carl laughed outright. "You and Mark Keller ought to hit it off."

"Why's that?"

"He loves to torment and tease Joanna about her cooking." His heart felt as if it were doing flips in his chest when he thought of the two of them.

"Yeah, well, I'm serious. Can you imagine a life where the highlights of a holiday meal consisted of boiled dinner, soda bread and lutefisk?"

Carl pictured the large family seated around a dining-room table, laughing, talking, complaining about the food. "Sounds great to me," he said.

"It traumatized me for life," Mick joked. "I don't think I could ever marry anyone but a French chef."

"Or a McDonalds cook," Carl quipped, reminding his friend of his real culinary weakness. Whenever they'd been partnered in any foreign country, the first thing Mick looked for was a fast-food franchise.

They were approaching Seventh Street, the main artery from the freeway leading to the downtown section. Carl signaled a lane change and reduced his speed to forty-five.

"I guess it sounds good to me because I was an only child," he said, lounging back in his seat now that he was free of the tension of freeway driving.

"It was great," Mick admitted. "I think the reason I've never felt the urge to marry is that I had so much family. I never really felt alone. We're all still very close, you know, and there's about a hundred nephews and nieces to satisfy any paternal urges I might feel twinges of now and then.''

The tension returned as Carl signaled a right-hand turn onto the bridge going across the river. A mixture of excitement and fear stirred in his bowels and stiffened his spine.

What if she wasn't glad to see him? What if she still thought of him as a cold-blooded killer? Would she listen to reason, give him a chance to plead his case? Worse, what if she was still the withdrawn, implacable stranger she'd been those last weeks before he left?

The house showed no sign of life. But then it wouldn't, for Joanna kept the front windows and door closed at all times. He took a deep breath and unclasped his seat belt.

Beside him, Mick did the same.

Ten minutes later they stood on the street and stared at the impenetrable house. Every window and door was locked. Nobody had responded to their repeated knocking and bell-ringing.

''Maybe they're at the doctor's,'' Mick suggested.

''Yeah, maybe,'' Carl said desultorily. Suddenly his face cleared. ''I know, I'll go over and ask Jack Smythe. He always knows what's going on over here.''

The shipping room foreman pumped Carl's hand, openly pleased to see him again, and then shook Mick's hand as Carl introduced them.

''You sure had me fooled, fella,'' Jack said, grinning at Carl. ''Guess that's part of why you guys are so good at your jobs.'' He took off his cap, scratched his head, put his cap back. ''Say, is that why you're here? More trouble?''

"No, Jack, no. I . . . well we wondered about the people next door. The Kellers. They don't seem to be home and I know—"

"You mean you didn't hear?" Jack interrupted.

Carl's heart gave a mighty lurch and his voice was reedy as he asked, "Heard what, Jack?"

Jack's voice lowered and his forehead furrowed. "The boy died. Two weeks ago, now. I went to the funeral." He shook his head. "Sad. That was one swell kid, you know. Watched him grow up from diapers. Never gave his mother a moment's heartache till he got sick."

Mick grabbed Carl's arm, sensing his friend's loss of equilibrium.

Carl began to shake and he leaned into Mick's shoulder. "What . . . what about the mother . . . Joanna?"

Jack nodded. "Yeah, that was the worst of it, the way Joanna took it. Like she was frozen, or something. Never shed a tear, never said a word. Her friend . . . you know, that dark haired model-type . . . she was with her. I guess they went back to wherever her friend lives. Saw them get into a cab with a ton of luggage."

Claire. Joanna was in New York with Claire. Carl plunged his hands into his pockets, curled into fists. Why hadn't Joanna contacted him, let him know about Mark? Even if she didn't want anything more to do with Carl, she had to know how much the kid meant to him.

He felt the tears loosening in his chest and turned away. "Gotta go, Jack," he mumbled. "Thanks."

Without speaking, Mick held out his hand as they walked around the building to the front where Carl's car was parked, and Carl handed him the keys.

Carl held on until he was seated in the passenger seat and then, oblivious of the other man's presence, he let the tears come in great, noisy gulps, bending his head to his arms folded on his knees.

Mick sat behind the wheel, feeling his own eyes burn with compassion. What did a man do when another man was hurting this way? He'd expected to have to comfort Carl if or when Joanna rejected him. But this was different. This was almost like watching a man find out he'd lost his son. Hell, it was exactly like that. During their weeks away, Carl had talked about Mark Keller as much as he had about Joanna, and with just as much love and pride.

Mick Johnson was enough of a family person to understand that kind of love, that special pride you could have for a family member who was a joy to be around. Much as he prided himself on his bachelor status, he always knew he'd like to meet a woman and have a family of his own.

He acted on instinct, the way he'd have acted if this were one of his brothers who'd suffered the loss. He put his arm around Carl's shoulder and pulled him over against his chest, offering the physical solace of brotherly love.

CHAPTER SEVENTEEN

CLAIRE STRAIGHTENED Joanna's collar as she moved up in the line with her. "You're sure you want to do this alone, honey? You know I could arrange to take the time off and go with you."

"We've been all over that, Claire," Joanna said, her voice heavy with fatigue. "I need to do this alone."

The man in front of her had put on his after-shave liberally. The heavy fragrance was beginning to nauseate her. She turned slightly, trying to escape the smell and caught the frankly intent gaze of the middle-aged woman behind her.

She put a trembling hand to her hair and turned back. "Let me get your boarding pass for you, Jo," Claire insisted, seeing her friend's discomfort. "You go sit down for a few minutes."

Joanna accepted the offer with relief. Would the exhaustion ever pass? She felt as if she were carrying fifty extra pounds around when, in fact, the opposite was true; she'd lost at least ten pounds in the past few weeks.

She went to a row of seats facing the long windows that gave a panoramic view of the airfield. Would she ever be able to lift a forkful of food to her mouth without hearing Mark's teasing comments about "gourmet goop"?

She took her sunglasses out of her purse and slipped them on, feeling the warning of tears scalding her eyes.

But they didn't come. They never did. Just that intense burning behind her lids and the heaviness in her bones.

"You'll be boarding ahead of the crowd, since you're traveling first-class," Claire said, coming up to her with her pass. "That will help."

"Yes," Joanna admitted. "It will be good to get settled for the flight."

Claire plunked down beside her, for once forgetting her perfect model's poise. "I feel so damned helpless, Joanna, as if there were a million things I could have done, and just didn't see."

Joanna put her arm around Claire's shoulder and hugged her. "You did just fine, Claire. If you hadn't been there, that last night, I don't think I could have survived. And it meant so much to Mark to say goodbye to you."

The tears poured from Claire's eyes freely. She wiped them with a tissue and then blew her nose. Joanna envied her the ability to cry. She, herself, seemed to see and feel everything through a layer of gauze, so that she couldn't connect with reality. At least in Great Britain, away from everything familiar, she might be able to find a new way to look at life, a new reality to focus on.

"Did I tell you, he called me his other mom," Claire said. She blew her nose and chuckled.

"I know. His words for us were, 'a motley pair of mothers,'" Joanna said.

"Why that little devil," Claire said, frowning. "Were we? Motley?"

Joanna shrugged. "Sure. I looked it up. It means 'an incongruous mixture.'" She grinned at her friend. "We are that, aren't we? That's how we decided we should become friends in the first place, remember?"

"Yeah." Claire's voice had softened, her eyes, still misty, looked off in the distance. "We were going to take the campus by storm."

They were silent, each remembering.

"You should have gone by ship," Claire said, coming back to the present. "It would have been so healing to be out at sea."

"Ships are too recreational," Joanna said wearily. "I don't want to socialize. Quite the opposite. Besides, my trip through the British Isles will give me plenty of sea air."

"You will keep in touch, Joanna?" Claire fretted, not for the first time.

"Of course. Postcards from everywhere, and maybe even a letter now and then."

Claire knew she had to be satisfied with that. She recalled the old adage, *she also serves who only stands and waits*. Her job as a best friend was just to be there whenever Joanna found her way back. Just as Joanna had always been there for her when Claire came home from New York, needing to get back in touch with her roots, or take a break from the rat race.

The loudspeaker announced the boarding of first-class passengers on Joanna's flight and Claire walked with her to the tunnel leading onto the plane.

They hugged, kissed, hugged again, and Claire pressed a fresh tissue to her eyes as she hurried away from her friend.

Joanna bit her lip to keep from calling Claire back, to beg her to come with her. She squared her shoulders, handed her ticket to the uniformed attendant and stepped forward onto the ramp.

She slept for most of the flight, the first real sleep she'd had in weeks, and was slightly disoriented as she stumbled down the steps to the airfield at Heathrow. But everything went smoothly. The rental car Claire had arranged for her was ready and waiting.

Claire had been a wonderful help, making all the travel plans through her own agent, just as she'd facilitated Mark's funeral arrangements. The car, a small, blue sedan, had an automatic transmission, air conditioning and a radio. All the comforts of home, Joanna thought, waiting for the attendant to load her luggage into what he called "the boot."

It took her a while to adjust to the right-hand wheel, and to driving on the left, but once she'd practiced, she found it no problem. She stopped, on the first leg of her journey, in a small village outside Leeds.

She signed the register at the desk in the lobby of the small, domestic hotel and looked around, finally appreciating that she was in a foreign land. She had agreed with Claire that she should drive through Great Britain first, and save London for the return trip, when she would be more rested. She was glad now for having made that decision, especially when she got her first glimpse of the charming hamlet with its quaint cottages and sparse population.

She'd made no reservations at other stops, wanting to have the freedom to stay longer in any one place if she chose, or to move on if she was uncomfortable or restless.

In this way she journeyed across Great Britain, driving along the coast with her window rolled down, breathing in the salty, invigorating sea air, stopping to look in tiny shop windows, or to pick wild heather, or to dawdle over a sumptuous high tea in a rain-dampened outdoor garden of a hotel in Newcastle upon Tyne.

She spoke to few people on her trip, other than to ask for services or to exchange comments about the weather. In Scotland she left the hotel she'd planned to stay at, because a large, American tour group was staying there, and found, instead, a quaint little pub with rooms to let upstairs. It was far more homey than the hotel and offered a lovely Scottish breakfast the next morning.

Sometimes she followed the guidebooks and maps that Claire's agent had compiled for her, and sometimes she just followed the road and let herself accept what came.

Her appetite had returned after her second day on the road, and she'd begun to look for out-of-the-way places to dine where she might enjoy authentic food of the region. She managed to find pubs and cafés where the food was well prepared and she began to regain the weight she'd lost.

Often she'd speak to Mark, as if he were there beside her in the small car, pointing out some place of special beauty or something unique that had caught her attention.

And she thought of Carl every day, missing him in an elemental way that went deeper than just surface memories. In an ideal world, she'd be making this trip with Carl, sharing the assorted bedrooms with him, hurrying him through his morning ablutions so they could be on the road before it became congested with traffic, feeding him bits of leftovers from her plate when he'd finished his own meal, teasing him about the way other women gawked at him when they entered a shop or café.

But Carl was far away, in a world she couldn't be part of. They would never have been able to make a leisurely, random trek like this together, for Carl would have been at the beck and call of the agency. Joanna knew she could never have tolerated a single moment of his work again.

In Glasgow she bought a camera and film, realizing that she wanted to record this time in her life. It was her first step back into society. Scotland merited the recording, it was breathtakingly beautiful country.

The picture-taking gave some substance to the trip, making it less aimless. She began to think of some future time when she would be curled up in her own front parlor, or on her own bed, looking at the pictures and remembering the trip. This was also a first—the first time she could envision herself at home without Mark, doing something that gave her pleasure rather than pain.

Thinking of herself alone in her house naturally led to thoughts of Carl there with her. She brushed these images away. It was never going to happen.

She sent postcards to Claire, and one to Jack Smythe. He'd come to the church for Mark's funeral and seeing his homely, sad face had made her feel very grateful. Like her house, he was a part of her history, a part of Mark's.

Despite the beauty of Scotland, it didn't feel like a place she could settle in for any length of time. Wales had a rugged, terrible beauty of its own, but there too she felt a restlessness that drove her on. She began making her way back toward London, looking for that special place where she might be comfortable for more than a few days.

Once she'd found such a place, she planned to write a long, chatty letter to Claire, sharing some of the thoughts that had begun to form in her mind, and the feelings she was beginning to have again. Not the ones about Carl, though. Those were too private to share with anyone. And too pointless.

CARL HIT THE RETURN KEY on the computer keyboard and sat back to wait for the information to come up on the screen. He'd been at it for two days, barely taking time to eat or sleep, determined to get a fix on Joanna's location.

Despite Mick's protests, he'd taken the first available flight to New York, without calling first, positive that he'd find Joanna at Claire Hanson's apartment. He'd been wrong on two counts: Claire lived in a brownstone she'd bought and renovated and Joanna was no longer there.

Claire had been wonderfully hospitable, offering him a drink and then dinner. They talked in her kitchen as she took a foil package from the freezer, unwrapped it and placed the plastic tray in a microwave oven.

"I get these from my favorite Italian restaurant," Claire told him. "They make them up in double servings for when I have a guest. I only have to nuke them for ten minutes and voilà!"

Carl sipped the ice-cold vodka martini she'd given him and felt the alcohol loosen muscles and nerves that had been tied up in knots for days. Now that he was here, in Claire's all-white and stainless steel kitchen, he felt closer to Joanna than he had in over a month. She might not be here, but, if anyone could help him find her, it would be Claire.

"You don't look so good, Carl," Claire said, frankly, squinting at him over the top of her own martini glass. "Wasn't the trip to the Island successful?"

"Joanna told you about it?"

"Uh-huh. Everything." There was no note of censure in her voice, it gave Carl fresh hope that she would help him find Joanna.

"We tied everything up nicely. The bad guys are all behind bars and the last bit of paperwork's been stamped and filed."

"Not *all* the bad guys," Claire said, reaching into the clear liquid for the olive at the bottom of the glass. She popped it into her mouth, licked her fingers and looked up at Carl.

Carl frowned. "Meaning?"

"Meaning my friend Joanna sees *you* as one of the bad guys."

Carl sighed and set his glass down on the white marble counter. "Still? Then time hasn't altered her feelings."

Claire shrugged, tapping her long, cherry-red fingernails on the side of her glass. Then she tilted it up to drain it. "You need to understand something about Joanna." She refilled their glasses from the tall, narrow pitcher and led the way to a breakfast nook with a white laminate table and benches covered with black-and-white cushions.

"Her life has been divided into brief spans of time, each marked by the death of a loved one. With each death, Joanna withdrew a little bit more until, by the time she knew Mark was going to die, she withdrew altogether."

She gave Carl a brief, bitter smile. "She came out of it when she met you. Apparently, you represented breathing, living, healthy life to her—a man who could make her feel all the vigor of life and forget the inevitability of death."

He was straining to catch every word, every nuance, everything he could learn about Joanna. "And . . . ?"

"And then you represented death to her. Worse, you delivered it with your own hands. You became the Grim Reaper."

Carl shuddered at the woman's choice of words. A graphic and terrible description of how Joanna viewed him.

His shoulders slumped and his jaw slackened. Futile. It was all futile. Even if she learned he'd left the service, there was little chance Joanna would want to have anything to do with him.

He said as much to Claire and was surprised by her abrupt burst of laughter. There was no humor in it.

"Oh, you do take on the guilt of the world, don't you, Donay?"

"What does that mean?"

"I just explained Joanna's problem to you, so you immediately assume you're not worthy. You haven't done anything wrong, Carl, you're not the one with the problem, so why are you acting like the villain in this piece?"

"So what are you saying?" His voice trembled with frustration. "I *do* have a chance with Joanna?"

She shook her head. "That I can't tell you. I don't know. Joanna may very well stay in her own emotional rut forever. All I'm saying is, why should you park your tail between your legs and slink off into the night? You have a right to go to her and present your case. If she's healed enough to listen to you, and if you know what words to say, and if she loves you enough..." She shrugged again and then got up in response to the chime on the microwave.

"Then you'll tell me where she is?" Carl asked, following her across the room.

She put the tray on a trivet and handed him two dinner plates with cutlery and napkins rolled up on top. "Can't. I don't know where she is."

Of course she knew where Joanna had *been*. Claire gave him the three postcards she'd received and told him the name of her travel agent. That had seemed a good starting place, but he'd been forced to return to the agency, to resort to the computer to follow the paper trail of credit card receipts that seemed to go off in no particular direction with no hint of where she'd go next. She left no forwarding addresses at the inns or hotels where he discovered she'd stayed, ostensibly because she didn't know, herself, where next she'd stop.

Five days after Carl returned from New York and began his computer and telephone search, he struck pay dirt. A week ago she had registered at an inn in Clacton, a small coastal city renowned for its resorts and, according to the person who'd taken his trans-Atlantic call, she was still there. He looked at the series of clocks on the wall and saw that it was three o'clock in the afternoon in London. That meant she wasn't likely to be checking out that day.

He shouted his victory as he punched a key that commanded the computer to print out the information on the screen and went tearing into Wisher's office without even bothering to knock.

"So you're off on your white charger to claim the fair maiden," Wisher quipped as he put down the phone after speaking briefly to his secretary. "We can get you on an airforce plane out of Fort Snelling at five o'clock this evening. Clacton is just a short distance from London. There'll be a car waiting for you at the airport." He was already redialing the phone to set things in motion. "And Carl," he called after the younger man's retreating back. "Good luck, son."

The flight overseas seemed endless. Normally Carl was able to sleep on trans-Atlantic crossings, but on this occasion his mind would not relinquish thoughts of Joanna and what he would say to her.

His seatmate was a small, neat, balding army colonel who was doing an inspection of American bases in Europe and who busied himself with paperwork from a bulging briefcase until he finally dozed off, a government form clasped to his chest. They hadn't exchanged more than a few words since boarding.

Carl resigned himself to the hours of idle solitude and concentrated on rehearsing his opening speech to Joanna.

JOANNA LOWERED THE CAMERA from in front of her face and stared, wide-eyed, at the woman who had popped into the frame, making faces and jumping around like a spastic monkey.

The woman's laughter was raucous, her face reddened by her physical exertions. "I couldna resist, deary," she said, on a trail of laughter. "You've been so solemn, going about your picture-taking as if it were the work of the devil himself. I thought you needed a little life in your pictures, a little fun."

"I—that was—" Joanna heard herself faltering, trying to put words to her reaction and then her own sense of humor, dormant for weeks, rose up and took over.

At first it felt good to be laughing again, especially when the other woman nodded and joined in. And then Joanna's laughter became uncontrollable, going on and on, becoming louder and louder until she realized she was almost screaming.

And then, finally, the tears came, and they wouldn't stop, either. Not even after the woman rushed to her side and swept her into her arms, clucking soothing sounds, patting her back.

They were in front of the pub where Joanna had been taking pictures of the old carriage pull-up that was now used as a driveway for delivery trucks. The woman eased her back to a bench that fronted the old stone building and down to the seat, still rocking her, still making those comforting, unintelligible sounds.

No thoughts crossed Joanna's mind. There was no self-pity, no anger in the crying; it was simply a breaking up of the chunk of ice that had so long rested in her chest, a spilling forth of feelings long buried. She cried because it was finally time, and because it felt so good.

She let herself be held against the motherly bosom of the strange woman, breathing in the comforting scent of lavender and starch, and hearing, over the sounds of her own sobs, the cooing sounds of sympathetic understanding.

She didn't realize, until she began to make out some of what the woman was saying, that her sobbing had quieted to weeping.

"There luv, there," was what the woman was saying. "Let it go, deary, and be done with it."

And when she lifted herself up, brushing her wet eyes with the palms of her hands, hiccuping her last sob, she knew she *had* let it go, and *was* done with it.

"You've lost someone dear, eh, luv?" the woman asked, as Joanna drew tissues from her purse and blotted her eyes.

Joanna nodded. "My son."

"Aye, that'll do it," the woman agreed, nodding, as well. "And you've been holding it in a long time."

"Yes," Joanna sighed, her voice quavering. "A very long time."

The woman held her own purse clasped on her lap with both hands and sat back against the stone wall. "You're staying at the inn, I've seen you there."

"You're staying there, too?" Joanna asked, surprised. "I haven't seen you."

The woman chuckled. "You haven't seen *anyone* have you, deary?"

Joanna looked rueful, shook her head wonderingly. "No, I suppose that's true, I haven't."

"Well. Time's right when it's right. And here we are now, and I'm May Perkins, if you're ready to take on a new friend."

Joanna grinned. "I'm ready." She held out her hand. "I'm Joanna Keller and I'm very grateful to you."

May took the younger woman's hand and shook it solemnly. "No need for gratitude, Joanna Keller. I'm glad to give comfort when it's called for."

She stood up, gathering Joanna's camera and camera bag along with her own handbag and took Joanna's hand. "Come. I get nippy if I don't have my tea on time. We'll have a proper English tea and I'll tell you the story of my life. After that, you'll sleep like a bairn."

Joanna let herself be led by the woman, enjoying the maternal fussing of the older woman after weeks of fending for herself. Suddenly she too was feeling a little "nippy" and ready for a meal. Besides that, she was suddenly aware that she was eager for company, happy not to be alone any longer.

They had tea in the dining room of the inn. When an elderly couple came in and took a table near theirs, May called out to them, "Come and say hello to Joanna Keller, my new American friend."

She introduced Harold Galsworthy as a retired vicar and his wife, Muriel, as a bridge master.

"I'm impressed," Joanna said. "I've never met a master before."

"You play?" Muriel Galsworthy leaned forward, grasping Joanna's hand with undisguised passion. "We've been losing our fourth almost every day. Nobody seems to stop for more than one night these days."

"I play only in the most amateurish fashion, I'm afraid, Mrs. Galsworthy."

"Please, call me Muriel. And don't be afraid of playing poorly. You'll make a most suitable opponent for Harry," his wife stated. "He only plays to make up a fourth. Really, Harry hates bridge, don't you m'dear?"

The vicar nodded and gave Joanna a reassuring smile. "It would be a pleasure to play opposite someone who doesn't take the game as seriously as these two," he said, including May Perkins in his gesture.

She shared their table in the dining room after their first meeting. May was at the same table. At night they played bridge in the lounge.

But Joanna spent most of her days with May Perkins, the two of them strolling along the high street or beside the quay or, when the weather allowed, on the beach in front of the inn, sometimes talking earnestly about life and places and people, and other times just walking in companionable silence.

May, Joanna learned, had been a school teacher in Swansea, Wales, and had never married. Joanna could easily picture her keeping a group of rebellious teenagers in line. She was amazed to learn that May had actually taught kindergarten for forty years. That accounted for May's ability to drop all the inhibitions most grown-ups were hampered by and do the most absurd thing at the drop of a hat. She was always surprising Joanna, making her laugh.

Joanna found herself talking about Mark to May, telling about the years when Mark had been well and they'd been closer than most mothers and sons because of Sam's death. She told her new friend about the years of Mark's illness, the waiting, and the knowledge that all there was to wait for was death. She talked about Mark's wit, his unusual intelligence, his acceptance of his own mortality.

May laughed heartily at Joanna's description of Mark's attack on her cooking ability and then sobered to say insightfully, "That must have been the best way he knew to cover his diminishing appetite."

Joanna was shocked. It had never occurred to her. "Why didn't I think of that?" she demanded, her eyes filling with tears. "I should have seen that, realized that's what he was doing."

May laughed at Joanna. "You should have done everything for him, even read his thoughts, right? You weren't two separate people, you were one person?"

Joanna was taken aback by May's sarcasm but she struggled to understand the woman's point. "I...I just thought, a mother should know—"

"A mother and child share a bond, they don't share a single mind," May said brusquely. "We are all mysteries to ourselves, so how could we not be mysteries to one another? Mark was happily busy untangling the mystery that was himself at the end, and that was where he unearthed the strength to give up this life and prepare himself to meet the next. You were so busy clinging to his life, trying to keep it part of your own, you didn't really see Mark as he was becoming, as he became."

They were walking along the wharf, the smell of fish and saltwater heavy in the air around them. Joanna dashed tears from her eyes and blew her nose. It was one of those deceptively warm mornings, making one forget it was early December. By afternoon it might well begin to blow and sleet, but for now the two women were able to enjoy their walk without being hampered by the weather. They sat down on the low stone wall and looked out at the ocean, silent for a time as Joanna absorbed May's words.

"I did want to hang on to him, what mother wouldn't?" she said at last, a little defensively.

"I saw it every year, when my new bairns came to class," May said, her eyes focused on the distance. "Mothers clinging to their babies, not wanting them to leave the nest. It took those children longer to adjust to our routine, kept them homesick, mother-sick, longer." She returned her attention to Joanna, putting her arm around the younger woman's shoulders.

"The first day of school is the first day of another life. Every new experience is another life." She put her hand on Joanna's face and turned it so that they were eye to eye. "Some of those lives we share with our parents, some with other people, some alone. Mark saw death as just another one of those lives. You were not meant to share it, Joanna."

CHAPTER EIGHTEEN

CARL STOOD ON THE PORCH of the Seaside Inn, his coat collar pulled up to shield his neck from the wind, and gazed down at the beach, his hands shading his eyes. Sure enough, he could see two women strolling, arm in arm, one distinctly middle-aged, the other, tall, slender, her hair a blaze of silver in the stringent morning sunlight.

"There they are," a voice said behind him. He turned and nodded at the proprietor of the inn who'd introduced herself as Mrs. Grass. She'd told him, when he'd asked about Joanna, that she usually took morning walks with Miss Perkins.

"Yes, I see them," he said, wondering if the woman could hear the barely controlled excitement in his voice.

"They usually come back up for the noon meal, unless they let me know they're going to lunch elsewhere," she said, shivering beside him, and rubbing her arms.

"Have you a vacancy?" Carl asked, striving to sound cool, contained.

"I do. How long would you be planning to stop?"

"I—I'm not sure—" Carl faltered. "Can we leave it open?"

"Aye. I'll just be checking to make sure the room's ready. Why don't you rest yourself inside, where it's warm, and I'll send the chambermaid, Tanya, to take you up in a few minutes."

She'd gestured into the lounge where a fire was blazing in the grate, but Carl stayed where he was on the porch, his gaze following Joanna and her companion on their trek along the sand.

She wouldn't be glad to see him, he had no delusions about that. But she was first, last, and always a lady, so he was sure she wouldn't make a scene. That would work in his favor, give him time to make her hear him out. If she chose to reject him after he'd had his say, well, that was the chance he'd known he'd be taking when he'd begun his search for her. All he could do was try.

He couldn't tell from that distance if the two women were talking or just walking companionably in silence. It didn't matter. It was enough to be able to see Joanna, to watch her, to be this close to her. In only a couple of hours he'd be able to see her face, hear her voice. *Beloved.* The word sprang to his mind, a perfect description of what she was to him.

He grinned at his romantic musings and then jumped, startled, as he felt a hand on his sleeve.

"Sir . . . sir, your room is ready now."

He realized the chambermaid had called to him more than once and he felt foolish as he stammered an apology. "I—I guess I was somewhere else for a moment."

"That'll be the jet lag, sir," Tanya said, her frizzled, brown hair bobbing as she nodded wisely. "Most take a time to get their legs."

He agreed that must be the case and followed her up the wide, open staircase to the second floor.

His room faced the ocean and he saw that he would be able to continue to watch Joanna from the window. He could hardly wait for Tanya to leave so that he could settle onto the window seat and gaze at his love to his heart's content.

He hadn't taken into account the toll the long trip had taken on his strength, or the week of nearly sleepless nights he'd endured; he fell asleep there in the window, his head resting against the lintel, his overcoat still on, his knees pulled up to his chest to accommodate the narrow space.

Joanna and May came up the steps that curved down from the front of the inn to the beach below, bending close to each other to shut out the wind.

"That jacket's not warm enough," May was scolding, as usual. "It's winter after all, even if we don't get piles of snow here."

"Don't bother fussing at me, May," Joanna said with a laugh. "I can't hear you over the chattering of my teeth anyway."

Suddenly she looked up, clutched May's arm and gasped aloud. "It can't be!"

May followed Joanna's wide-eyed gaze to the second-story window where a strange man appeared to be asleep, his head almost resting against the pane. But no stranger to Joanna, it was clear. And yet, for all of their shared confidences the past week, Joanna had never mentioned a man, except for her husband who had been dead for years. From Joanna's suddenly pale face and haunted expression, it was clear this man was somebody important in her life.

"And who is it, it can't be, lass?" she asked, nudging Joanna gently forward.

"It's—I—" Joanna stopped dead in her tracks and stared upward. At first sight of him she'd felt numb, and then her body seemed to go into overdrive. Her blood was rushing through her body, her heart pounding furiously, her breathing heightened. *Carl, here!*

She wanted to rush up the steps of the porch, up the stairway to that room and into Carl's arms. But of course that was only her first reaction. Sanity followed quickly.

"A friend of yours?" May asked. "Someone you weren't expecting?"

Her eyes were dazed when she turned to May. "Expecting? No—no, I—I don't know what he's doing here . . . how he found me."

"You were hiding from him, then, deary?"

Is that what she'd been doing? Hiding from Carl? Surely not. She'd had only to tell him she never wanted to see him again, to make him disappear from her life. There would have been no need to hide from Carl. No, it was more likely that what she'd learned from May was true: she'd been hiding from her own feelings. Did that include her feelings about Carl?

She shook her head, sensing that May was waiting for an answer. "No. I just hadn't let him know where I was."

He looked exhausted. As she moved up the path, she felt a familiar aching in the area of her heart, the ache she'd felt every time she'd looked at her sleeping son.

"Do you want to talk about it?" May asked as they climbed the porch steps.

"Not now, if you don't mind, May." Joanna smiled at the other woman, grateful for her new friend's concern. "I think I'll just skip lunch and go up and rest for a bit."

May's hand on her arm stopped her. "You'll have to face him sooner or later, m'dear," she said softly.

"Yes. But not now, May. I'm just not ready. It's too much to take in without some preparation."

She was pleased to see that Tanya had put a match to the coals in the grate in her room, the chill of her walk suddenly striking right to her bones. She sat in the upholstered chair in front of the fireplace and rubbed her hands together, trying to restore warmth to them. If she was going to stay over here much longer, she'd have to add to her wardrobe; she'd brought no real winter clothes from home, and jeans, sweaters and a windbreaker weren't enough to fend off the coastal winter winds.

She chuckled wryly as she realized her mind had gone off on a mundane tangent to keep from thinking about Carl in that room just down the hall. Obviously her defense mechanisms were still in good working order.

She got up, put the Do Not Disturb sign on the door, slipped out of her jeans and sweater and climbed into bed. She stared up at the canopy over her head and let her mind wander through various scenarios of coming face-to-face with Carl.

If he'd followed or tracked her here, he'd obviously made up his mind to have another go at winning her back. Her female ego sent up a tiny smile over that thought that was quickly squelched by a frown of disapproval from a more practical side of her mind. She had the right to try to get over him and that wasn't going to be as easy with him right here on the premises. She wondered what May Perkins would think of him. Probably like most women, she'd be swept off her feet by his good looks and easy charm.

She was barely conscious of the sound of the lunch bell as she fell into a light doze. She dreamed again of her last moments with Mark.

"I think it's time to say goodbye, Mom," Mark said. He sounded almost cheerful and she wanted to grab him by those thin shoulders and shake him, demand that he give up his foolish idea that death was just another dimension of life, that he fight it with all his might.

But she knew he had no might. He'd grown so frail in these last weeks that she could see all his veins through his skin and his eyes seemed huge in his narrow face.

She looked helplessly around the sterile hospital room, as if hoping to find an answer in the very walls.

She turned back to him as he clutched her hand. He was in pain again. His suffering made her feel guilty; would she really want him to endure this pain a moment longer than he had to?

"Mom, will you do me a favor?"

"Sure, hon, you just name it." She leaned forward and dabbed the sweat from his forehead with a tissue.

"I want you to give Carl a message for me."

She didn't hesitate to agree. Carl was lost somewhere in the far reaches of her mind. Only a name. All she could think about was Mark and what Mark needed. It was easy to agree when Carl was buried so deeply behind her pain that her heart couldn't feel him.

"Tell him . . ." Mark's breath was ragged as he tried to speak again. "Tell him that he was the best buddy a guy could have asked for."

Words of high praise from a teenager. It would have been okay with Mark to say, "Tell him I love him." Mark was that kind of kid. But he was mature enough, sensitive enough, to know that it would be easier on Carl to hear the message the way he'd worded it. Joanna understood that immediately and knew Carl would know exactly what the message meant. For a moment her heart wanted to relinquish the lock it had on Carl's image, but Joanna fought it, concentrating again on her son.

"Claire . . ."

"Claire will be here any minute, Mark," Joanna said. "Just hang in there." It took such an effort not to plead with him.

"I wish..." Mark swallowed, smiled weakly, began again. "I wish you could...know how...easy this is...for me, Mom."

Despite her determination to suppress her tears, a sob escaped. She nodded. "I know, Mark. I do understand, believe me. It's just..."

She didn't get a chance to finish her sentence for just then the door opened and Claire came swiftly into the room, bringing the exotic scent of expensive perfume mixed with the acrid smell of tobacco smoke.

As she bent to embrace Mark, he gave her a weak thump on the shoulder. "I thought you'd...given up the deadly...weed...Aunt Claire." He fought for control of his voice. "Are you trying to...shorten...your life?"

Claire sat on the bed and took Mark's hand. "I couldn't handle this without a cigarette, kiddo," she admitted frankly.

Mark nodded. "S'okay, Aunty Baby."

Claire's laugh hung on the edge of a sob. "I'm going to quit again when...after... Oh, hell, kid, you know what I mean."

"Yeah." Mark's smile faded and his eyelids quivered and closed. "Tired, Mom," he said.

Claire got up and reached for Joanna as the boy fell into a medicated doze. They held on to each other, letting the tears fall openly now that the boy was oblivious to their grief.

"How...how soon?" Claire blew her nose into a monogrammed handkerchief as Joanna wiped her own on a tissue.

Joanna clenched a fist to her mouth and whispered, "Any second, I guess. He thinks it's time. I honestly think he was waiting for you."

They wept quietly as they stood and watched the sleeping boy, each thinking of the wonderful times they'd shared with Mark.

And then he opened his eyes and smiled. "Thanks, Mom," he said. "I really... loved..."

He died with the word still formed on his lips, and in the days that followed, Joanna kept remembering the way the word sounded stronger than any he'd spoken in a long time. "I really loved you. I really loved my life." He could have meant either. Either would mean the same. He was saying she'd been a good mother to him and he'd appreciated her. It helped her accept his going a little.

She was standing beside his grave two days later when she suddenly heard his voice.

"I really loved your cooking, Mom."

Her mouth fell open and her eyes widened in shock. And then she began to laugh. When Claire came running to her side, protesting that Joanna was hysterical, Joanna shook her head and told her haltingly what she'd just imagined she'd heard Mark say.

"That sounds like the brat," Claire said solemnly, wiping at teary eyes, but then she laughed, too, and nodded. "Just like him."

The laughter was a gift from beyond the grave, a last reaching out from the boy to his mother. Joanna clasped it greedily to her heart and began to make plans to continue with her own life.

She awakened suddenly, aware that she had just relived Mark's dying. She always dreamed it the same way, exactly as it had happened. Odd, when she was awake and thinking about it, it only came in fragments, mixing with thoughts and memories of better times in his life.

She sat up against the pillows and pushed her hair back off her face. But Mark never differentiated between living and dying as she did, she reminded herself. It was *all* good to Mark.

She remembered then that he'd given her a job to do for him. Sooner or later she was going to have to deliver his message to Carl.

She shivered and scooted back down under the covers. Later. Time enough to face Carl when she was feeling more rested and better able to keep her emotions in check.

IN THE DINING ROOM all the guests looked up as the tall, handsome man entered the room, his gaze quickly sweeping the area, obviously looking for someone in particular.

May Perkins gave only a brief nod to the knowledge that she was meddling and waved the stranger over. "Won't you join us?" she invited. "We're friends of Joanna's, if that's who you're looking for."

"Yes," Carl said. "I saw you walking together when I first arrived. The proprietor told me you're Mrs. Perkins?"

"Miss. Yes. And you're...?"

"Carl Donay. How do you do, Miss Perkins."

He put his hand out and she hesitated briefly before taking it. Once he was seated, she introduced him to the Galsworthys.

"Joanna knows I'm here, then," Carl observed, putting his napkin in his lap and keeping his eyes lowered in order to hide his disappointment that she wasn't at the table.

"We saw you napping in the window as we came up the walk," the woman admitted.

Carl's grin was sheepish, lighting on his three companions. "Jet lag." He cleared his throat and picked up his soup spoon. "Joanna's late."

"She felt a bit unwell, decided to skip lunch today," May told him. "But I'm sure she'll be fine after a wee rest."

"Ah, I see." What he saw was that Joanna was avoiding him. Of course, she wouldn't want their first meeting to be held in public where she'd be forced to listen to him politely. He covered a burgeoning smile with his napkin. She'd given him an idea. Two could play at that game; from now on he'd make sure she didn't come face-to-face with him until they were surrounded by other people.

With that in mind, he shared his smile with the three at the table and began to pump them subtly for information about Joanna's daily routine.

May waited as Tanya cleared their soup plates and set down the entree in front of each of them, and asked, "And what do you do, Mr. Donay?" using his surname pointedly.

"I'm unemployed at the moment," Carl said cheerfully, returning his attention to his meal. He forked a small, overcooked carrot and popped it into his mouth.

"I plan to open my own law firm soon, though," he added hastily, after he'd chewed and swallowed the vegetable.

"You weren't expected, Mr. Donay," she blurted suddenly.

"No, that's true, May." He put a gentle hand on her arm. "Do you mind if we call each other by our first names? I'd like us to be friends."

"We don't know each other well enough to be friends," May snapped. "Why did you come here?"

"You're a loyal friend, May," Carl said softly. "I'm relieved that Joanna has made friends here."

"And why wouldn't she? There's no finer girl than our Joanna."

His smile was gentle. "I couldn't agree with you more."

Carl went on eating, hardly tasting the food, tuning out the conversation of his companions. Maybe he should go up after lunch and knock on Joanna's door, face her down, as it were. But if he did that, and she slammed the door in his face, he might not have the nerve to keep trying to see her. After all, she knew he was here, and she'd very clearly made a point of ignoring his presence.

On the other hand, maybe she really wasn't feeling well and he'd only be adding to her discomfort by confronting her. He was beginning to question the wisdom of his having tracked her down.

He thought of Claire, envisioned her expression of disdain at his sudden clutch of uncertainty. She'd consider him a real wimp if she could see him in this indecisive state.

He was still lost in thought when Tanya returned with a tray of custard cups, and was surprised to see she'd already removed their luncheon plates.

He looked over at May Perkins who seemed to be studying him thoughtfully. "I'm afraid I lost the gist of the conversation," he apologized.

"Aye," she nodded. "But that's understandable. You've obviously much on your mind."

"Yes." He found he liked the woman, despite her apparent hostility, and he especially liked the fact that she'd befriended Joanna. "I'm not sure I had any right to come," he admitted, deciding to be open with her. "And I'm wondering if I should just leave without seeing Joanna."

May's gaze was penetrating, as if she were looking right inside of him, at his soul. She shook her head. "You're here now. Perhaps you'd best leave it to Joanna to decide if you go or stay. She just needs a little time to figure out what it is she does want.''

Yes, of course, the woman was right. Carl would simply be there, doing whatever it was people did on a cold, blustery afternoon in Clacton, and let Joanna come to him when she was ready.

JOANNA WAKENED ABRUPTLY, as if someone had shouted her name, and lay still, listening. She could hear the sound of her heart pounding and, in the distance, the constant rumble of the ocean, but no other sound close by.

"Must have been a dream," she muttered, turning over to snuggle back into the warmth of the bed.

And then she remembered that Carl was here, in Clacton, in this very building. She shivered, this time not from the cold, and sat up and reached for her chenille robe at the foot of the bed. Her watch said three-thirty. Almost time for tea. Would he be there? Had he slept through lunch? He must have or else he'd have come looking for her.

What would she say to him? How would she act? She went into the bathroom and turned on the bath taps, adding a handful of scented salts from an apothecary jar to the water.

She slipped into the warm, fragrant bath and submerged herself in the cocoon of water. What was it May had said on their walk yesterday? Oh, yes. Each new experience is a new life. Well, Carl was a reminder of the old life and she almost resented his showing up here. She'd just begun to come to grips with the present, was just beginning to think about all the possibilities for the future. There was no future with Carl, so why did she have to deal with him at all?

She'd been thinking about the future more, lately, thanks to her long talks with May Perkins. May didn't believe in "mucking about in the past." As she said, "You miss too much of what's at hand if your mind is busy mucking about in the past."

Joanna thought about what the future might hold in store for her if she was truly able to cut herself free from the past. She could finish the university education her marriage to Sam had interrupted. Or take a job that would eventually lead to a career. She might even meet a man who was her perfect counterpart—a man who wanted the same kind of safe, quiet life she wanted.

She tried to visualize such a man. Tall, because she was taller than average. And with a good build. She liked big men, always had. She could see his hair, the color of old gold in the light, warm brown in shadow. Eyes the color of sea when a storm was brewing, a kind of gray that could be light as pewter or dark as charcoal, depending on his mood. He'd have a large, sensuous mouth that made her lips tingle and her skin sing and he'd . . .

"Oh, damn you, Carl Donay," she fairly shouted, splashing water with her fist as she realized who it was her mind was describing. She took a couple of deep, even breaths and tried to steady her racing pulse. Carl hadn't been here more than a couple of hours and already he was making her crazy.

She breathed in the scented steam and ran her hands through the silken water. "Petulant," she said. "You're being petulant, Joanna." She giggled and pushed lower into the water until just her face was exposed to the air, her hair streaming out behind her.

She closed her eyes. What if they'd taken a shower together the night they'd made love at her house. The fantasy became a picture behind her closed lids, like a film

passing through a projector in her mind. She'd be unable
to tell where the water ended and his hands began, so
gentle would be his touch, so erotic the feel on her sensi-
tized skin. Her body would thrum with excitement and she
would feel herself opening, needing to be filled with his
maleness. He'd accommodate her with a smooth thrust,
leaning against the stall and lifting her onto his hips and
she could imagine how the water would pour over their
faces, bubbling into their kisses.

Gasping a little, she opened her eyes as she realized her
body was remembering as vividly as her mind was, the
ache at her loins already becoming a driving need.

She sat up and began to wash her body hurriedly, willing the hunger away, making herself grasp on mundane
thoughts, like what she would wear for tea.

Carl was here and that was a fact she couldn't change.
She'd be polite to him and firm about the fact that he was
no longer part of her life. He'd give up and go away and
she'd get on with whatever it was she'd set out to do when
she'd come here.

But as she buttoned the front of her blouse and tucked
it into the waistband of her skirt, she couldn't, for the life
of her, remember what it was she'd expected to achieve.

CHAPTER NINETEEN

CARL WAS DISCUSSING the weather with Mrs. Grass in the lobby. As he glanced up toward the stairway, his words trailed away, midsentence.

Joanna was halfway down the stairs when she looked toward the reservation desk and suddenly her hand clutched the rail and her foot halted, midstep.

Their eyes met, held.

She's more beautiful than I remembered, Carl realized.

He's so handsome, so...actually here, Joanna thought.

"Ah, Mrs. Keller, there you are," Mrs. Grass called out. "And look who's here to surprise you."

"Carl," Joanna breathed, hoping she sounded calm, cool.

"Joanna." Carl's voice sounded rusty to his ears and he cleared his throat.

"You...you're looking very well, Carl," Joanna said.

"You too, love," Carl said softly, his gray eyes glinting like burnished metal.

Her foot felt around, found the next step. She took it, and the one that followed, and then she was standing in front of him, looking up into his solemn face, her head tilted slightly back to accommodate the difference in their height.

"Why are you here, Carl?" she asked, even as she wondered why she could never be near him without wanting to enfold herself in his arms, to breathe in his special scent, feel the strength and warmth of his body next to hers.

He looked down into her lovely face and wished he had the nerve to sweep her up into his arms, to kiss her until they were both delirious. "I had to see you, Joanna. There was so much left unsettled between us."

Loose ends.

But that wasn't what her life had been made up of until now. No, all the other endings in her life had been clearly defined; they'd been tied up and put out of her reach forever.

Had she been avoiding a showdown with Carl to keep this relationship from becoming one more final ending? The sudden insight shook her, both physically and emotionally. She put a hand out to steady herself and found she'd grasped Carl's arm.

"I need more time," she said in a near whisper, shaken by her latest self-revelation.

He studied her face and then nodded. "But I'm not leaving until we talk," he warned. The feel of her hand on his arm sent a shock of excitement through him, but he wouldn't let himself think the gesture was meant as a promise of further intimacy. In any case, just then she withdrew her hand, using it to brush her hair back.

"Yes. All right. I agree."

"I was just about to ring the bell for tea. Will you be joining us?" Mrs. Grass asked from behind the registration desk.

They turned in unison. "Yes, Mrs. G.," Joanna said, smiling tightly. "I'm sure Mr. Donay would enjoy one of your special teas."

He did. They joined the trio he'd lunched with and this time he had an opportunity to see, firsthand, how popular Joanna was with the other guests. Everyone made a fuss over Joanna, and with her in the limelight, Carl was able to sit back and observe her to his heart's content. There was something different about her though he couldn't quite put his finger on what it was. She'd always been poised and gracious. And with Carl and Mark she'd often been playful, capricious. Those aspects of her personality were a pleasure to behold, but they weren't new.

As he watched her interact with May and the Galsworthys, he realized there was a serenity about her now he'd never seen before. Would that work in his favor? Had she finally come to accept that there were things in life she had no control over, things she would have to give up fighting?

She laughed softly at something May said and Carl's stomach lurched with the old familiar excitement her laughter always engendered in him. Maybe it wasn't so much that she'd acquired serenity as that the look of desperation was gone from her face, he thought.

"You're very quiet tonight, Mr. Donay," May said, turning to him.

"I'm just enjoying the view," Carl quipped, arching an eyebrow at Joanna.

Joanna felt the color rise in her cheeks and looked away from Carl's frank stare. "Vicar, perhaps after tea you'd like to look at those pictures I took last week at that little church in Ipswich?"

Carl ate two cucumber sandwiches in two bites and swallowed them down with his tea. He'd hoped Joanna would opt to spend some time with him after tea, but he'd promised to give her time and he'd have to honor his promise. "I'd like to see them, too," he said, joining the conversation. "I understand you've become an accomplished photographer."

Joanna's eyes fairly glowed at the compliment. "I'm really an amateur but I'm finding it's incredible fun all the same." Lowering her eyes modestly from his probing gaze, she found herself staring at his arms. He was wearing a blue sweater, the sleeves pushed up to just below his elbows and she realized she'd always thought he had the sexiest arms she'd ever seen. Not to mention the broadest shoulders, the most masculine legs, and overall a perfect build.

Muriel poked her husband with her elbow. "Remember when Joanna told us she was an amateur at bridge? Jo, dear, I'm beginning to think you underestimate yourself drastically."

"It's just that I'm not used to trying new things, I guess," Joanna said, hoping no one had noticed her preoccupation with Carl's physique. "And truly, I haven't played bridge since my mother d...died. I was sure I'd be very rusty."

Carl noticed that no one else at the table seemed to have caught Joanna's hesitation when she pronounced the word "died."

"Well, I for one am very grateful that you didn't forget what you'd once learned," May said cheerfully. "This is the first time I've ever beat Muriel at bridge." She turned to Carl again.

"Do you play, Mr. Donay?"

"What's with the 'mister'?" Joanna asked, with a puzzled look at both Carl and May.

"I asked Miss Perkins to call me Carl, but she seems to prefer observing the formalities," Carl said, helping himself to two more of the small sandwiches as the plate was passed to him. He passed the plate on to May who was seated to his right. "I meant what I said," he told her in a low tone, "I'd like for us to be friends."

"Perhaps . . . Carl. Perhaps."

Her wait and see attitude was no surprise to him, she was clearly in Joanna's camp, not ready to accept him until she was sure he wasn't Joanna's enemy. He liked her for that.

He winked and tilted his head so that none of the others could hear him. "My intentions are purely honorable, ma'am, I assure you."

Joanna smiled at his comment in particular and the table in general and buried her face in her tea cup. Carl certainly had these people eating out of his hand. It was almost fun to watch how easily he charmed May out of what had first appeared to be a very strong reservation about him.

He had the social graces of a diplomat, but then she supposed an agent would find himself in all sorts of company that would require him to be a consummate actor. She almost giggled as she thought of how her new friends would react if they knew what he did for a living. A flash of memory assaulted her mind and sobered her. This man across the table who was calmly eating his sandwiches and smiling benignly at everyone was capable of dealing death in a most cold-blooded fashion. She recoiled from the thought, her stomach lurching unpleasantly.

Carl had been watching Joanna surreptitiously. He saw her look of amusement turn suddenly to one of aversion and knew instinctively that she was having a flashback. Despair swamped him. How could he ever banish that memory from her mind?

Both Joanna and Carl were uncommonly quiet as they finished the meal and adjourned to the lounge to look at the photos Joanna had taken.

They had no time alone from then on. When they got up a bridge game, Carl begged off saying he'd rather sit on the sidelines and observe.

Carl was thinking about packing it in, maybe going for a lone stroll along the beach and then going up to bed, when Joanna got up from the table and came over to him.

"Are you bored?" she asked politely, sitting in the corner of the sofa.

"No, just a little tired. I was thinking I'd take a walk and then hit the hay early."

"Yes, that seems like a good idea. You do look tired." She studied his face, frowning at what she saw there.

"There hasn't been a right moment to say this, Joanna," he said, leaning forward slightly so that she alone would hear him. "But I wanted to say something to you about Mark."

She put a hand up to stop him and her hair swung forward as she shook her head. "No, Carl, please, I really don't want to hear any more condolences. I know you feel sad about Mark's...passing."

He drew back, mindless of how his voice might carry, and fairly growled at her. "Condolences? Is that what you think I was going to offer you? Like some polite, distant relative who shows up at all the family funerals and makes the appropriate sympathetic noises?"

Joanna would have moved farther from him if she wasn't already backed into the corner of the sofa. She couldn't recall ever seeing such anger in another person's face, and certainly not Carl's. "Carl...I...shh..." She glanced quickly at her friends at the bridge table. They didn't seem to have noticed anything amiss.

"Don't shush me, love," Carl hissed. "You're way out of line here, and you know it!"

"I just thought—"

"You didn't think at all, Joanna, or you'd have realized that Mark left behind *two* grieving parents!"

"Wh-what?"

His eyes had darkened and were glinting dangerously at her. Joanna shivered.

Carl put a hand to his eyes and then rubbed his forehead, willing himself to calm. He hadn't meant to attack her. "I miss him more than you could ever know," he said, his voice scratchy with feeling. "I don't think I could have loved him more if he were my own and I'd raised him from infancy."

There was no doubt in her mind that Carl spoke the truth, and hearing a pain so comparable to her own, she reached out to him, instinctively, her hand grasping his savagely.

"I know Carl, and I . . . I'm sorry, so sorry."

He raised pain-darkened eyes to hers. "We should have shared those last moments with him, Joanna, should have shared the grief when he'd gone."

Joanna nodded, afraid if she spoke, she'd cry. Their hands clung, as if they had a life of their own.

"You should have let me know," he accused. "You knew you could reach me through Chief Wisher."

He was squeezing her hand so hard it hurt, but the pain in her heart was worse and she said nothing.

"There was no need for you to suffer alone, or for me to find out secondhand, as I did," Carl continued. "I would have been there in just a matter of hours if you'd have let me know."

She nodded again, letting his pain, his anger, punish her, knowing she deserved it. He was right. She'd been totally insensitive to his feelings about Mark even though she'd known he really loved the boy. Theirs had been a special relationship, separate from the relationship Carl and Joanna had had.

He let go of her hand, to run both his hands through his hair. She remembered the gesture, she'd seen it so often when he was disturbed or frustrated.

And now, as then, she ached to take him into her arms, to offer him solace, to give him something of the tenderness that filled her being when she saw his pain.

They stared at each other for a long moment, each letting the other see the depth of their sadness. And then Carl stood up, shoving his hands into the pockets of his slacks. "You go back to the game," he said, his voice weary. "I'll just say my goodnights and go on up."

Joanna watched Carl leave, mindless of the desperate hold she had on her cards until May pointed out that she was bending them. She cleared her throat, forced her eyes to focus and bid two spades.

She didn't have a single black card in her hand.

THE SUN'S RAYS were feeble this time of year, providing plenty of light, but little warmth. What they did do was cast a sparkle over everything they touched so that sand, sea, air fairly glistened. The air was thin, sharp in their lungs as May and Joanna breathed it in.

"That was some game you played last night," May said, taking Joanna's arm for support as they started down the steps to the beach.

"Yes, I guess you could say that wasn't my finest hour," Joanna admitted, smiling sheepishly.

They reached the bottom of the steps and started across the sand. "You skipped breakfast," May said conversationally.

"Yes. I wasn't hungry."

"Apparently your young man wasn't, either."

Joanna kicked at a piece of dried wood in her path. "Funny, he usually eats like a horse."

"Aye? Well, he didn't even show up at table," May said, stealing a glance at Joanna's profile. "And of course he went to bed before supper last night."

Joanna shrugged and looked out across the vast expanse of ocean. The sparkle of sun on water almost hurt her eyes. "He must have needed sleep more than food."

"I think what he needs can't be found on a pillow or at table," May commented. She felt the stiffening in Joanna's arm but ignored the signs. "Truth is, that young man strikes me as someone who's felt more pain than is good for a body."

"And delivered more," Joanna muttered.

"Aye. That's the way of it, girl. Them that carries guilt feel the most pain." She used her free hand to turn up the collar of her down coat as a draft of wind chilled her neck. "I reckon you've never done anything you wished you could've undone?"

"I never killed anyone!" The words were out before Joanna could realize they'd formed in her mind. She stared at May, her expression as stunned as that of the older woman.

"I didn't mean—I shouldn't have said—"

"You're telling me that warm, charming lad killed someone?"

"No! I mean yes, but it wasn't exactly—" She broke off and went over to the sea wall, leaning against it for support.

May came up beside her and waited quietly, looking out at the rolling sea.

Joanna sighed heavily. "I guess I should tell you all of it."

"Not unless you need to unburden yourself, lass. It's no my business, else."

"I guess it would help," Joanna admitted. "I've never really talked about it to anyone else, not even my best friend Claire though I think she understood without my going into detail."

May nodded, her eyes still focused on the nebulous horizon.

"Carl is an FBI agent," was how Joanna began. When her first words wrought no reaction from the older woman, she went on, unfolding the story of how they'd met, how he'd become entangled in her life, how they'd fallen in love, and finally, how she'd felt when she'd seen him take the life of another man.

Throughout the telling, May was silent, the only sign that she was listening, an occasional nod of her head.

"So, when he left, I made up my mind that that was the end of our relationship," Joanna finished.

May was silent a moment longer and then she turned to Joanna, her face a study in perplexity. "You made up your mind and didn't include Carl in the decision?"

Joanna was confused by the question. "What do you mean?"

"I mean, my young miss, you've told *me* your feelings, your decision, but did you bother to tell *him?*"

Joanna said nothing.

May nodded. "So you let him go off, believing you'd be there for him when he returned, *knowing* he believed that, knowing all the while you'd done with him. Is that about the way of it?"

"I . . . I was preoccupied with Mark's illness, for one thing," Joanna cried, searching frantically for a defense.

"And with his dying," May snapped.

Joanna stared at her friend, shocked. May was always blunt, honest, sometimes sarcastic. But never cruel. She bent her head to her chest and stared, unseeing, at her hands.

"Aye," May went on. "It's easy to see why you began to believe life is about dying, Joanna, the Lord knows you've had a huge taste of it in your life. But that's a distortion of how it really is." She cupped Joanna's chin and turned the younger woman's face to her own.

"Joanna, you see Carl's killing that man as being about death—I see it as Carl's attempt to preserve life. Yours, first of all, and not to mention all those unknowing folk who'd have had a murderous taste of that poisoned saffron."

Joanna looked into the clear, blue eyes of her newest friend and saw the truth emblazoned there, shining out of May's eyes with startling clarity. It was like looking into a mirror at her own soul, Joanna realized, as if May had insight into Joanna that Joanna had never found the key to unlock for herself.

As if she'd read her mind, May nodded sagely and smiled. "You'd have discovered all these things yourself, given enough time, dear heart, but you see you don't have the luxury of that time any longer. Carl is here now, and he's a strong, loving man, but he won't wait forever. He has needs of his own and if you send him away again, he'll get over you and he'll find someone else to fulfill those needs."

"No!" The anguished cry echoed on the crisp, morning air.

"Aye." May put her arms around Joanna and held her close a moment. Her voice was muffled a bit when she said, "I know something about that, Joanna. I lost such a man myself when I was a lass, and spent the rest of my life regretting the deed.''

Joanna drew back but slipped her arm back through May's. "You didn't mention this before, May. Wasn't there ever anyone else for you?''

"No one I could love enough to spend my life with. The irony is, I hadn't loved him enough to give up my way of life and go off with him, and then my life wasn't worth a pin without him.''

"But May, you seem so happy, so... so free.''

May's chuckle was a bitter denial. "So childlike, you mean. I threw myself into my work with the wee ones and spent my whole life in their kindergarten world.'' She shook her head and moved to resume their walk. "Easy to blot out the loneliness when you spend your life wrapped up in other people's children, playing children's games all day. But that was my mistake, lass, it doesn't have to be yours.''

Joanna halted her steps and turned to May. "I don't know if I can just go back there and pretend nothing happened, just shut my eyes to who and what Carl is.''

"Maybe not. Maybe not,'' May agreed. "But you can give him a chance to speak his piece, to hear him out. You can grant him the courtesy of listening to his heart. And then, if you still think you canna make a life with him, you can bid him an honorable farewell and make your peace with him and more importantly, with yourself.''

CHAPTER TWENTY

THE SUN HAD GIVEN WAY to dark clouds that burst open as the wind picked up momentum. By three o'clock it had begun to sleet and rain and even the fires in all the grates did little to provide adequate warmth to those sitting more than three feet away. All the guests wore sweaters, jackets or shawls, and went about their games, or reading, or visiting as if the weather was of no matter.

When Joanna and May returned from their morning walk, Joanna had gone directly to Carl's room, planning to ask him to meet with her before lunch. There was no answer to her knock. Tanya, coming out of the room across the hall with her cleaning cart, told her Carl had gone into town on an errand and said he might miss lunch.

Joanna, eager now to have her talk with him, chafed through lunch and couldn't unwind for the nap she tried to take afterward knowing she wouldn't be able to concentrate on anything as demanding as bridge, she took a book down to the lounge and pretended to read.

She had fallen into a soft doze when she sensed a presence looming over her. She bolted upright in her chair, knocking her book to the floor, and let out a sharp cry of surprise.

Carl bent to retrieve her book and handed it to her with a rueful smile. "Sorry. I didn't mean to startle you."

Embarrassed, Joanna snapped, "Where on earth have you been all day?"

He arched an eyebrow at Joanna and then glanced at his watch. "It's only three o'clock. I can't have been gone more than four hours. I take it you missed me, love?"

His teasing smile made her feel foolish about her irritability. "I just wanted to talk to you and I couldn't imagine what business you'd have in town all . . . for so long."

"Well, I'm here now," he said cheerfully. He pulled a chair over and sat down. "Shoot."

Joanna looked around the lounge. "Not here. Somewhere more private."

"Your place or mine?" he asked, leering comically.

"I was thinking more along the lines of a walk on the beach," she said, ignoring his innuendo.

"In this weather?" He pulled the collar of his leather jacket up and shivered. "I almost froze just getting from the car to the building."

"We're from Minnesota," she scoffed. "We ought to be able to handle a little weather."

"We have things like central heating in Minnesota. We get a chance to warm up before we face the elements. I haven't been warm, indoors or out, since I got here."

"Okay," she agreed reluctantly. "We'll go to my room."

Carl felt his heartbeat accelerate as he followed her up the stairs. The fact that she'd asked to speak to him privately, this soon after his arrival, could bode ill or well. Either way, he wasn't sure he was emotionally prepared to deal with her decision.

"Do you want me to order up some tea?" she asked, when he was seated in front of the fireplace.

"No, thanks." He saw that she was nervous now that they were alone and it added to his own anxiety. "Let's cut to the chase, Joanna. I don't think I can handle any more of this waiting."

She sat across from him and twisted her hands in her lap. "You said you wanted to have a chance to settle some things between us, Carl. I thought it was time we do that."

Carl cocked his head and studied her face. "You said you needed time. Is this it? You're ready?"

"I think so," she said, nodding. She read the doubt in his eyes. She leaned forward, her own expression earnest. "May and I had a long talk this morning. She pointed out some things to me I hadn't seen before. There's no point waiting any longer, Carl. Some things are never going to change and others need to be dealt with right now."

"What things aren't going to change?" he asked softly.

She took a deep breath, swallowed hard and plunged ahead. "My love for you, for one," she blurted.

"Ahh." His soft, relieved sigh was accompanied by a tender smile. "If that hasn't changed, then we can handle anything, Joanna."

She shook her head. "The other thing that hasn't changed is my feeling about what happened at Argylle...and your work...and...and..."

"And we're right back where we started." He was angry. He stood up, restless, frustrated.

"No, I don't think we are," she said, almost pleading. "At least we're talking about it now."

"Listen, what you're saying is, you love me but you can't forgive who I am, what I am," he snapped, pacing toward the window. He spun around. "What if I were an accountant, or a mechanic?"

"What do you mean?"

"I mean, if I had any other kind of job, we wouldn't be having this discussion, right?"

She looked confused. "I guess."

"Would you take me to work every morning and pick me up every night?"

"Huh?"

He went to her chair and knelt on one knee in front of her. "It would be the only way you could guarantee I'd get there and back safely." He ran a hand through his hair. "But then, how could you be sure I'd be safe during my eight hours of work?" He frowned and then his face cleared. "Ah, I've got it. Maybe the boss would let you hang out, sort of keep an eye on me."

She gave him a shove that toppled him onto his behind and stood up herself. "Very funny, Donay, your humor is . . . is . . . totally awesome!"

She began pacing, now, her arms wrapped around her waist. "You obviously think I'm some kind of wimp, Carl. But I'm not." She glared at him where he was still sitting on the floor, his knees bent, his arms behind him. "I'm not! I've been losing people all my life and I've survived every loss, and gone on with my life, no matter what. I'm getting on with it now, as a matter of fact, and I didn't need your help doing it!"

His laugh was a short, bitter gasp. "You call hiding out in the middle of nowhere in a strange country, surrounded by strangers, getting on with it?"

"This is only temporary. I just needed some time to gather my thoughts."

He shook his head. "Let's face it, love, you're doing the same thing now you did when you decided I was wrong for you—running away instead of dealing with it head-on." He got to his feet and came over to her.

"I don't think you're a wimp at all. I just think you have some warped idea that there's a safety factor built into some people's lives that's missing in others." He grasped her arms and kept her from turning away.

"We take less risks in the service than the average guy on the street does. We're trained to avoid risk, given weapons for our own protection, taught to reduce the risk factor. I'm not saying it's a pretty job, or that there is no danger whatsoever. But you're overlooking the everyday statistics—an accountant can get hit by a car crossing the street, a mechanic can take a plane to another city and crash. Joanna, last week I read about a small appliance repairman who spilled coffee on his workbench while he was working and electrocuted himself!"

She pulled out of his grasp and went to the window. "I know all that, Carl." She sighed and laid her head against the frame. "But when I close my eyes at night, I see you shooting that man, see his face, feel his dead weight falling on me." She turned to face him and her eyes were bleak. "I'm not sure I'll ever be able to erase that image from my mind, Carl."

"Let me give you new images to replace that one," he said softly, his expression solemn.

"Until you have to kill someone else," she sighed. "Or worse, someone kills you."

"The bottom line is, we love each other and we should be together," Carl argued.

"For how long?"

He squinted at her and lifted his arm to show her his watch. "For however long we have."

Joanna laughed bitterly. "Right!"

"I mean it. If it's only five minutes, or an hour, or five years, that's a whole lifetime. If I died tomorrow, I still would have loved you for what there was of my lifetime, wouldn't I?"

"Clever reasoning, Carl, but I don't want to settle for five years and I don't want to face the fear again of losing someone else I love," she shouted.

"Joanna," he pleaded softly. "What if you'd have met, fell in love with and married that small appliance repairman?"

"Don't be absurd." She blinked, shook her head, felt around for a chair and fell wearily onto it.

Carl nodded, a tight smile on his lips. "You get it now, don't you, love?" he asked. "There are no guarantees. Babies die in their cribs for no apparent reason at all, and fathers die in battle and mothers die from cancer."

"Like mine," she said softly, nodding.

"Like anybody's. I don't know why there's been so much death in your life— I suppose there's some cosmic explanation for it if you believe in that sort of thing. But I do know one thing for certain—it's better to share whatever time you have with someone you love, than never to have had that time at all. Mark was the best example of that."

He went to her and pulled her up into his arms. She came, unresisting, and rested her head against his chest.

"I am so grateful for the months I knew Mark, love," he said in a near whisper. "I'll never forget him, I'll always love him and he'll always be a part of me, a part of my memory that will shape everything I ever do. It horrifies me to think that you might have chosen not to have Mark if you'd known there'd be time limits on how long you'd have him."

These were the things he would have said to her when Mark died, if he'd been allowed to be there. These were the thoughts they should have shared. Joanna felt the last shards of ice melt from around her heart and she let the tears flow to wash them away.

They clung to each other, weeping silently, missing Mark, missing the weeks they had been parted from each other.

Drawing back from her for a moment, Carl said, "I'm going to be practicing law from now on, darling," he murmured. "And I can't guarantee that some disgruntled client won't shoot me for the size of my bill, but if you're willing to take a chance, I'd like us to get married, to start a family."

"Yes, oh yes, my darling," she said, just before their kisses spun out of control.

When he looked into her face a moment later, he saw the love written there, the acceptance. He used his thumb to dry her tears and she laughed and reached up to do the same for him. Their lips met, then, and they began the timeless journey into the future.

Following the success of WITH THIS RING, Harlequin cordially invites you to enjoy the romance of the wedding season with

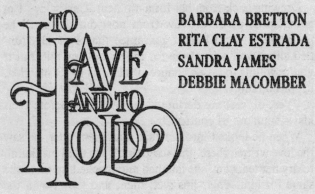

TO HAVE AND TO HOLD

BARBARA BRETTON
RITA CLAY ESTRADA
SANDRA JAMES
DEBBIE MACOMBER

A collection of romantic stories that celebrate the joy, excitement, and mishaps of planning that special day by these four award-winning Harlequin authors.

Available in April at your favorite Harlequin retail outlets.

THTH